REVENGE SCHOOL
SAN FRANCISCO

PRAISE FOR REVENGE SCHOOL

"'Revenge School' announces the birth of a franchise and a made-for-the-big-screen series. There is much to cheer for in this debut, especially Pay Back, a big-hearted big man, who is much more than just quick fists and fast dialogue. Reading 'Revenge School' will keep readers glued to the page until the early hours and finishing it will leave them watching the calendar for the next installment."

—Steven Gore, Author of *Night is the Hunter*

"A fast-moving tale in an original, appealing voice."

—Joseph Finder, New York Times bestselling author of *Suspicion*

"Evokes memories of Andrew Vachss and Lee Child."

—Jon Land, USA Today bestselling author of *Strong Darkness*

"I like Knapp's Spillane-Cain style."

—Neil Russell, Author of *Beverly Hills Is Burning*

"A hugely thrilling novel with a fresh group of charismatic heroes that will appeal to fans of Jack Reacher, Joe Pike and my own Joe Hunter books."

—Matt Hilton, Author of *The Lawless Kind*

"'Revenge School' will appeal to fans of Robert Parker."

—David Morrell, creator of Rambo and New York Times bestselling author of *First Blood*

REVENGE
SCHOOL
SAN FRANCISCO

MYLES KNAPP

GRIT-LIT
PUBLISHING

GRIT-LIT
PUBLISHING

REVENGE SCHOOL: SAN FRANCISCO
© Myles Knapp, 2015 & 2018
All rights reserved.
The author's moral rights have been asserted.

Previously published in 2015 as Revenge School
This new edition has been re-edited based on suggestions and advice
from both readers and professional editors.

Visit the author's website www.RevengeSchool.com for book extras, free stories, and more.

Editing, cover, and interior design by ArgosEdits.com

Right now, you are thinking, "Is this book going to be a fun read?"

The decision about a novel is seldom whether it is worth the money. An eBook or a paperback costs less than a tumbler of good bourbon. But entertainment time… relaxation time….That time is precious.

If you like stories where the bad guy's ass ultimately gets kicked…

If you love Jack Reacher…

If you like evil, sick, twisted villains who make the devil look a nice guy…

If you like the Equalizer, both the TV series and the movies with Denzel…

If you don't want to have to work at reading to be entertained…

If you wish Rambo lived in your neighborhood…

Then this is a book you'll enjoy.

If you are someone who loves larger than life heroes and twisting plots that keep everything moving without requiring a road map or a character list for you to keep everything straight—you will love the Revenge School books.

I hope this one keeps you up all night.

Myles

"Justified acts of violent, personal enforcement make me feel good."

Pay

The weekend in North Beach was moving at a full drunken lurch. Pay loved his neighborhood's vibrant nightlife even as he felt bad for a hard-partying college kid puking in the gutter.

Two attractive, middle-aged women, whose cheap black and gold I ♥ SF sweatshirts clashed with their designer linen shorts, stood giggling and pointing at dildos in a sex shop window. Catching his reflection, they turned toward him and powered up their smiles. He grinned back, wondering if tourists would ever learn to dress for the skin-puckering cold of San Francisco's foggy summers.

Pay slowed as a group of tonight's victims-in-waiting hustled by. Businessmen—wrinkled suits, starched shirts, loosened ties, and faces red with booze, ogled a top-heavy raven-haired babe—braless nipples standing at rigid attention, wearing nothing but an extra-long man's dress shirt, six-inch heels, and two armfuls of goose-bumped tattoos—and completely missed both punks trailing them. Punks scheming to separate them from their smart phones, watches, and cash.

Pay wondered if he should warn them but decided against it. *Too drunk to listen.* He shook his head sadly, continuing toward home, but then reversed course and followed.

Can't let them get hurt even if they are too stupid for their own good.

Five feet in front of Pay, the lead punk held a six-inch chrome hunting knife low, alongside his thigh. The second asshole pulled a piece of pipe from his backpack, the ripping sound of Velcro hidden by blues, rap, and stripper music blaring from open club doors.

Windows vibrated with the beat. Every Friday night, full moon or not—rare balmy summer evening or freezer-burn cold—the energy level on Broadway was frantic.

A woman's scream pierced the chaos. "Get off me. I'm not giving you anything."

Fifty-feet up Broadway, underneath Centerfolds' blue neon sign, Pay spotted a brunette in a plaid ultra-mini, her blouse unbuttoned to her navel, upper right arm strangled in the grip of a steroidal brute wearing a tux at least two sizes too small in the waist. Knowing in North Beach that cheap tuxes were the standard uniform for strip club security and their stupider, even more violent bouncer sidekicks, Pay figured him for a bouncer.

The mugger with the knife took a deep breath, nodded at his follower and murmured, "On three."

Pay took two quick steps forward, rested his right arm on the lead punk's shoulder, leaned into his ear, growled, "One," and slammed him head first into Centerfolds' brick wall. The knife clanked to the cement and his unconscious body crashed down, quivering alongside the now benign weapon. The second banger dropped his pipe and ran, one look at Pay convincing him it was the only smart move to make.

Pay swiveled up the street toward the stripper.

"Rock, let me go!" She swiped at the bouncer's eyes with her nails.

Pay admired the girl's guts. Rock was a beefy six-three; not as tall or built as Pay, but more than twice the little girl's. Two teenage boys ran forward, smart phones thrust above the gathering crowd. Pay figured they were hoping to capture a viral-worthy video of the stripper's boobs or a bloody beating.

Closing on the girl, a rush of adrenaline jolted Pay, followed by a confident grin that didn't reach his combat-ready eyes. Next to teaching victims how to kick the shit out of the assholes who tormented them, nothing felt better than taking down a deserving prick. And in Pay's book, any man beating a woman was more than deserving.

Rock yanked the brunette's ponytail, jerking her face toward him, and smacked her with an open-handed right. A ripping backhand sent her crashing to the sidewalk, writhing on the ground, blood dripping from her nose, red splotching her white blouse.

A woman's voice screamed, "Call 9-1-1."

Rock dumped the girl's backpack on the sidewalk. Everything fell to the ground—cell phone, wallet, make-up, loose change, books, a sweater, a thumb drive, and dark glasses—landed on the concrete alongside a Porsche idling at the curb. Its driver took one look at Rock's enraged face and floored it through the red light.

Rock yanked the cash from her wallet and grabbed the thumb drive.

She snatched at his hand. "That's mine. I need it!"

He laughed and slapped her hand away.

The girl took a deep breath and hooked a fist at Rock's balls. Blocking the blow with his thigh, he kneed her in the face. She went woozy, slumping toward the curb.

Now ten-feet away, it took Pay less than a second to evaluate the situation: Two-hundred and fifty pounds of enraged asshole who wouldn't have made it as a bouncer without being a decent fighter. Sure, the guy was smaller than Pay, and on the doughy side, but he was high. Stupid high. Putting hands on him to take him down with a pressure point hold or an arm lock would be damned dangerous.

Releasing a steel police baton from the spring-loaded holster in his sport coat sleeve, Pay whipped it open and smashed Rock's shoulder joint. Bones crunched, as he howled and collapsed.

Pay's ferocity warned the other bouncers not to come to Rock's aid.

The girl snatched the wad of cash and the thumb drive from Rock's limp hand, then scooped up the rest of her stuff and crammed it into her pack. She bolted up the street, waving at an oncoming taxi. Between the shrieking of the crowd and Rock's wails, Pay barely registered her yelling, "Thank you, mister," as she slammed the cab's door.

Cradling his broken shoulder, Rock rolled onto his back and slammed a double mule kick at Pay's legs.

Sidestepping the flying heels, Pay whipped the baton at Rock's butt, landing a crippling blow on his exposed hipbone. Rock bellowed and went limp.

The crowd shouted encouragement and screamed for more.

Pay glared at the pathetic voyeurs and they began to scatter. He didn't see any new threats, just the faces of women showing fright or gratitude, and the backs of men who'd realized their own cowardice.

It was time for Pay to get going. In a few minutes, sirens would be screaming toward Centerfolds, and witnesses would be telling the police about the big guy with a club. He didn't want to hang around for that; it would be a pointless annoyance. Rock wasn't going to press charges. And if he did, it wouldn't be the first time the cops came looking for Pay.

Across the street from Centerfolds, standing in the entrance of an abandoned nightclub, Morano watched the fight. When Rock slammed the girl to the ground, he smiled. *Looks like money well spent.*

But when that asshole Pay got involved and the girl escaped, Morano's pleasure turned to disgust. If Pay didn't kill that stupid bastard bouncer, Morano was gonna tap Rock himself. He hated wasting money on incompetent help.

Morano tossed his cigar into the gutter and hustled after the girl's cab, already a block ahead; his size fourteen Nike's squashed flat with every step, and the jolt of his four-hundred and fifty-seven pounds made his gut fat bounce.

In less than fifty-yards, sweat streaming into his eyes, heart slamming in his chest, he was cursing the girl and the taxi.

Fucking Rock. After I kill him, I'm gonna shit on his unmarked grave.

The crush of Friday night traffic kept the cab from moving much faster than a normal-sized man's walking pace, but Morano was now almost two blocks behind.

Not in shape for this crap anymore. Running after Rock's screw-ups is going to give me a fucking heart attack.

The cab pulled to a stop in front of Starbucks and the girl got out. Morano staggered to a bus shelter bench and collapsed.

As his pulse slowed, anger turned to calculated thinking. He didn't care about the girl. She was just another pole slider. But he couldn't have his operation destroyed by a renegade bitch blackmailing him.

And Pay. Pay could be a problem. He'd spent most of the last four years doing time in a federal pen thanks to Pay.

Morano pulled out his phone and activated the fingerprint reader. "I need a full update on a guy named Pay Back. Get me anything there is about him since I went to prison. Yeah, that Pay Back, idiot, the Caucasian vigilante ass-hole in San Francisco that put me in prison." He thumbed the phone off.

Rubbing the inside of his right thigh, feeling scar tissue and a golf ball sized hole of missing muscle, Morano remembered blood spurting from his crotch and the bullet that almost killed him. Pay's bullet.

If Pay showing up was anything more than a coincidence, his multi-mil-lion-dollar operation could be destroyed. Worse, if Pay got involved and things got fucked up, the feds would slam him back into Pelican Bay and he'd end up doing laundry for ten-cents an hour.

3

Pay had barely gone a block and a half when two police cruisers and an ambulance, blue-red lights strobing, accelerated past him toward Centerfolds.

Seeing no point in making it easy for the cops to find him, he ducked into his favorite neighborhood liquor-store/mini-mart, grabbed a blue plastic basket from the stack, and started filling it. A one-pound bag of M&M's went in first. They were out of Wild Turkey, so he grabbed a bottle of Knob Creek. Ice. Soda. He started toward the register, looked at the basket, sighed, and replaced the M&M's with a bag of low-salt jerky and a snack-sized bag of fat-free baked chips. At the last minute, he tossed in the smallest bag of peanut M&M's on the rack.

His Revenge School team was after him to eat better. He knew they were right. But it sucked. The baked chips were like toasted newspaper, and the jerky had all the taste appeal of unsalted rope. Alone they were awful, but they'd be okay with the bourbon.

Daleep looked up from his position at the register, slid a pair of mangled and duct-taped glasses off his forehead onto his prominent nose, and patted his flat stomach. "Still eating that crap? Thought you'd have given it up by now."

In all the years he'd been in the neighborhood, Pay'd never seen anyone but Daleep working the register. He was there eighteen hours a day, seven days a week. Christmas, New Years, Hanukah—no holiday seemed to matter. "If I was as thin as you, I could eat whatever I want."

"Hey, at least you got all that great hair." Daleep's scalp was ringed with a thin fringe of grayish-white.

"Good hair, tall, slender, or handsome, most men are lucky to get two out of four. A few get three. Get all four and you're a movie star."

"So, when are you heading to Hollywood, big guy?"

Pay laughed. "You better get new glasses, old man. If you don't, you're going to have to start putting the prices in braille."

Daleep made change and waved him out the door. "Stop eating all that snack food crap. Let my wife make you some good vegetarian curry. That's what you need. Crazy Americans eat too much meat."

Avoiding the scene at Centerfolds, Pay took the long way home. Up the steep cement steps cut into the sidewalk on Romolo Place—more an alley than a street—the angle of incline was so radical that everyone, including the craziest skateboarders walked it.

In two blocks, Pay had left behind the chaos of Broadway and entered a quiet neighborhood of two-and three-story multi-family buildings. He turned right and began the steep downhill trudge home. A left took him past Henry's Hunan Restaurant and its strange paint job—almost, but not quite, army green with burgundy red paint framing the windows—toward his home, a three-story, gray cement tilt-up. If he'd known when he moved in that the building would wind up being the Revenge Team's headquarters, he'd have hired a professional to make it more functional and comfortable.

Originally a parking structure, most of the ground floor was still a parking lot of sorts with a constantly changing selection of high-performance, nondescript, surveillance vehicles. Over the front door the original neon parking sign, now permanently set to "FULL," provided light and concealed the security camera.

Pay pressed his thumb against the scanner and was met with an Angelia Jolie voice that breathed, "Hi, Pay. Welcome back."

He was glad to hear her. Brad Pitt's voice meant the security system had been breached.

Locks snapped open, the door slid back, and Blade, Pay's charcoal gray Great Dane-English Mastiff mix, rubbed against his thigh. Blade ran up the stairs while Pay took the elevator to the second-floor kitchen where he filled a half-liter British beer mug with ice, bourbon, and soda. After knocking back a big swallow, he tore off two hunks of jerky: a small piece for him and a bigger one for Blade.

Blade sniffed at the jerky like it was diseased. Pay laughed. "I know, dog. It's nasty stuff."

Blade and Pay took the elevator to the third floor, the only route to Pay's personal living space. As the door opened and the bourbon kicked in, Pay's shoulders dropped and his breathing deepened. Sparse, decorated in black, white, and cobalt blue, the living room consisted of a couch, coffee table, bookcase, and an oversized black leather recliner for reading.

Settling into his favorite chair, Pay chewed the jerky, then followed it up with a swig of bourbon and soda. Wishing Brooke or Chase was around so he could tell them about the girl and Rock, he pushed the recliner back, kicked off his shoes, and five minutes later was out.

Mary Ellen winced, sitting gingerly on a chair at the Starbucks across the street from her apartment. Her knee ached from being slammed to the ground and she knew there was going to be a giant purple bruise on her butt. One that would look horrible on stage because it would be impossible to cover with makeup.

Sucker is really going to cut into my tips.

She pulled the sweater from her bag and began transitioning from Destiny the stripper, to Mary Ellen…financially stressed student.

Still wired from the fight, she sipped decaf and practiced deep breathing, watching her building's entrance. Once in a while, some overheated guy would follow her home or some weirdo would be hanging around. Half an hour and one bathroom break later she felt better.

Mary Ellen pawed through her stuff, disappointed, but not surprised to find her pepper spray missing.

She returned to the counter. "One extra-large black coffee to go, please."

"Decaf again?" The barista turned toward the pot without waiting for an answer.

"Whatever's hot. And you can keep the lid."

With keys poking out between the fingers of her right hand—just in case—coffee in her left, Mary Ellen headed home, wishing she'd complained more about the building's lack of security. The entry door lock had been broken since Wednesday, and most of the stairway lights had been burned out for weeks. Peering into the darkness, she limped up the staircase, grateful for the one dim bulb ahead on the landing.

The coffee roiled uncomfortably in her empty stomach. She paused near her downstairs neighbor's front door, listening for music or conversation… anything to indicate he was home and awake.

She still had the key from feeding his fish last week.

Maybe I should go in and wait for him. Tell him about the fight and that I'm scared to be home alone. She shook her head at the silly idea and frowned.

At the club, I can lead guys around by the nose. But not out here. Can't just use a guy's spare key and make myself at home.

As Mary Ellen turned toward the last flight of dark stairs, a black-gloved hand seized her throat, cutting off her breath. She jerked back, slamming her head into the man behind her. Starbucks spilled from the paper cup, scalding her hand.

Over her shoulder, she felt more than saw, a tall, fat man; his soft belly pressed into her back and shoulders. With his right hand clamped over her mouth and left hand crushing her throat, it wasn't going to be long before she passed out.

"Be quiet."

Out of the corner of her eye she couldn't see much but a gray hoodie.

"I want the videos."

She tried to answer, but what came out sounded more like a snort.

His hand relaxed slightly on her mouth and throat. "Don't scream." She gulped in a ragged breath. "Videos? What are you talking about?"

"Ah, shit. Open the fucking door."

Fumbling through the ring, she found Richard's key and willed her shaking hand toward the lock.

Thank God there was only the one deadbolt.

As the lock clicked, Mary Ellen heaved right, throwing her Starbucks directly into the fat man's face.

He screamed and clawed at his eyes, as she rammed the door with her shoulder.

Whirling into the apartment Mary Ellen ran toward the kitchen. Three steps in she reversed and threw her weight against the door, slamming it shut. Then realized he was already inside.

Shit.

Scalded by coffee, her attacker stumbled over the end table, sending the aquarium crashing to the floor. Slipping in the water, he tripped and took a nose-dive.

Mary Ellen clobbered his head with her bag and one of the textbooks inside smashed his nose.

"Ow, fuck!" Dazed, he blinked, tears streaming from his eyes as he struggled to his knees.

Swinging the backpack up from the floor like a golf club, she whacked his face. He collapsed, as the force of the hit made the bag's zipper split open and stuff flew all over the room.

Mary Ellen raced down the hall toward the bedroom, screaming: "Help!

Rape! Rape!" Slamming the door, she dove across the bed toward the fire escape.

The fat man lumbered down the hallway and bashed the door with his fist. "You think that flimsy ass thing is going to stop me?" The door burst from its hinges and he thundered into the room. Mary Ellen grabbed the reading light, twisted to her left, and swung at his head. He roared, blocked the lamp with a forearm, and delivered a right to her gut. Her ribs crunched. She puked. A left hook broke even more ribs, and an overhand right crushed down on the crown of her head.

Is this how I'm going to die?

5

Pay'd been asleep for about an hour when the office phone roused him from his unplanned nap. He pulled himself out of the recliner and stumbled toward the third-floor extension. "Pay."

"Hear you've been busy playing proactive citizen at Centerfolds."

It had been a couple of years, but Pay recognized the voice—Emir Tabb, SFPD Violent Crimes Inspector; mid-forties, muscular yet going a little soft, with medium gray hair and tired eyes. Emir and Pay had a brief history. Not a good one, not a bad one, just brief.

Pay had nothing against cops. Who else were people going to call when they couldn't handle something themselves? Too bad the rules kept them from being much help when it came to preventing crimes or getting vengeance.

"Kinda late for you to be working, isn't it?" In San Francisco, inspectors typically worked office hours.

Tabb grunted. "Mayor's all hot about cleaning up violence on Broadway. The brass says this one can't wait till Monday."

"Lucky you."

"Yeah. Goes with the job. Listen, I just finished interviewing the bouncer you thrashed at Centerfolds. Stephen Andrew Duncan; goes by Rock. Guy was high on ice. Has a full sheet. Mostly petty theft and drugs with a couple of heavy-duty violence beefs. Got a broken collarbone and a hip pointer. What did you hit him with?"

"Baton."

"Can't find the girl to make a statement and he declined to press charges against you. We cut him loose. I can't guarantee he won't come after you."

"Don't care if he does."

"You might want to. His record shows he's good with a knife and he hangs out with some exceptionally bad people."

"BFD. Can't find the girl?"

"Centerfolds has a number, one of those prepaid cells. She's not answering. I was hoping you'd know how to find her."

"Don't know her. Last time I saw her, she was getting in a cab on Broadway."

Tabb droned out the standard speech. The one Pay'd heard a million times. The one that always ended with, "When are you going to stop sticking your nose in police business?"

6

Streaming cold water into the apartment's bathroom sink, Morano ripped off his coffee-soaked sweatshirt and plunged his face into the bowl.

Damn, how'd I let a little girl hurt me so bad?

Once the burning subsided, he assessed the damage in the medicine cabinet mirror. Though painful, the singed parts of his face were mostly pink, not cherry red. And his bleeding nose wasn't broken.

Back to normal in a couple of days. A week, tops.

But he couldn't go out on the street wearing his blood-spattered sweatshirt. It only took a glance in the closet to realize everything was too small. Fortunately, there was no blood on his T-shirt.

The girl rolled over with a groan and Morano slugged her in the temple. She needed to be out until he was gone.

No point in killing her. That would just force the cops into a full court press.

He wasn't worried about her identifying him. He'd given brain-rattling beatings to dozens of people and not one had ever accurately described him. The turmoil and agitation after a violent hammering led to witness descriptions that were crap. All anybody ever remembered was a 'fat man in a hoodie.'

Time to find that thumb drive. Morano spent almost fifteen-minutes searching through her shit, which was spread all over the chaos of the front room, when he heard a key in the lock. Sliding to the hinged side of the door, he pressed back against the wall.

A slight, mid-twenties male, backpack over one shoulder, pushed the door open. Morano figured he was no threat. Just another wimpy metrosexual. He'd take one look at the mess and run over to Starbucks before calling the cops.

Instead, he turned and closed the door.

Can't let him get a good look at me.

Morano threw a left that missed the jaw, following it with a thundering right cross to the chest and an out of control left that scraped the smaller man's ear. Grabbing him by his polo shirt collar and belt, Morano heaved him over his head and flung him into the wall.

Been here too damn long.

Booting the wimp in the gut just to make sure he wasn't going to come after him, Morano left the unconscious body in a puddle of aquarium water and blood.

7

What the hell?

Dizzy from the attack, Richard struggled to his knees and crawled toward his bag, groping for his pepper spray. The kitchen table was on its side, fish tank shattered, wet papers everywhere. Pepper spray now clutched in his trembling hand, Richard sobbed, shuddered, shook his head in an unsuccessful attempt to clear it, and staggered through the living room, bouncing off the hall wall and reeling toward the bedroom.

In his bed sprawled a girl wearing laceless black Converse platform sneakers, a neon pink thong that barely covered her Brazilian wax job, and a sweater with the Centerfolds logo. Her face was covered by his blood-spattered sheets.

Richard leaned over, probing her neck for a pulse with his left hand, and using his right hand to pull the sheet from her face. It slid back and he collapsed to his knees.

Forcing several deep breaths, he wobbled to his feet using the desk chair to support legs that didn't want to fight gravity anymore.

Come on Richard, you can do this. You can do this. You have to do this.

Careening down the hall to the living room, tears dripping from his cheeks, he grabbed his cell and dialed 9-1-1.

■ ■ ■

"SFPD coming in."

Richard, hand holding a towel to Mary Ellen's forehead, slumped down in the chair beside the bed, his heart slowing to a still faster-than-normal thud. "Back here."

An officer appeared in the bedroom door, pistol and eyes aimed at Richard.

Eyes burning with fear, Richard blurted, "Not me. Don't shoot. Don't shoot me."

A second officer yelled from the hall, "Apartment's clear," then stood, gun drawn, with her back to the wall where she could watch Richard and monitor the apartment.

The first cop motioned Richard up. "I need to pat you down for weapons for our safety."

"Huh?"

"Palms on the wall. Feet spread. Now." Richard struggled up and reached for the wall.

Grabbing the back of his shirt, the officer kicked his feet apart and back, simultaneously pressing Richard's chest forward so his weight was on his hands.

Richard flinched when the man's hands ran over his crotch.

Satisfied that Richard was weaponless, the officer directed him back into the chair.

"I'm Delgado. She's Rhodes." He holstered his weapon, then pulled on latex gloves and reached to check Mary Ellen's pulse. "She's breathing, you stopped most of the bleeding. Not much we can do now." Using his gloved fingers, he spread her eyelids and blipped his flashlight across her face. "Pupils are reacting. Major size difference."

Rhodes grimaced and notified dispatch. "Victim is alive, unconscious, extensive blood loss, unstable pulse, likely concussion. Need that ambulance ASAP. What's the ETA?"

The radio squawked. "Two minutes."

Mary Ellen whimpered, "Help."

Delgado leaned back over the bed. "Ambulance is on the way. Who did this to you?"

"Big fat guy."

"Did he do this to you?" Delgado thrust his chin at Richard.

"No." She snuffled, slumping against the pillows.

"Did you see the guy's face?"

"So fast."

Wailing sirens filled the room. "The ambulance will be here soon."

"Great big fat man. Not Richard." She labored. "Richard is my friend." Her eyes glazed. "Great big...huge...fat man," she whispered, passing out just as the siren ground to a halt.

Rhodes moved to the front door to guide the EMTs in.

In minutes, the two of them bandaged Mary Ellen's head and moved her onto a gurney. One attendant secured an oxygen tube under her nose. "We're taking her to SF General."

Richard wiped his palms on his slacks, staring at the sweat stains they left on his Dockers. "Is she going to be okay?"

The EMTs rolled the gurney toward the bedroom door. "We'll do everything we can. Won't know anything until we get her to the hospital."

"Rhodes will follow you down in a little bit to get a statement." Delgado turned to Richard. "Docs will take good care of her. Tell me what happened."

"I opened the door and he jumped me." He licked his lips, tried to stop his trembling hands, but couldn't. "Guy hit me a bunch of times. I kind of remember being thrown into the wall." Richard waved in the direction of the bathroom. "Uh—could I get some water? Please?"

Delgado filled a glass from the tap. "Sweating and excessive thirst is a side effect of extreme stress. It'll go away. Can you identify him?"

"All I remember is a big fat dude hitting me."

"How long has it been?"

Richard looked down at the floor to the shattered remains of his yoga clock. It read 9:48.

Delgado glanced at his cell, checking the time. "So, about an hour and a half?"

"I guess."

Delgado frowned and looked at Rhodes, "He had plenty of time to get out of the building."

"Better check his ID."

"We need to make sure this is your apartment."

Richard pulled his wallet out and sorted through credit cards until he found his driver's license.

Delgado scanned it and made some notes in a spiral notepad. "Remember anything about this fat guy?"

"No. I just remember black hair and a T-shirt with some kind of printing on it."

"C'mon. You can do better than that. What color was he?"

Richard closed his eyes, twisted his face into a grimace and rubbed it with both hands, trying to visualize the attacker. "Um, white? I'm pretty sure he was white."

"Short?"

"He was tall."

"How tall?"

"When he picked me up over his head just before he slammed me into the wall, I kinda bounced off the ceiling."

"So about six-foot." Delgado smiled. "Now we're getting somewhere. Age?"

Richard closed his eyes, breathed deep. "I don't know."

"You know he was white, tall, and had black hair. Picture that."

"Maybe mid-thirties. And one big fat mother."

"How big?"

"Like one of those TV wrestlers."

"Like a football player?"

"Bigger than that. Way bigger than that."

"What color were his eyes?

"I don't know."

"Did you see any tattoos or scars?"

"It was just seconds. And then he slammed me into the wall."

"So, this," he referred to his notes, "Mary Ellen is your girlfriend?"

"No. She's my neighbor. I was kind of thinking about asking her out or something, but it just never seemed like the right time."

"How'd she get into your house?"

"She's got a key. I gave her one to feed my fish and bring in the mail when I'm out of town."

"Any idea why anyone would want to do this?"

"I wish I did."

"She looks like a hooker or a stripper."

"Never. Not Mary Ellen. Couldn't be."

"What do you know about her?"

"She's a student. Lives upstairs. To make extra money she takes care of people's pets and stuff. That's about it."

8

As the two AM alcohol cut off passed at the North Beach hot spots, lucky clubbers paired off. Others, wallets shrunk from a night of ten-dollar imported beers and fifteen-dollar martinis, straggled home where the drinks were cheaper.

By the time the police were done with Richard, the partying crowds had been replaced by immigrant workers sweeping up storefronts and piling trash bags in the alley for early morning pickup.

One thing Richard knew for sure, even if the cops had been willing to let him—and they weren't—was that he wasn't going to stay in a bloody apartment or sleep in that bed.

Never again. Never.

Exhausted, numb, feeling like he was going to vomit, all he wanted to do was go somewhere safe and sleep. He stuffed some clothes in his backpack along with his Mac and headed for the Hyatt. It was a little pricey, but he could afford it…and he hoped he'd feel safe there.

■ ■ ■

Richard collapsed into the hotel bed, tossing and turning, until a nightmare where a hairy hand jammed the barrel of a pistol into his right eye scared him awake.

Great. I got an entire fifteen minutes of sleep.

Will the monster that beat me and Mary Ellen come back? Maybe he'll come back and kill us both. Could he have followed me to the hotel? Was he waiting downstairs to kill me right now?

God, I'm scared.

Fear was nothing new for Richard. He'd lived with it for so long it felt normal. Like a small anchor dragging behind a sailboat, fear made doing everything harder. The wind blew and the boat moved. Then the anchor snags and everything slams to a stop. Richard's fear was like that. It made him tired, it made him careful, and when shit happened, it paralyzed him.

Richard knew why he was afraid. He was a man, but not one who could take care of himself. At least not when it came to stuff like this. His Berkeley anti-war activist mom had told him over and over, "There is always a better way to solve things than fighting."

So, while other kids played football or practiced martial arts, he spent his afternoons with the chess club.

Guns of any kind were off limits at his house. No BB guns. No cap guns. Not even a water pistol was allowed. His first spanking came the day he chewed his peanut butter and jelly sandwich into the shape of a gun and "shot" his little brother.

Richard knew he had to do something about the fear. He also knew, deep inside, the way you know there is a God and your mother loves you, he had to find the guy that beat Mary Ellen. Otherwise, he was going to be a scared little boy forever. But he didn't know how. Now, he sat at the Hyatt…scared. Was that freak going to come back and kill him? Why? What had he ever done to anyone?

Maybe that fat bastard was after Mary Ellen. Or maybe it was some horrible, random, slap-in-the-face from the universe.

For the last three weeks, every morning over his herbal tea he'd been using Anthony Robbins's positive visual affirmation techniques to conjure a beautiful girl into his life. His new mantra was, "I live a wonderful life. I am full of health and happiness and joy. I am sharing it with a lovely woman."

Maybe I needed to ask for a woman who wasn't beaten half-to-death in my bed.

The only thing he was sure of was it had been pretty brave and very foolish to stay in his apartment armed with nothing but pepper spray. For the first time in his life he'd been brave. And what had it got him? He'd heard the cops describe him as "bruised and confused," but it was the only thing he'd felt really good about for a long time.

The fat man could have killed them both and didn't. But that didn't mean he wouldn't. He could come back any time and finish the job.

If he decides to kill us and I don't get some help, I'm dead. And so is Mary Ellen.

Deciding that sleep was impossible, Richard powered up his laptop and searched: "I'm tired and scared."

The top results offered:

"I'm tired of being scared all the time"—Anxiety Message Board anxietyissues.com

I'm tired « Parent Who Writes While Others Sleep sleeplesswriter.word-press.com

I'm really tired but I'm scared to go to sleep? - Yahoo! Answers answers.yahoo.com

Forty minutes of searching led to nothing useful. Frustrated, he typed in exactly what he wanted: 'I'm scared; I don't know how to protect myself. A monster beat me and my friend up and I need to get him before he finds us.'

The result definitely caught his eye. When You Need Help Getting Even: www.RevengeSchool.com

There wasn't much to the site. No pictures. No links. No FAQS. Just a single page. In the center were two boxes. In the first, blood red words read:

You or someone you know has been wronged. Like most adults you don't know how to protect them or yourself. Fill in the box below with a short description of your problem. We don't need your whole damn life story. If we want to help you, we will contact you. If you don't hear from us in seventy-two hours look somewhere else.

Richard filled out the second box and hit 'Send.' He had nothing to lose but fear.

J ust before dawn, Pay was sitting at the team's second floor worktable putting an edge on his Blackie Collins switchblade when the security system announced: "Chase has entered through the front door."

Fifteen seconds later a six-foot-ten-inch two hundred and ten pound, forty-one-year-old man with a shaved head, a brilliant blue sapphire piercing his left ear, wearing red Italian motorcycle racing leathers, stepped out of the elevator. "Figured you'd be in bed."

Pay tested the knife's edge on a sheet of newspaper. "Had a busy night. Couldn't sleep."

"Came by to pick up the Ducati from downstairs and these new bone con-duction headsets." He grabbed a fist full of black wires off the table and waved them in Pay's direction. "I reserved time this morning to try them out at Sears Point Raceway. If I can talk on my cell doing a buck sixty on the straight away, they're good enough for us. You being busy mean there's work coming up? There are a couple of toys I've got my eye on."

"You made millions playing in the NBA. You can buy anything you want except maybe a Gulfstream." Pay knew Chase lusted for his own private jet.

"I never spend my capital on toys. I use the money I earn with you for that. Looking at a new Victory Vision."

"What the hell do you want a big, slow motorcycle like that for?"

"My Ducati's great for the track, but the seat's hard as a rock, and with legs as long as mine there's no room for a passenger."

"Ah, those big Harley clones all ride like a Winnebago."

"Girls like the cushy heated seats, and my jazz-filled soul loves the built-in audio."

"Get a Goldwing. Rides better and women love them."

"Not my style, big man. You need me for anything?"

"Nothing right now."

Chase frowned. "Damn. It's been kind of boring around here. I was hoping for some excitement. Well…I'll be back for the staff meeting." Punching the elevator button, he was gone.

Pay shook his head, thinking about how much he hated people standing around waiting for him to somehow magically create work. In his business, you couldn't make work. It wasn't like he could hire a bunch of salesmen and have them knocking on doors, cold calling, and spilling martinis on their ties.

In order for the Revenge Team to have work, something truly awful had to happen to somebody.

Chase got back from Sears Point; bug guts on his leathers and smelling like grease and hot tires, he barely made it in time for the eleven AM staff meeting. A Saturday ritual where Pay, Brooke, and Chase divvied up the following week's work.

Pay settled down with a double espresso, while Brooke sorted through her notes, and Chase opened his laptop.

To say Brooke was the best looking member of the team was like saying Michael Jordan was a 'pretty good' basketball player. Long, lithe, and lovely—a svelte redhead with green-gold eyes just slightly darker than Pay's, Brooke carried the beauty and mystery of a mature woman. Usually standing almost five-ten in heels, she'd tossed the chic garb away, choosing instead a comfortable white Gap T-shirt, light gray slacks, and blue-gray Nikes. She sent a smile in Pay's direction. "What have we got on schedule for tonight?"

"Pretty quiet. Just my turn with Sam Hong."

Sam was a reclusive inventor who claimed his best ideas came during the middle of the night as he walked around town. For years he had wandered the city streets unmolested. A slight, quiet, elderly Asian, even panhandlers ignored him. But a couple of months ago his picture had appeared in Fortune magazine, with the caption: "The World's Most Anonymous Billionaire."

Some punk realized Sam was the perfect kidnapping victim. The guy was loaded, defenseless, with a loving wife, kids, and grandkids. His wife would cave with the first ransom call.

Which is exactly what happened.

Sam had been out half a million the day Pay met him on the waterfront near Red's Java Hut. "Hear they took you for a big ransom. You want help getting it back?"

Sam shook his head. "I'm not sure. Haven't decided yet."

"Then why'd you call me?"

Sam smiled and quietly explained his need to wander.

"That's it? You just want me to follow you around?"

"For right now. But I've got to come up with a better option. It isn't wandering if some big guy is always following you wherever you go. You'd probably want to share coffee and donuts, or beer, and talk about something."

"Sure you want to leave half a mil on the table like that?"

"Losing five hundred thousand dollars won't change my life much."

"I could teach you to use a knife."

"I learned how to use one in the military. The men who took me were big and young." Sam frowned. "There is no way I could take them with just a knife."

"How about a gun?"

"I'm a slow old man. They'd just take it away and use it on me."

"How 'bout pepper spray...or a Taser?"

"That might work if it was only one person. I was jumped by two."

Ever since then, several times a week Sam went walkabout, but the only way his wife would let him go was if someone from the team provided security.

"Where's he going tonight?" Brooke asked.

"Just said meet him at eleven PM at the usual spot in the Marina."

Chase looked up from his laptop. "Pay, you had a long night. All I've done the last couple of days is race my bike. Let me take Sam."

"Thanks, but I'll be okay. Just need a nap. Plus, Blade needs the exercise."

"Let's move on to some potential new business." Brooke glanced down at her notes. "There might be something going on at my club."

Like all the team's members, except Pay and Chase, Brooke had a regular job. Nights she worked at San Francisco's most exclusive private club. Not a strip joint, but a businessman's social club so private, it didn't have a sign or even an official name. The members just called it "The Men's Club." It was the kind of place where the entry-level bottle service scotch was an eight-hundred dollar bottle of Johnny Walker Blue, with French La Pouvade champagne starting at a thousand. A place where billionaire CEOs and investment bankers cut deals.

"Let's hear it."

"Several of the men are acting strange. They've been hiding, whispering in the private VIP rooms."

Chase shrugged. "What's unusual about that?"

"Without girls? I'm talking about the players. The ones who think monogamy is only for wives."

"Are these guys normally happy to see you?" asked Pay.

"Yes, and that's what's strange. Members who would normally be delighted to see me are upset if I don't knock before I enter. Knocking is mandatory if someone's in a VIP room with a girl, but when it's just three or four guys sitting there with the door closed drinking more than normal and looking morose, I have to think something is going on."

"They figure out you're not single?" Pay asked. Brooke had recently gotten engaged to Denny, a popular local bartender and the team's newest member. "They find out you're off the table, might make 'em act different."

"No. Nobody knows. And it's not everyone. Just the mega-rich, mega-players. The guys on their second or third wives. Members who would never think of showing up without arm candy are suddenly arriving and leaving alone. Two of the guys have started spending their regular date nights at the club—alone—mistresses not welcome. There's definitely something that's not right."

Chase had closed his laptop and was dismantling one of the bone conduction mics. "If somebody's bleeding them, there could be millions of dollars at stake. What do you think, Pay?"

"Let's check it out; maybe offer to help. Quietly, in a way the cops can't."

"Publicity is the last thing my members want."

"Anybody I could talk to?"

Brooke's face showed her concern. "Is there a more discreet way? I could lose my job. Getting another one that pays like this isn't going to happen without me moving to someplace like New York or Dubai."

"Don't want that." Pay hated it when a team member moved away. It took forever to find someone with the skills they needed. But it would be worse if Chase or Brooke left. They were his closest friends and the only two people he trusted to know about everything.

"I can get Chase into the club tonight as a guest, maybe he could hang around, get to know a few of the guys?"

"Not me?"

"Please don't take this wrong, but at my club you'd stand out like a destruction derby car at the Concourse d'Elegance."

"Chase is six-ten and bald. I'm gonna standout?"

"He's also a rich, educated, urbane, retired NBA champion. He doesn't have to blend."

"And don't forget exceptionally good looking." Chase laughed.

"Ah, hell. So I got Sam tonight and tomorrow if he wants to go out. Chase, who you gonna take to the club? You might need someone to watch your back. Maybe Amy?"

"Amy would be fine. How many girls do you think we need?" Chase's eyes flicked to Brooke.

"You're a first-time guest, so I'd suggest discretion. Two nice young women would be ideal."

"Two adoring females sounds good to me." Chase chuckled. "If Amy is one,

I don't need anyone else to watch my back. We just need another lady who is young, beautiful, and, of course, interested in being attendant to me."

"How 'bout Amy's friend Keira?" Pay suggested.

"I don't think I know her."

"Sure you do. First time you saw her, your eyes all but popped out of your head. Tall, slender girl. Long strawberry blonde hair with the great—"

"Moves?" Brooke jumped in.

Now it was Pay's turn to laugh. "Yeah. At least…it kinda, sorta rhymes with 'moves.' That Irish girl."

"She'll fit in just fine. And something tells me she won't have to work too hard to play a party-girl out for a good time."

S aturday afternoon at 1:30, Morano was at Brandy Ho's. He went nearly every day for his first meal. For his money—a phrase that always
made him laugh because his money was never really his money, it
was always somebody else's money he'd stolen—Brandy Ho's had the best food
in town.

Morano was addicted to one of the restaurant's house specials, Hot Smoked
Ham with Fresh Cloves of Garlic. One time he'd even tried to count the garlic,
but lost patience when he got to twenty-two cloves.

A waitress served his first Tsing Tao beer before his butt had hit the seat.
Then, she ran to the cooler and set a six-pack aside for him. He'd drink four or
five with his meal and they knew better than to run out.

He pulled out his phone and checked his email, looking for updated information on Pay. Morano didn't need to order. Everyone knew his choices by
heart.

The cook started things going before Morano had swallowed his second
gulp of beer—twelve pot stickers, two orders of ham with garlic, and bean
sprout salad with extra peanut sauce. The servers' mantra at Brandy Ho's was:
"Medium is hot here." But for Morano 'extra spicy' was no problem. Once, to
win a bet, he'd chugged an entire bowl of their black bean hot sauce. Suffice to
say, he won the bet.

The report on Pay Back wasn't good. Before the busboy had delivered ice
water and chopsticks, Morano had found the key part. "Looks like Pay has
branched out and added to his team. In addition to Chase, he leads something
called the Revenge Team and runs vigilante mixed-martial arts classes at a
low-profile place called the Revenge School. One of my cellies from Pelican
Bay told me Pay said, 'We help good people when the law can't,' just before he
broke my guy's jaw."

The waiter set down pot stickers, soup, and a fresh beer.

Morano grimaced. Pay might be a problem. He'd crushed that fool, Rock. But it worried him that Pay might have stumbled on to his new operation which was generating cash faster than a cheap hooker could drop her thong.

Waving at the waiter, he pointed to his chair, and mouthed, "I'll be right back."

He headed out the front door to Columbus Avenue where four lanes of city traffic and clamoring crowds of tourists generated more than enough noise to cover his phone call. "Put guys on Pay, twenty-four seven. I want him followed everywhere. Have them report back on anything he does that touches my operation. And if anyone gets a shot at taking him out there's fifteen large in it for them."

After the meeting with Chase and Brooke, Pay got a quick nap. Yawning, stretching, still sleep deprived, Pay was counting on several double espressos to get him through a long night with Sam Hong.

It was a quiet evening at what the team referred to as, "Pay Back World Headquarters." The outside of the building was the essence of bland. Except for the color of the neon parking sign everything else—walls, front door, even window coverings were cement colored or charcoal gray.

Inside was the stuff they needed for work: mixed martial arts set up, weights, a rotating selection of surveillance vehicles, weapons locker, several computer worktables, Pay's living space, and, of course, Blade.

The mammoth dog scared everyone who saw him. His missing ear and scars left no doubt he'd been trained to fight, and Pay had figured he'd belonged to a drug dealer at one time. It wasn't until later that he learned Blade was a retired War Dog, who'd honorably served in the military.

Blade was so intimidating that animal rescue couldn't give him away. But when Pay had offered up half of his beef jerky, the beast had rolled over and begged for a belly rub. They'd been watching each other's backs ever since.

Pay scanned his email, trashing spam and searching for people who deserved assistance, deleting messages from whiners who wanted help killing the guy whose cat peed in their yard. Or the ones who complained about neighbors parking cars in "their" section of the street. Pay wondered if people really thought he'd school someone over cat pee or a friggin parking problem.

One email started out right. "I need help. I'm frightened for my life. Last night this monster hammered me and left me unconscious. And I found my neighbor beaten nearly to death in my bed. She's a girl I don't know very well, but I like. I looked right in his face, but it happened so fast that I don't think I'd recognize him if I saw him again. But he won't know that. Will he want to kill me now? I'm too terrified to go home. I want to find out who hurt Mary Ellen, but I don't know how. I don't want to be scared anymore."

Richard Johnson.

Guy sounded good.

In Pay's world, a client's commitment to getting personal justice was key. Pay never turned anyone away for lack of cash, but he regularly refused clients who didn't demonstrate the motivation and dedication required to get revenge.

Pay grabbed the phone.

"Hello, this is Richard."

"Richard, name's Pay. You put some information on my Revenge School website. Sounds like you got a problem."

"Uh."

Pay could almost see him shake his head in confusion.

"What did you say your name was?"

"Pay. I'm a guy who helps scared people like you."

"Mr. Pay, I really need some help. There's this girl and she was beaten."

In Pay's mind a picture started to form; slight, frightened, mid-twenties male, most likely born in California. Stuff anyone could hear in a voice if they paid careful attention and knew what to listen for. "It's Pay, not Mr. Pay. Got your email, read it. You don't need to repeat it."

"Okay, sir. I am sorry. What should I do?"

"It's Pay, not sir. Just be quiet. You've got to learn to protect yourself. This evening a package containing a key will be delivered to your room. Which hotel and room?"

"I'm at the Hyatt Regency Embarcadero, Room 2217."

"Tomorrow, take the key to the UPS store on the seven-hundred block of California. Open mailbox number twenty-one. Inside will be a package. Take it and leave me a key for your apartment.

"Don't open the package in public. Inside there'll be a bottle of Phase Four Grizzly Bear Pepper spray. It's eighty times more powerful than regular pepper spray. Along with it will be a shoulder holster, pistol, and ammo. The gun is clean. Call Old West Gun Range in South SF. Ask for Matt. Schedule lessons and range time. Right now, you can't defend yourself. By the time we're done, you'll be able to."

Pay paused to breathe. And to see if the guy had enough stones to jump in.

"Um…Pay, are you done? Could we meet first? Someplace safe, like the Hyatt lobby? I'm not sure I'm ready for a gun."

As Richard talked, the picture in Pay's head continued to fill in. Based on vocabulary and clarity of voice, which lacked the throaty distortion common to people in their late thirties, a vocal characteristic that grew with every ciga-rette, year of life, or extra pound, Pay figured Richard was a college educated, non-smoker. The quiver in his voice was fear.

"You want to get even?"

"I want to find out who beat me. And I want to be safe. But shooting someone? I don't know."

"Violent self-aggression is your only option."

"Can't the police help me?"

"If the guy is a real pro, the cops can't really help. If they find the guy you might be safe for a while. But he could kill you before they find him. Or they could find him and he'll pay someone to knock you off while he's awaiting trial. Only sure way is for you to take him out."

"K-k-kill him?" Richard stuttered out.

"I know. It's a hard thing to come to grips with. Right now, you don't have to. But to be safe, you need to learn how to use a gun."

"Um. Okay. I guess."

Pay could hear the reluctance in his voice. "Tell me about the guy who beat you."

"He was a huge fat man. I kind of remember a black beard. Caucasian. Maybe a little over six-feet tall. Mostly I remember he picked me up and bounced me off the ceiling, then tried to throw me through a wall."

"And what do you want to do about that?"

"I'm not sure. I just want to be safe."

"What we do is not about justice. My team will help you get revenge. And I don't mean an eye-for-an-eye. The exact level of retribution is your decision, but most people eventually want more. Like two eyes for an eye. Or two eyes and a leg."

"That's disturbing."

"It is. And it's a lesson I learned the hard way. Listen, if you want to be safe but can't commit to growing a pair and handling the messy parts—and there are always messy parts—don't waste my time." Pay paused to let that sink in. "The fastest way to help you is to change the way you think. And the first thing I have to do is teach you skills so you are no longer completely defenseless."

"All this scares me."

"It should. But it's the only way I know to get rid of the fear."

"What's this going to cost me?"

"Five hundred dollars for the gun and the lessons. That's our cost. You can leave cash in the box with the key. It's just to cover expenses and prove you're serious. Your choice. Hire us or spend the rest of your life scared." With that, he hung up.

Richard wanted to find out who hurt Mary Ellen. And thinking 'brave' sounded good. But he didn't want to risk his life on a guy he knew nothing about. He called his friend, David Hunter—a reporter at the San Francisco Chronicle.

"Hunter."

"David, its Richard Johnson."

"Richard! Been too long since I heard from you. How are things?"

"They could be better. Last night my neighbor was beaten and left in my bed. I got pretty badly mauled, too."

"That was you? I read our police reports this morning. There was something about a stripper in North Beach, but I didn't make the connection."

"It was me. I'm still in shock. The guy might come back. I think I'm going to need someone to protect me."

"How can I help?"

"I found this guy online who calls himself Pay. He runs something called the Revenge School and says he can help me."

"I think I've heard of the guy, but I don't remember anything specific. Let me search our files and talk to some of the other reporters. I'll see what I can find out."

"Thanks, David. That would be great. Could you get me something soon?"

"I'll get right on it."

"Anything you can do, I appreciate."

"If there's a story in it, I want it."

"I really need you to hold off on that. I saw the bad guy's face. Anything you print could get me killed."

"Sure, I understand. I'd never put a friend in danger."

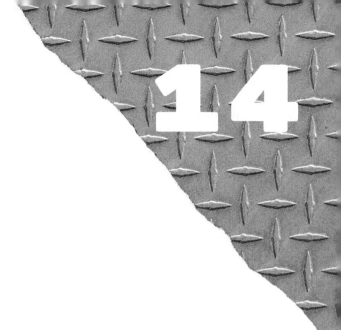

Chase and Pay sat in the team's lounge—pool table on the left, Formica worktable on the right, and six big green chairs lined up around the plasma. Pay had permanent dibs on the extra-large one. He'd had more knife wounds stitched up in that chair than he cared to count.

Pay was curling a thirty-pound medicine ball. He'd start with twenty standard curls then switch to reverse curls, palming the heavy ball like a basketball. He made it look easy. So easy everyone who saw him thought they could do it, too. But everyone who'd ever tried, even Chase, had failed.

Every now and then he'd put the ball down, switch hands, and take a big hit from a quart of purple Gatorade.

Chase was at the worktable, jeweler's loop screwed into his eye, fiddling with a tiny screwdriver and swearing at a non-performing gadget.

To Pay, it looked like a surveillance recorder, but he could never be sure what Chase was working on. Sometimes a candy cane was the latest in hi-tech microphones, and sometimes it was just a candy cane.

"You okay with tonight?" Pay switched hands.

"Sure. Why not?"

"Could be dangerous."

"How? Visit an exclusive club and enjoy adult beverages with a group of wealthy, white gentlemen. A few of whom are trying to figure out if they can steal my money and my women. It'll be just like hanging with a bunch of NBA owners."

"Whom?"

"What?"

"You speak English better than I do."

"Actually, I speak English more correctly." Chase chuckled. "Could be because, unlike you, I actually went to class, graduated cum laude—that's 'with honors,' for you Neanderthal lineman types."

"Just don't want anyone hurt. All those rich guys with concealed carry permits and no experience."

"Wouldn't be the first time I got shot at."

"Can't believe Brooke thinks you will fit in better than I would."

"Course I will."

"Crap. You guys think I'm a total redneck."

"If you hadn't insisted on marrying your sister." Chase laughed. "Come on, Pay. Even if we could get a decent designer suit in size fifty-four double long, I'd still have to tell everyone you're my friend, a second-rate WWE wrestler."

"Whatta ya mean, second rate?"

"I keep telling you. Steroids are the secret."

"Six foot five and 285 isn't big enough?"

"Well, it isn't just the size."

"What?"

"Successful wrestlers have entertaining personalities."

Pay laughed and flipped the medicine ball at Chase. Chase caught it, tried to do a reverse curl, and for what must have been the thousandth time, dropped the ball, barely missing his foot. He snarled and kicked it towards Pay.

Brooke walked into the room as Pay moved to the door. "You boys ready to plan this thing?"

"I'm in," said Chase. "Pay, you staying?"

"Little tiny, second rate redneck wouldn't be any help with this."

"Jeez, Pay. Tonight's a simple 'meet, greet, look real sweet.' Way more me than you, big guy. When it gets serious we're still going to need help from our favorite wrestling has-been."

"Five minutes and I've been demoted from second rate to has-been. I'm gone."

Brooke smiled at Chase. "There's not really much to plan. Tonight, it's you, me, Amy, and Keira."

"What have you got in mind, gorgeous?"

"We'll all ride over together. The membership committee has instructed me to make sure you have the absolute best possible experience."

"Mighty white of them."

"With a half million membership fee they've got motivation. Plus, you represent a market segment the club has had trouble reaching."

"The club wants brothuhs?"

"No, they want rich, charming sports and entertainment personalities. They're hoping you'll bring a little fresh excitement to their ambiance."

"And by excitement you mean they're interested in me bringing in a new group of ho's."

"Yes. But only in the classiest sense of the word."

An hour later, Pay called Chase. "How'd the planning go?"

"It isn't going to be hard."

"Brooke's told you who the likely victims are?"

"She'll introduce me to the guys she thinks have a problem. I'll chat about my NBA days. Sophisticated guys like that always want to know what kind of thinking is required to win a championship. Like you can think your way to winning."

"They won't drop the blackmail thing on you because you played ball."

"I'll visit a few times, invite some of the guys over to the house. Could take a while."

"Could be big bucks at stake. Some mean players."

"Relax, Pay. You know guys like these never shoot anyone on their own turf."

Pay split his PowerBar with Blade, washing it down with strong, black coffee from his thermos. Cursing under his breath, he wondered what the hell good it was to be the boss if Chase got to hang out in the world's most exclusive club while he followed an eccentric old man all over the city.

Christ, it was freezing. Even Blade was shivering.

Pay pulled his leather jacket tight, wishing he'd brought gloves. Damn! San Francisco fog was colder than hell.

Following Sam was usually easy work. Just enough aerobic activity to keep you warm and loose. Sam wanted Pay close enough to help if there was a problem, but not so close as to encourage conversation.

Uphill or down, Sam normally didn't stop. But tonight wasn't normal. A little after midnight, they'd wandered into the financial district which was empty. Nothing but a few homeless guys sleeping in doorways and a few rats prowling the trash.

Pay figured Sam would follow his usual pattern—hustle through the empty streets until ultimately turning back toward North Beach. He'd wind up in Chinatown at some dive bar for his ritual one forty-five AM beer. But not tonight.

For the last hour Sam had been quietly talking to an old wino and petting the guy's dog; a pitiful, shivering Chihuahua, head barely peeking out under the bum's filthy blanket. It seemed like Sam knew the guy. Pay couldn't hear the conversation, but from the body language it started out friendly, moved to intense, and ultimately transitioned into low key, companionable silence.

Pay stood there, shivering, watching, and cussing his luck.

About one thirty, Sam smiled sadly, emptied his wallet into the guy's hand, nodded at Pay, and took off.

Pay followed, figuring Sam was about done for the night. Usually, they parted company at some randomly selected bar. Sam would have that normal beer and then catch a taxi home. But tonight, instead of waving goodbye, Sam motioned Pay into the bar.

Blade took up his position just outside the front door.

Sam picked an empty window booth where Pay could see Blade, and perhaps, more importantly, Blade could see Pay.

The cracked red vinyl creaked and the table rocked as Pay wedged himself into the seat.

Sam ordered a Coors Light.

Pay went with his usual. "Wild Turkey, rocks. Harp back."

"Tonight, I wish I could drink like that."

"You could."

"My size, at my age, couple of those would put me on my knees in the men's room." Sam glanced at the dirty neon lights that barely illuminated the grunge covered bar. "Don't think I'd even want to take a piss in their john."

"What's got you?"

"That guy."

"The wino?"

"My first boss. He gave me my big chance. And he's probably the reason I'm rich. Brilliant, with an incredible grasp of technical things, he's one of those rare people who could talk to an engineer, understand what he was saying, and then translate the concept into something a normal person would want to buy. One of the smartest men I ever met."

"What the hell happened to him? Booze?" Pay slugged back some Wild Turkey and chased it with a gulp of Harp.

"He was so smart he couldn't work with regular people. His management teams kept blowing up."

"What'd you talk about?"

"Old times. Then I offered to help him out." Sam's voice faded.

"Didn't take you up on it."

"I didn't think he would. He's too proud."

"Saw you give him some cash."

"He wanted a cell phone so he could let his kids know he was okay."

"How much you give him?"

"Little over two thousand."

Pay's surprise must have showed.

"It was all I had," Sam said with a frown.

16

ay watched as Jon D parked his three wheeled electric chair alongside the team's heavy bag.

Jon D was the team's armorer. A retired cop, shot in the spine by a serial killer, he was partially paralyzed from the waist down and tormented by frequent bursts of uncontrollable pain. Once, he'd been a valued team member and leader, second only to Pay. But his injury made him bitter and angry. And the pain medication could make him twitchy and secretive. Now he was loved, but often barely tolerated. Since the injury, Pay thought Jon D was a little too likely to kill first and not be bothered to ask questions later.

"Need to arm Sam Hong."

"Guessed that was what you wanted to talk about," Jon D grumped, pushing a button on the chair's left handle bar. There was an electronic 'whir' as the chair's bucket seat transformed itself into a recliner. Nothing on the chair was stock. Jon D had hyped up the motor, painted the body British Racing Green, and put Aston Martin logos on every available surface.

Pay was sure that when Jon D died, whoever inherited the chair would find all kinds of surprises. Hell, for all Pay knew, the left fender hid a grenade launcher. "I can't follow him all the time."

"Does he want to kill somebody? Or just protect himself?"

"Not sure. I just know he doesn't want to get kidnapped again."

"He used to be a marine or something, didn't he?"

"Been a long time since his military days. He's a little old man now." Pay shaped the air with his hands, approximating Sam's slight stature.

"Old, small people need to rely on surprise. They gotta hit first and they gotta hit hard."

"I don't think Sam could hit a guy hard enough to do any damage. He only weighs about a buck-ten. How about a Taser?"

"Only works on one guy." Jon D sneered. He hated non-lethal solutions.
"Last time he got jumped by two."

"If all he wants is to punish someone and run, he might want this." Jon D
pulled a furled black umbrella from a tube on the side of the chair and waved
it in Pay's direction.

"What's he going to do with an umbrella?"

"I'll show you." Backing his chair up until he was ten-feet from the heavy
bag, Jon D slapped the joystick forward. He rocketed toward the bag and
whacked it with the umbrella. The bag swayed like Pay had mule-kicked it.

"Meet the unbreakable walking-stick-self-defense umbrella. Perfectly legal.
Lethal in the right hands." Jon D broke out what passed for a smile. "Even a
banged up old asshole like me can kick the shit out of a couple of punks."

"So, Sam whacks them with the umbrella and runs like hell?"

"Or shoots the shit out of them. That'd be my preference."

"So we get him a gun, too. I could get him a forty-five but he'd have a hard
time getting a carry permit."

Jon D waved off Pay's concern. "Concealed carry permits aren't important to a rich guy like him. You're a big, violent vigilante. How often have the
police frisked you for a gun?"

"Twice. At crime scenes."

"But they never just stop you and search you, do they?"

"Not yet."

Jon D fingered his pocket, feeling for the pipe he'd given up in the hospital
after his injury. "A rich guy like Sam, he'll never get searched. And if they try
to hang something on him, his attorneys will get him off. Forget the carry
permit. And the forty-five. Too big."

"What would you suggest?"

"Something loud and scary. Two shots, the umbrella and maybe a backup
piece should be enough. Most street crooks are stupid cowards. They pick on
the weak and run like hell when someone pulls a gun. Punks that don't run
right away take off the minute a trigger gets pulled."

"Sounds right."

"The bad guys brace Sam. One of them says something dumb like, 'your
money or your life.' Right?"

"You've been watching too many old movies."

"But I'm right."

"Yeah."

"He takes them down with the umbrella and runs like hell."

"What if that isn't enough?"

"There's an old derringer holster that fits in your hip pocket."

"Like a wallet?"

"Yeah. It has a hole in the center that practically forces your finger onto the trigger. All Sam needs to do is act real scared, say something like, 'you can have anything…just don't hurt me,' then reach for his wallet. Bam, bam. Two bad guys down."

"Okay."

"Long time ago, the thing was made to hold a High Standard mag derringer."

"Sounds pretty effective."

"So effective, the holster's illegal in California. And most of the rest of the country."

"Great. A solution we can't get." Pay groaned.

"Ah, hell, it's easy to make. I can get my leather man to make one in a few hours." Jon D penciled out a sketch of the rig. "Guy Sam's size would be better off with a version that fits in his breast pocket."

On the chair's LCD screen, Jon D pulled up a picture of a small pistol. "That's a Bond Arms Snake Slayer. It shoots two big, loud bullets. Get him one for the wallet and one for an ankle holster."

"Why not something smaller like a Lady Derringer?"

Jon grimaced in agony, twisted his face away, pounded his fist on the table. "Shit. Why the fuck you call me if you aren't going to take my advice?"

He gulped in several ragged breaths and turned back to Pay, pain overflowing in his eyes, and trying but failing not to cry. "Damn pain makes me a real shit. Lady D's okay. But the Slayer is better for Sam. Unlike most derringers, it has a trigger guard. Less chance of him shooting off his foot."

"And?"

"And you can load it with different kinds of ammo. You want to put somebody down, it shoots a full forty-five caliber load. But, for Sam, I'd load it with four-ten buckshot shotgun shells. Thing makes a hell of a bang. Very scary. Very damaging. And you don't need to be real accurate. So, he won't need any special training."

"Sounds perfect."

"One problem. It's legal in lots of states, but not in California. Here, they consider it a sawed-off shotgun. Got several in my gun safe if you want 'em."

"What's the risk?"

"If Sam kills someone with one he could get hit with felony weapons possession."

"But if he uses a regular pistol and misses he could wind up dead."

"Easy choice for me."

"Get him two, ASAP."

"It does have one other interesting feature."

"Yeah?"

"Pansy ass pacifists like them because you can use non-lethal ammo. Shoots a black rubber thing looks like a champagne cork. Stings like hell.

Won't stop a pro unless you hit them in the eye or maybe the throat. And definitely won't stop anyone wearing body armor."

"I don't need rubber bullets. Neither does Sam. I'm gonna teach him if he points a gun at someone he'd better plan on killing 'em."

"Always a good policy, son. Always a good policy."

"When can I give it to him?"

"Couple of days."

As Jon D rolled out the door, Pay watched the twin oxygen tanks bounce in the rear holder. He thought about asking, again, why Jon D carried oxygen he didn't use. But the last time he'd been told to "mind your own fucking business."

Maybe it was time to have Chase figure out what the hell was in those tanks.

17

I t was almost three on Sunday afternoon when Inspector Tabb called Pay. "You might need to know this. Friday night a squad car found Destiny, the missing stripper. Real name Mary Ellen Samuels. Beat real bad. She's in intensive care. They don't know if she's going to make it."

Pay winced and wondered what kind of shit the girl had been into. And if this was the same Mary Ellen their new prospect mentioned in his email.

He heard a keyboard click. "She was found at the North Beach apartment of one, Richard Johnson."

The keyboard stopped clicking. "Mr. Johnson was also beaten. Currently, he's not a suspect, but that could change. Initial investigation uncovered evidence of a violent struggle. That's it. You learn anything about this you better let me know."

18

Early Sunday evening Richard got an email from David Hunter.

No one really knows much about this Pay guy. Attached is an article from the paper; everything else was pulled from our internal files. I've highlighted quotes that I thought you would be interested in.

Richard scanned the quotes first.

Pay and the Revenge Team helped me when no one else would.

The lessons were arduous and sometimes painful. But with their help I got justice. And now I can take care of myself and help other people.

But the quote that stood out for Richard was: I'm not scared anymore.

The article provided additional details about a vigilante group. Eyewitness reports mentioned a large Caucasian man, a tall, slender, African-American man, a statuesque redheaded woman—race unspecified—and a dog.

The team was reported to have left a man naked and handcuffed to a tree in Washington Square Park. Nailed to the tree was an envelope with enough evidence to convict him of multiple capital crimes. The message read:

This murderous son-of-a-bitch mutilates and tortures women and children. With the help of people he abused, we have taken the first step towards justice. Three of his victims verified his guilt. He remains alive at their request. They want him legally prosecuted. We think the world would be better off with him dead.

For Richard it was a moment of agonizing clarity. He'd never been a physically brave man. Now, to protect himself, he needed to be one…and he didn't know how. The police had told him to stay out of it, but he had to do something. And it was clear he couldn't do it by himself.

This Pay guy was obviously violent. Unfortunately, Richard didn't know anyone else who would help him.

19

Late Sunday evening, Chase called Pay. "I've been checking out Richard Johnson. There's an account at Bank of America, two credit cards with zero balances, and an e-trade account."

"That's it?"

"He's registered to vote and has a driver's license but doesn't own a car. Works as a freelance computer guy. Looks like he designs games."

"Can he pay us?"

"His checking account shows an average balance of four grand. E-trade account is in the low five figures."

"So, we've got a client?"

"Well, he can pay us."

"Good enough."

"Anything else you want me to do?"

"Yeah. Remember the bouncer I roughed up?"

"The guy beating on a stripper?"

"Turns out the stripper is the girl found in our new client's bed."

Pay heard the concern in Chase's voice. "Interesting. What did you get in the middle of?"

"I don't know."

"Anything else?"

"There's a chance the bouncer was the last guy to see her."

"Want me to have a talk with him?"

"No, let's go together."

"I'll let you know when I find him."

"Good. And tell the rest of the team to be careful."

Morano spent Sunday night watching the video footage from his honey traps. The idea was simple. Morano had bought it, sort of, from a cell mate at Pelican Bay.

His cellie had been a pro wrestler wanna-be. But got started on 'roids and then gone down hard behind drugs, gambling, a weak work ethic, and a violent temper.

Paul Scully, aka Monster Paul, had been stripping an original old master off the library wall in a rich asshole's Nob Hill mansion when the homeowner came back early. Monster shot him and got caught. A violent three-time loser convicted of felony burglary with a discharged weapon, who stabbed a guard his first week on the yard—he wasn't going to get out until he stopped breathing. By the time Morano met him, Monster had ten years to figure out the perfect crime.

"Video blackmail." Monster cracked his knuckles.

"Blackmail's mostly penny ante crap. Too much risk getting paid." Morano wasn't buying.

Monster switched to gnawing on the knuckle of his left index finger.

Morano watched as blood dripped down his chin and landed on the blue prison shirt stretched over his distended belly. *Guy definitely was not well.*

"Not my way. My way, a guy could take down a million, two million a hit. A year or so, you could take in thirty, maybe forty million. Over and out. You only hit middle-aged, rich pussy guys. There's no risk."

"I'm listening." Morano thought Monster was full of shit. But, what the hell, he had the time.

Monster glanced down, surprised at the blood on his belly. Then began furiously rubbing the swastika intertwined with the '666' tattooed on his right hand. "You get out, you do this. Then I need you to do something for me."

Monster stuttered it out. Even the worst cons in Pelican Bay were scared of Morano.

"What?"

"You gotta promise me you'll send me the max cash they allow, every week, for smokes and stuff. And the max of those mail order packages from the prison supply place. I want underwear, deodorant, toothpaste, books, and stuff I can trade."

"That it?" Guy was flippin' crazy.

Monster was back to stuttering again. Probably because his index finger was jammed halfway up his nose.

"And you promise to send ten percent of everything you get to my momma. Sort of like a commission. Momma's sick and ain't got no insurance."

Jeez, yeah, like that'll ever happen, Morano thought. "Okay." Knowing as he said it he could always stiff Monster in the end. Wasn't like the guy was going to sneak out of level-four security one night and come looking for him.

"Keys are video and the right victim."

Morano nodded encouragement.

"You only hit real rich dudes; guys who think of a million bucks the same way you and I think of a couple of Gs."

Morano nodded again. He didn't want Monster to get off track. He didn't know if Monster had taken too many head shots or just done too damn many drugs, but the guy had trouble concentrating. "Rich. Sounds good."

"Hell, that's not it." Monster's eyes drifted sideways and he snorted a stream of wet, yellow snot out his nose. "You want rich guys who just went through a messy, expensive divorce. A divorce that cost them millions."

"Rich, divorced, millions." Morano was worried. Monster's eyes were starting to dart rapidly—randomly back and forth, up and down, three flicks every second or two. Left, right, up, left. Jerk to the right, then down. Worse, they were glazing over. When Monster got agitated sometimes you couldn't get him to refocus for weeks.

"After the divorce, guy marries a new, younger wife."

"Trophy wife. Got it."

Monster's eyes stopped flitting and he looked dead-on into Morano's gaze; which was something no smart con ever did. His smile got so big Morano could see the scars where the prison docs had hacked out his tonsils. "This is the absolute key. New wife has to have a family member that's a hot shit divorce attorney." Monster snorted. "Video the target with a bimbo. It's a setup. High-def with audio. Once you've got the goods, send the guy a copy and offer to sell him everything for about twenty percent of what a divorce is gonna cost."

"Why's the new wife gotta have a family attorney?"

"More chance of an expensive, ugly divorce and less chance of a pre-nup."

Morano was amazed. Here, he'd mostly been entertaining himself. And it turned out Monster actually had a real plan. A plan that could work.

For the first time in Morano's experience, Monster was totally focused. "The attorney can raise hell with a mega-millions divorce and it won't cost her nothin'. Your victim will practically kiss your ass you'll be so cheap compared to the divorce. Not that he'll ever see your ass, if you're smart."

"Why only take him for twenty percent?" asked Morano.

"Get greedy and the guy might hire somebody to knock you off instead. A million is big money to you and me, but chump change for the right guy. Christ, I ripped off a house in Pacific Heights. When I hocked a painting from the job, the fence told me it was a Jackson Pollock. Thing was worth two and a half mil. Dude I ripped off had it hangin in the crapper."

Pay picked at the worn red Naugahyde in the diner booth and waved at the waitress for another Red Bull. He hated it, but the diner's coffee was lousy. Stale, burnt, cold, and weak. Pay thought there might be an excuse for stale coffee—even cold coffee. But weak coffee just meant someone at the restaurant was a cheap bastard.

Rubbing at his stubble, Pay breathed deep, struggling to generate some energy. Exhausted, he chugged the drink and waited for Sam, wishing he'd gotten more sleep.

Up most of Friday night with the cops. Up most of Saturday with Sam, and now he'd be up again all night. With the weekly meeting, and the beginnings of the Richard Johnson case, he hadn't gotten more than a nap in days.

Sam walked in, as Pay knuckled back a yawn. "What's so special tonight that we have to meet? I'd like to get moving." Sam twitched impatiently.

"Talked it over with my team. You go some sketchy places. So I got you some protection."

"One of you guys follows me all night. That seems like it should be enough."

"Hope it is." Pay handed Sam the umbrella and played a self-defense demo video from the manufacturer's website on his phone. "If that isn't enough I got you these," he said, handing over wallet and ankle holsters. "Both derringers are loaded with buckshot. Just point, shoot, and run. If nobody chases you, after a few blocks you can stop and call us."

After asking Pay where to get help with his long dormant shooting skills, Sam shoved the wallet in his jacket pocket, strapped on the ankle holster, gave the booth a good whack with the umbrella, and hustled out the door, with Pay jogging along behind.

▪ ▪ ▪

At four in the morning, Pay was still yawning and chasing Sam. Uncharac-
teristically, Sam had headed straight for the financial district where he began
walking a search grid looking for his former boss.

Finally, Sam stopped at the mouth of an alley where the financial district,
Chinatown, and North Beach, all sort of merged together. "Looks like I'm not
going to find him tonight."

"Guess not."

"Any ideas where else to look?"

"You gave him a couple grand. Probably got off the streets for a while."

"I'm going to look again tonight."

"Okay. You done for now?"

"As soon as I find a cab."

▪ ▪ ▪

With Sam safely away, Pay gave Blade the hand-sign for "relax, we're off duty"
and turned up the alley towards home. Blade followed, never more than fifty-feet behind, stopping occasionally to sniff. Eyes barely open, practically out
on his feet, Pay fantasized about sleep.

Yawning, he glanced over his shoulder, checking on Blade as he turned the
corner. A minor, thoughtless movement…that saved his life.

The lead pipe that would have crushed his skull instead glanced off his
shoulder.

Pay whirled right, his elbow snapping up to shoulder level. Fueled by 285
pounds of pissed off, scared, confused anger, Pay knew anything he hit, even accidentally, would go down. The pipe wielder's nose shattered and he screamed,
before crashing to the ground. Continuing his spin, Pay glared at two assholes
with guns. The closest one held a chrome-plated pistol just inches from Pay's
chest.

Pay grinned at him the way a lioness smiles at a baby antelope separated
from the herd. Slapping the gun across the smaller man's body, he pulled him
into his chest using the goon to shield him from the second shooter.

Blade, trained to disarm, then kill, soared at the remaining gunman; 170
pounds of twisting, writhing dog—shredding muscle and crushing bones—
met his gun hand. Dropping his weapon, the thug turned to run. Blade leapt
and rode the punk to the ground, clawing at his eyes and ripping chunks of
flesh from his face.

Snapping his right hand toward the ground and ramming his left up, Pay
dislocated his goon's elbow, ripped the gun from his hand and ran him face-
first into the wall.

The guy on the ground whipped the pipe at Pay's legs. Pay jumped, but the pipe clipped his calf toppling him backwards. As he slammed his head on the wall behind him, the last thing he saw was Blade lunging for the creep's neck.

Morano was trying to sleep when his phone pinged with an urgent text from the guys following Pay. Dave had been with him since almost the beginning, a low-level, twenty-something, no brains and no potential—only slightly smarter than the rest of his team who were dumber than drunken cattle.

"Tried to take Pay out. Went bad. Heading to the warehouse." Morano debated texting back but decided this was one of those things better handled by phone. "What the fuck happened?"

"Alberto's dead. Bled out. Pay's damn dog ripped out his throat."

"Ah, shit."

"Ravon's got a broken arm and a bunch of big ass chunks missing from his face. Damn dog nearly bit off his nose. I got a dislocated elbow, a fucked-up face, and a shredded gun hand."

"Where's Pay?"

"Left him out cold on the sidewalk near Chinatown."

"What?"

"Dog's the fucking devil. We barely got away alive."

"Jesus fucking Christ. What a goddamn mess. Give Ravon whatever painkillers we've got. Give him lots of them."

■ ■ ■

On his way, Morano stopped at Café Me on Washington for food. Not because they made great breakfast sandwiches. In his mind breakfast sandwiches were bullshit. Breakfast, if you were stupid enough to be up at that time of day, should be biscuits and gravy, or corned beef hash, or some kind of truck driver mega meal full of carbs, protein, and fat. He stopped at Café Me because it was, unbelievably, one of the few places in SF not named Jack in the Box or Denny's where you could get food at five-thirty in the fucking morning. And because he needed coffee and time to think.

Morano bought the warehouse on the cheap—surrounded by decrepit sheds, a couple of tired wheelbarrows, and other castoff supplies a bankrupt contractor had left behind. The metal walls were pockmarked with rust and riddled with holes. Located in the worst part of the Richmond industrial waterfront, it had been foreclosed and empty for years. The bank was more than happy to take his low-ball cash offer.

At first it was a place where he used cash and occasionally his fists to convince call girls, dancers, and bouncers that they needed to work with him. Less than a month after the sale was complete, he'd realized that having a single location to meet with the supporting cast was stupid. It made him too easy to find.

Now he used the warehouse as a place to park his deep-sea fishing boat and to lift weights. And he used a series of flunkies to run errands, make pickups, and keep the girls in line, making sure to never let any one guy hang on too long or learn too much. He met them in bars, restaurants, and parks, contacting them via pre-paid cell phones and changing locations randomly. There was no way any of the new ones could trace anything back to him.

But Dave was his first hire. And he'd been to the warehouse.

Dave met Morano as he pulled up in his truck. "What we gonna do?"

"Load Alberto's body in the boat. Set it up to look like we're fishing. When we get out around the Farallones, we'll toss him overboard. Lots of great whites out there. They'll like him."

"What about Ravon?"

"Bring him along. Keep him doped up. After we get rid of Alberto we can get him some help."

One glance and Brooke knew Pay'd had a rough night. Because he seldom slept in the big green chair, and because Blade lay beside it, sniffing Pay and looking worried. Normally he'd have greeted her at the front door.

Pay's calf sat on a blue rubber ice bag. His head rested on a second bag and a bottle of Wild Turkey was on the end table next to his hand. She fingered the ice bags. *Room temperature. He'd been there a while.*

Brooke refilled the bags and gently slid them back in place.

Pay moaned but didn't waken.

She'd been with the team long enough to know Pay was tough. And also to know that if he believed he had suffered a serious injury he wouldn't have opted for ice therapy. The team had several medical professionals, all past clients, who would provide painkillers, first aid, and even outpatient surgery without dragging the police into things that were better left in the shadows.

Settling into the chair next to Pay, she dialed his favorite MD. "At the moment he's asleep. There are fresh scabs on his jaw, along with bruises and scratches on his hands."

She could hear his frown through the phone. It wasn't Doc's first Revenge Team phone call. "How's his pulse?"

Brooke reached over and felt Pay's wrist. "Ninety-one and steady."

"If you can keep the big guy off the bourbon, that would be good."

"Yeah right. If I could do that, the President would be calling me for advice. You know Wild Turkey is his 'go to' painkiller of choice. That, and beer, and whatever OTC pain relievers are handy."

"Jesus! How many times have I got to tell him those things don't go at all well with possible concussions or internal bleeding?"

"What's that saying about teaching a pig to sing? Doc, what's done is done.

Is there anything I can do right now?"

"If he starts vomiting or his pulse kicks up, text 9-1-1 to my cell and I'll be there stat. If I don't hear from you before, I'll be there by lunch."

"I'll order in. You still hooked on Wimpy's black-and-blue burger, extra blue?"

"Medium rare with onion rings. Couple of those and I might forget to send you a bill."

They both laughed at the ridiculous thought that his visit would result in paperwork of any kind.

24

Halfway to the Farallones, Morano decided he was going to toss both Alberto and Ravon to the sharks. Alberto cause he was dead, and Ravon because he was a whiny piece of shit who was going to need real medical help from a real doctor. That left him wondering what to do with Dave who could connect him to the warehouse and a dead body.

A six-foot swell appeared out of the fog, and Morano adjusted his line to take the wave head-on. Beside him, huddled shivering in the passenger seat, nostrils and lips twitching, eyes blood shot, skin greenish where it wasn't covered with purple bruises from Pay slamming him into a wall, Dave looked worse than Alberto.

"Feel like shit."

"Almost there. Rides smoother on the way back. How's Ravon?"

"Curled in a ball down there in the cabin, crying and moaning."

"You should take some Oxy, it'll help with the pain. Give the rest to Ravon. Don't want him hurting. I'll get more when we get back."

With fog making line of sight navigation impossible, Morano watched the GPS. He wanted to stay far enough from the islands that there was no chance the bodies would wash up on shore. Although he wasn't really too concerned. There were more great white sharks around the Farallones than any other area in the world, outside of South Africa. And the breakers in the area had been described as 'trying to swim in a turbo-powered washing machine full of boulders.'

■ ■ ■

Twenty minutes later, fog coating everything, Morano throttled back and yelled for Dave to bring Ravon on deck. He then checked to make sure the forty-five pound Olympic barbell plate Dave had hung from Alberto's ankles was secure—wired, roped, and duct taped as he'd directed.

Dave bent and grabbed Alberto's collar with his good hand. "That stupid fucker Ravon took eight Oxy 80s. He's barely breathing. I left him down there."

Morano grabbed the rope around Alberto's ankles in one hand, the weight in the other, and hurled both over the side, hoping the momentum would yank Dave overboard and save him a decision. Dave yelped, as Alberto's corpse leapt from his grasp, sailed over the gunwale, splashed into the whitecaps, and disappeared.

"Let's get Ravon up here. Fresh air might be good for him."

Morano squeezed his bulk down the narrow ladder into the cabin. Bending over, he did a quick feel for a pulse. *Eight greenies could stop a rhino.*

Feeling a thready pulse, Morano slapped him hard on the forehead—right-left-right. No response. Not even a whimper.

He yelled up to Dave. "Shit. He's dead. Oxy must have got him." Morano figured it would be better if Dave thought they were tossing a dead guy overboard. Morano pulled Ravon over his shoulder, turned, took two quick, jerky steps, and pinned his body against the ladder. Shoving Ravon's arms overhead, Morano yelled, "Pull hard on three."

Morano squatted and took several fast, deep breaths. "One, two, three." He exploded upward. Ravon's not-yet-dead body shot through the narrow door, smashing into Dave, who flailed backwards, out of sight. Morano heard a thud and a splash, followed by Dave screaming, "Help! I can't swim. Help!"

Lumbering up the short cabin ladder, Morano glanced to port and saw Dave floundering. Chucking Ravon over the starboard side into the waves, Morano pulled out his forty-five but when he turned to put Dave out of his misery he had already slipped below the surface.

Morano jammed down the throttle hard and roared away. Glad to be rid of the three losers, he was looking forward to killing Pay himself.

25

The gun shop was about what Richard expected; a bland cement building with two windows in front and a small sign. The low profile was probably smart. Liberal San Franciscan's were not likely to welcome a gun range in their neighborhood.

He took a deep breath, examined his shaking fingers, pushed the key fob to lock the door on his rental car, and headed inside. Pulling open the door decorated with police decals from nearby cities and a small sticker of a smoking gun that read: 'These Premises Protected by Smith & Wesson'—the first thing he noticed was the smell. Evidently gunpowder smelled a lot like asparagus-scented urine.

The left wall was filled with glass showcases displaying pistols surrounded by police supplies: Tasers, batons, combat knives, and other special equipment. On the right, were rifles and hunting supplies: camo outfits, waders, and various kinds of animal urines.

Over the central counter a small sign read, "Rentals," with the glass case under the sign holding a small selection of pistols. Security cameras mounted near the ceiling monitored the floor from all four corners.

The two guys closest to Richard appeared to be off-duty policeman. Fit, with close-cropped hair and eyes that briefly scanned Richard before refocusing their attention on a group near the pistols. They were thugs with bloody dagger prison tattoos, shaved heads, and do-rags offsetting straggly facial hair. Each group watched the other while pretending not to.

One of the counter guys, name tag 'Matt,' pointed at Richard. "Come on back," and waved him toward the range entry. Medium tall and plump, with silver hair and a lush white beard, Matt looked—except for the pistol in his hand—like he could play Santa in the community Christmas play.

"Before we get started. I have a few questions."

"Sure, what?"

"What do you know about this Pay Back guy? Can he help me?"

"Never met him. But his money's real. A few times a year I get a call. This voice snarls— 'I got a new one for you. Teach 'em how to shoot.' The next day a courier shows up with cash."

"How come you've never met him?"

"Because he doesn't need or want to meet me. My guess is a lot of what he does is illegal." Matt slid a magazine into a dull gray metallic pistol and racked the slide.

"And you don't care?"

"Nope. Not my issue. I just teach people to shoot."

"What if they go out and kill someone?"

"Always possible. But doubtful. Not the kind of people he sends me."

"What kind of people is that?"

"Pay sends me victims."

"Victims?"

"Mostly guys like you. Occasionally a woman. Pay doesn't send me any 250-pound bikers or Green Berets."

"What do you mean like me?"

"Mostly quiet, non-violent types. No one he sends me is your typical gun store customer. After the first few, I figured out they all wanted some kind of help; help they weren't going to get from the police. What's he doing for you?"

Richard shook his head and looked away. "That's a long story. Maybe after the lesson."

"You're just like the others, tight-lipped. Now, I need to know, have you ever shot a gun before?"

"Sure I have. Why?"

"Most people Pay sends here haven't. And most guys who walk in the front door with an S&W Air Weight in a shoulder holster don't carry it unloaded. So, I'll ask you again, have you ever shot a gun?"

"Just a cap gun, a super soaker, and my neighbor Timmy's BB gun."

"A plain old 'no' would have sufficed." Matt paused and looked Richard directly in the eyes. "The hardest part about using a gun is making up your mind you intend to kill someone. Never, ever, draw a gun and point it at anyone you aren't going to kill. If you pull out a pistol to scare some gangbanger or drugged out burglar, you might get away with it. But if you pull one on a professional or someone with military training and don't pull the trigger right then, they will. One moment's hesitation and 'bang,' your corpse is the lead on tonight's news.

"Here's your second lesson. If you point a weapon at me, even accidentally, I'll break your finger when I take it away from you. And I won't ask first. So don't point it at me. Got it? Now, do you think you can stop your hands shaking long enough to load the one in your holster?"

"I don't know. This whole thing is scary."

"Okay." Matt rolled his eyes. "Let's start with a little breath control. Close your eyes and take three deep breaths. You need to be calm to shoot accurately, and holding your breath makes everything worse. Deep breathing makes it better. Good. Now do it again. Okay, open your eyes and look at your hands."

"They're not shaking so much."

"Still too much, but better." Matt loaded Richard's revolver and gave a running description of the gun. "Smith & Wesson Air Weight titanium with the two-inch barrel. I'm loading it with the .38 Special Plus P load. Almost the stopping power of a .357 magnum. A good choice for you."

"It looks awfully small to me."

"It is. Makes it easy to carry."

Matt used the control wire to move the target closer. Richard stared at a life-size, full-color picture of Osama Bin Laden holding a .44 Magnum Desert Eagle.

"How far away is that?"

"Thirty feet."

"You don't have to move it any closer. Even a blind man could hit that."

"Wanna bet? Fifty bucks says you don't hit the Bin Laden with your first shot."

"It may be my first time, but I think anybody could do that."

"Put your money where your mouth is." Matt put a fifty on the counter.

Richard pulled three tens and a twenty from his wallet. Matt handed him a headset. "Hearing protection."

Richard slipped the big, gray plastic cups over his ears, as Matt put the gun on the shooting counter that separated them from the range. Pointing at the target, he shouted, "When you're ready, pick up the gun and go for it."

Richard stared at the gun like it was a cobra. "Don't I get a practice shot first?"

"Nope. That's not the bet. You think it's so easy. Go for it."

Ignoring Matt's initial suggestion that he hold the small pistol with two hands, Richard held it up with his right hand and took a deep breath. Carefully aiming at the target, he pulled the trigger.

BOOM!

His hand jerked towards the ceiling, like it was controlled by a puppeteer on speed. He opened his eyes. God, the noise!

Matt folded the cash into his pocket. "Congrats. You hit squat. Want to go double or nothin?"

"Uh, no."

"Okay. Let's get started."

Matt taught what Richard decided was the Zen approach to shooting.

"Hold the gun firmly but not too tightly. Trust your hands; your hands know what they need to do. Your hands are smart. Thinking doesn't help you shoot. When it comes to shooting, your brain is dumb. Dumb. Dumb. Dumb."

Thirty minutes later Richard discovered with careful concentration he could breathe deeply and shoot without jerking the trigger. But he was still having trouble keeping his eyes open. In the last batch of bullets, he'd barely grazed Osama.

Now, he had one last bullet. And despite Matt's advice to aim at central body mass he was determined to shoot Bin Laden right between the eyes. It was his final shot and he really wanted to score. One deep breath, another, a third. He emptied his mind and concentrated on squeezing slow.

BAM! Richard opened his eyes and saw a hole right where Osama's nose had been.

Matt grinned. "Good shot. Always good to end on a high note. You did okay today. You think too much and trust your hands too little. But you'll get there."

26

Doc was finishing lunch when Chase arrived. "Ah, damn. Wimpy's Black-and-Blue? I don't suppose you've got one of those for me?" Smiling, Doc drained the last of his no-alcohol beer. "Just finished my second. Was thinking about a nap."

"What's with the near beer stuff? You take the pledge?" Chase laughed.

"Nah, I'm on call this afternoon."

"How's Pay?"

"Asleep right now. He's been through worse. My examination probably took longer and hurt more than whatever happened to him. Biggest injuries are a bone bruise to the skull and a painful, but non-threatening one on the calf."

Chase groaned. "Any permanent damage?"

"I can't tell for sure without an MRI. Maybe a minor concussion. There's minimal swelling. Everything else is incidental. Painful, but incidental."

"Any idea what happened?"

"He talked with Brooke before I got here. Best if you ask her; I'd just as soon not know."

Doc's iPhone made a siren noise. "Ah, crap. That's the hospital's emergency notification system. Gotta go." He grabbed his backpack of medical supplies and ran out the door yelling, "I left a few days' worth of Lortab pills for when he wakes up. Tell him, no booze with the pills for at least two days—three would be better."

Chase laughed and put the bottle of pills with the rest of the team's emergency medical supplies, absolutely sure that Pay would never use them.

When a case got really dangerous, Pay had a recurring series of nightmares. He'd met a "dream therapist" once who said lots of people had stress dreams. Ones where they dove into a swimming pool from the high board, only to have the water suddenly disappear so they either crashed into the pool bottom or were sucked down the drain, were common. In another popular one, you arrive for an important school test wearing only your underwear.

Pay would have been delighted if his dreams were so benign.

In one, he was chased through dark, deserted streets by a pack of Hells Angels riding hideous orange Barcaloungers which had somehow been turned into three wheeled, turbo-charged choppers. Racing through town on his Goldwing, barely keeping ahead of the pack, his motorcycle slipped on rain slicked cable car tracks and crashed. The Angels beat him for hours.

Then, their leader pulled out a big, foul smelling cigar...and an even bigger knife.

He lit the stogie and told his henchman to, "Haul his ass up against that telephone pole." Pay was forced to hug the pole, hands overlapping, while the leader grinned around his cigar and slammed his knife through both of Pay's hands, pinning him to the pole. That's when Pay screamed awake, heart pounding, teeth clenched, jaw muscles cramping, dripping in sweat, knowing there would be no more sleep that night.

He'd have been glad if that was his only recurring dream. The worst was the one where the team began to doubt him.

First, they talked among themselves, worried about the way he was acting. None of them could pinpoint anything wrong, but they avoided him whenever possible and agreed he'd been acting strange. Then, Jon D would pick up a gun, spin the cylinder, and say: "If he were a horse, the trainer would say, he's off his feed."

The end was the worst and it was always the same. The team would be attacked by an unnamable horror. "Shoot. Shoot. Shoot," Pay would scream. Then there was a stumbling hesitation where the team members decided whether or not to follow him.

Everyone ended up dead. Everyone, except him. Pay worried one day…that dream would come true.

"**B**etween the shot Doc gave him, the beating, and his self-medication, Pay's pretty much out of it." Brooke looked up from her paperwork. "He remembers walking home through Chinatown and getting mugged. The last thing he remembers is Blade hauling some guy off him."

"One of the best street fighters in the world and a self-defense expert got mugged in his own backyard? Going to be real hard for him to live that one down." If it had happened to anyone else, the irony would have Chase rolling with laughter. "How'd he get home?"

"Says he limped."

"Could it be related to Sam?"

"Sam said everything was fine when he and Pay split up."

"Any chance it was the guy who beat up Mary Ellen?"

"I thought about that. But I don't think so. Richard said that guy was a huge, fat man. Pay didn't remember anything like that."

"Anything taken?"

"Nothing, and he had more than five thousand dollars in his money clip." Brooke smiled wistfully. "You know what he says."

"'If the shit hits the fan you don't want to have to go looking for an ATM.' Are the cops involved?"

"Haven't heard from them."

"Guess Blade saved Pay's ass."

"It certainly looks like it."

"Jon D and I'll see what we can do about finding some badly mauled punks. If Blade got a hold of them they're going to need serious medical attention."

"Or caskets."

I t had taken Morano almost a year to figure out how to get out of Pelican Bay. It wasn't a new idea that finally got him out—just a twist on something that had been done before.

Douglas, the ancient trustee who snuck Morano extra library materials in exchange for protection, brought him a new Time magazine.

"Anything good?"

"Other than the article about Operation Midnight Climax and the centerfold of Halle Berry doin' Jennifer Aniston, not much," Doug chuckled.

"Operation Midnight Climax sounds like it would be about them doing it."

"Nope. It's about a bunch of my old government coworkers doing shit. Worse shit than the stuff I'm in here for."

Morano'd heard about Dougy's "days" as a forensic accountant with the FBI and his nights washing money for a Miami drug ring, and he didn't need to hear it again. But prison could be a lonely place. "So…Operation Climax?"

"Back in the 50s and 60s the CIA had safe houses in New York, San Francisco, and Marin."

"So? CIA's always had to hide rats."

"Places weren't for informants. CIA used 'em to test LSD on USA citizens. Even dosed some FBI agents."

"Why?

"Article says the official purpose was to test the effects of mind-control drugs on non-consenting individuals, but who the hell knows? CIA in the 60s? Nobody was watching that hen house. Your elected officials were too busy using the FBI and CIA to spy on each other and everyone else. Shit. As long as J. Edgar wasn't accusing you of being a commie or a fag or smoking marijuana, you were golden. Who the hell cared about a CIA safe house full of hookers?"

"Hookers, too?"

"Article says they operated three deluxe bordellos in the Bay Area complete with government paid whores and acid-laced cocktails."

"No shit?"

"Yep. Your tax dollars at work. The Telegraph Hill operation supposedly had panoramic water views, one-way mirrors, and no-cost, acid-free martinis for the FBI agents working the covert video recording equipment."

"What?"

"FBI guys apparently like to get drunk and watch ho's fuck people."

"Sounds just like you, old man."

"You telling me you wouldn't give me ten grand for a martini and a hooker right now?"

"Aw, get out of here." Morano rolled over on his bunk and began to read.

■ ■ ■

In the end, it had turned out Dougy wasn't making it up. Government paid prostitutes had lured carefully selected men to a penthouse apartment at two-twenty-five Chestnut, in San Francisco's upscale Telegraph Hill neighbor-hood—just a short taxi ride from North Beach's rowdy nightlife. The suite's walls were adorned with photographs of tortured women in bondage, and provocative posters from French artist Henri de Toulouse-Lautrec.

Once there, the unsuspecting johns—selected because they would likely be too embarrassed to go public for fear of ridicule and exposure—were served those acid-laced cocktails while agents swilling martinis monitored video equipment and watched the action from behind a one-way mirror.

Later the CIA would say that the program led to many key operational tech-niques, including useful research about the use of sexual blackmail, improve-ments in surveillance technology, and possible benefits of using mind-altering drugs in field operations. Two weeks after Morano had finished researching Operation Midnight Climax, his lawyer delivered a sealed letter to Homeland Security. The envelope contained a proposal offering Morano's services to fight domestic terrorism. It suggested taking advantage of an unexploited terrorist practice: male suicide bombers were often treated to a celebration at a topless bar or brothel a few nights before a Semtex loaded vest was strapped to their chests.

In the letter, Morano proposed installing covert video recorders with facial recognition in San Francisco's "Adult Establishments" to watch for rag heads. He'd also incentivize doormen, bouncers, club security, and dancers to report any suspicious activities.

The idea was simple. Identify 'about to die' terrorists so the government could haul them off to Guantanamo, or some other dungeon for fresh water facials before they screamed Allah Ahkbar and rocketed themselves to a date with ninety virgins. And it was none of HLS's fucking business if he used the same network to fish for marks he could bleed with Monster's video blackmail scam.

One month after Homeland received Morano's proposal, he received a formal letter. Three crisp pages of bureaucratic legalese that essentially said, "No fucking way."

Apparently, covert facial recognition video of upstanding citizens getting lap dances was so odious, no government bureau would officially touch it. But the idea was clearly good, and Morano wasn't surprised when, a week later, Dougy delivered a Newsweek with a flimsy off-white envelope tucked inside. The single sheet looked like a ransom note—the letters cut from a magazine and pasted to the page: "You will be released on Mon. Go to Elk Hotel SF. Paid room waiting."

At the hotel he was handed a key, and an envelope containing a contract that said he would provide anti-terrorist activities as agreed. Such activities were to be limited to potential terrorists, and non-violent in nature. Nowhere on the "agreement" did it indicate who he worked for.

Per the accompanying instructions he signed the agreement with an illegible scrawl, licked closed the pre-stamped, pre-addressed envelope going to Memphis, and waited for the next contact. Three days later he received a box with fifty grand in small bills and another ransom demand-style note.

"More $$ if u prove this works." It ended with a phone number he was required to report to every day. Usually all he got was a message machine that said, "Leave your message at the beep. Call this new number tomorrow." Not only did the number changed daily, so did the voice on the machine.

For two years, from an encrypted desk phone in his warehouse, Morano had made his nightly calls, providing information about what appeared to be rag head nut cases. On the side, he quietly ran a blackmail operation that was bringing in cash faster than a stable of gorgeous, horny, bisexual whores.

At two AM Tuesday, Morano made his call for the day. "No towel heads." He slid his thumb over to punch the disconnect button, but got a surprise when a live person picked up.

"Your operation has helped prevent several significant terrorist incidents. Management wants you to expand the program to New York."

"Fuck 'em."

"Wrong response. Stupid, too. My boss's boss could order an operator at the U.S. Army's Nevada drone facility to fly an electronic butterfly in your bedroom window, spray a fast-dissolving, quick-killing gas on you while you sleep, and replace you with an even bigger asshole by midnight tomorrow."

"Gonna cost."

"They thought you'd say that. Here's the response I was told to give you, and I quote: 'Fuck you. Use the money from your unauthorized activities.'"

That was the moment when he realized that in prison he hadn't been anyone's bitch. Now, he was a government whore.

Pay and Chase were deep in the chaos that was Mary Ellen's studio apartment. Mounds of paper, medical books, and magazines overwhelmed the desk, spilling onto a TV tray. Pay sat in the desk chair, bruised calf elevated on an open drawer, deciding what to do next. Examining every piece of paper, one at a time, would take the rest of his friggin life. Or he could douse the whole mess in lighter fluid and toss a match.

On hands and knees in the sleeping alcove, Chase was rooting around under the queen-sized bed looking for anything that might help them figure out who mugged Mary Ellen. So far he'd discovered paperback romance novels, old issues of Cosmo, wadded up tissues, and three boxes of tampons. Pulling his hand out from under the bed, he found a lacy, lavender bra hooked on his index finger. It looked dainty and out of place in his huge mitt. Shrugging, he tossed it in the general direction of the closet. "Has this Richard guy paid us yet?"

"Five hundred for the gun and lessons. Haven't discussed the rest yet."

Chase groaned and stretched, wind milling both arms overhead. Even kneeling, at full extension his hands almost hit the ceiling fan. "You sure we shouldn't get paid before we start searching?"

"Ah, you know me. Better if he pays us, but if everything keeps looking legit we're gonna take the case whether he can pay us or not."

"Yeah, I know. If he can't pay us we always end up at your version of that convicted felons' line. What is it? Oh yeah— 'A man with a gun should never be hungry or broke.'"

"If he can't pay, we'll take whatever we can from the bad guys."

"Like Robin Hood."

"Exactly."

Chase blew a cloud of dust off the nightstand. "Thought women were supposed to be the neater sex. You know…take care of the home, clean, organize stuff." Glancing at the clothes spilling haphazardly out of the closet, and a dresser with drawers stuffed so full that two of the three would never close, he sighed. "This could take forever."

Pay laughed. "Wanna trade? You know how I feel about paperwork."

"Oh, hell no." Chase scanned the tower of paper. "Fire Marshall sees this place he's going to declare it a hazard."

"Isn't as bad as the frat house I lived in. No moldy pizza crusts. No rats. What do you want to do with the laptop?" Computers were always left to either Chase or Jon D.

"Jon D's got time on his hands. I thought we'd give it to him."

"Okay." Pay yanked the power cable from the wall sending a stream of paper crashing to the floor, uncovering a small pink notebook with a drawing of a rose on the cover. A cute little padlock hung from a tab on the front. Pay snapped the lock open with his fingers and scanned the first few pages. "Diary. Looks pretty up to date." He tossed it on top of the laptop. "I'll give it to Brooke."

Chase finally gave up feeling around the mattress edges and flipped the mattress against the wall. "Well, lookee here…old mail and a thumb drive."

"Give that stuff to Amy." Pay looked at his Tag Heuer. "We've been here almost an hour. Could spend another month just on this paper. Let's do a quickie on the bath and then take whatever we can carry to some place where the police aren't going to bust us for burglary."

"What about Richard Johnson's place?"

"I'm hungry. And thirsty. Let's drop this stuff in the car, get some food, and then search Richard's place."

"You worried the cops might find this stuff in my Bugatti?" asked Chase.

"Naw. Takes a pretty good reason for a cop to search a rich guy's car."

"Being black, my experience is a little different."

"Can't tell you're black if the car's empty."

"Okay. Rock-Paper-Scissors for the lunch check?"

"Why not?" Pay laughed. "I gotta win one of these days, don't I?"

▪ ▪ ▪

Lunch was broiled fresh halibut, steamed vegetables, and a King Estate Pinot Gris for Chase; two large meatball subs extra cheese, extra peppers, extra sauce, and two creamy pints of Harp draft to wash it down for Pay.

"Anything you want me to do about the guys who mugged you?" Chase had searched the area where Pay was attacked, but all he'd found were blood stains and a cheap Saturday night special. "Kinda surprised Blade didn't kill at least one of them."

"Probably too busy protecting me."

"When are we going to go after those guys?"

"On this leg I'd have a hard time catching them. Have Jon D keep on the cops and the hospitals. When he gets a lead you and I can decide what to do."

"Not like you to leave guys like that walking around."

"Don't think any of them are going to be walking much. Pretty sure I broke one guys face. Fucked up the other guy. Plus, the damage Blade did."

"What if I see a dog bitten scumbag or two when I'm out walking with Sam?"

"Make sure Sam's safe, and then do whatever you need to do to convince the little bastards to give up their life of crime." Pay laughed.

"Break their trigger fingers? Their necks? Give me a little help here."

"Break their collarbones so they can't wipe their own asses. Kick 'em in the nuts till your foot gets sore. Break a bunch of ribs and maybe a leg or two. I find 'em, I'm going to do to them what they were going to do to me. But I'm not going to ask you to do my killing for me."

Chase ordered a non-fat cappuccino sweetened with Splenda for desert. Pay got a Godiva chocolate brownie and a double espresso, no sugar.

After Rock-Paper-Scissors, Pay pulled a hundred-dollar bill from his money clip and set it on the tray, sipping the dregs of foam off his second espresso.

"Why do you do that?" asked Chase.

"What?"

"Drink espresso black. No sugar, yuck." Chase gagged at the thought.

"Gotta cut calories where you can."

"Could have skipped the brownie."

"Mom always said it isn't a meal without dessert."

"Could have skipped the extra cheese, or the extra sauce, or the entire second sub. Could have even skipped the Harps."

Pay gasped in mock terror. "Skip the Harps? Skip the Harps? Thought I was being good only having two."

"You saved about fifteen calories by not putting sugar in your espresso. Then added about two or three thousand between the cheese, the extra sub, and the beer."

"What are you, the black Richard Simmons? Give me a break." Pay grabbed his change and they headed out.

31

After lunch, Pay decided it was time to call Richard. "Hello, Richard."

"Hello, mister…uh, Pay."

"Matt says you made it to the range."

"Guess I did all right. Shooting's harder than it looks."

"Gets worse when the targets shoot back. We searched Mary Ellen's studio. Got her diary, laptop, a couple of USB drives. It will take a while to go through everything. We also searched your apartment."

Pay paused, waiting for the panicked intake of breath he was expecting.

Richard's whine started up, right on cue, and it all came out in one continuous rush. "You what? You searched my house? Why did you do that? Don't you trust me? Why didn't you ask? Why my house? I mean, it is my house. A man's house is his castle." Richard took a series of shallow, rapid breaths.

"Richard, chill. Slow down. Slow, deep breaths; slow, deep breaths. In slow. Hold."

"What do you mean you searched my house? Why? Why would you do that? I don't understand." His voice had become a little more controlled, but he was still reeling.

"Too fast. You'll get dizzy, Richard."

Pay heard a slow, deep breath; then a second. Just as he thought things might be calming down, Richard's whining started back up.

"What were you thinking? Searching my house? It's my house. I've got private stuff in there."

"Richard, you gonna get all pissed off every time I tell you something?"

But Richard kept right on whining—each time just a little bit louder.

Pay thought he might be growing a pair. Taking a first tiny step towards manhood.

"You searched my house. Without my permission."

"Shut up and listen." Pay'd had it. "Who do you think you hired here? A new accountant or something? It isn't like you hired Batman and Robin, either. I'm no freakin consultant you tell what to do. I do what I do. I don't ask anyone's permission." He could tell Richard was getting ready to whine some more. "Take a deep breath. I'm going to explain this to you. One time. You still have a problem after that, you can fire me."

The other end of the line grew quiet.

"I had to know you were real. The team has lots of enemies. You could be a plant or a setup. And you might not even know it. You might be the nicest guy in the world. Hell, you could be Jesus, Mary, and Joseph all rolled into one. In my world you only trust people once you have proof. The team and I could wind up in jail or dead."

"You could have just asked me what you want to know."

"People lie. I can't take that risk."

"Okay. I'm sorry. So how is my place?"

"The good news is the front door still locks. Police released the crime scene. You can go back if you want."

"I'm not sure I'll ever be able to go back there. I'm pretty sure I'd be too scared."

"That'll fade. Stuff we teach you will help. Give it a while. Place is a wreck. Fingerprint powder, yellow tape, everything turned upside down. Lots of dried blood."

"No."

"Yeah. We're still searching through the stuff we took from Mary Ellen's. Later today, I'll talk to the cops and see what they can tell me about any progress they've made."

"Hey, I know their names."

"They're out of it now. Case has been given to the inspectors."

"Inspectors?"

"That's what they call a detective in San Francisco."

"What happens next?"

"The team finishes looking through Mary Ellen's stuff and talks to the cops. You keep visiting the girl. We need to know as soon as she regains consciousness."

"Last time I went to the hospital they wouldn't let me in."

"I've got a friend there. Mary Ellen's in room five twelve. Just dress nice and act like you belong there."

"It doesn't seem like I'm doing enough."

"Stop by Mary Ellen's twice a day and keep working on the shooting. It'll get busy and bloody soon enough."

32

Tuesday was a typical workday for Morano. It started about eleven AM with calls from greedy whores, texts from whiny pole sliders, and sleazy stupid crooks spewing mounds of bullshit trying to wheedle him out of a few dead presidents, drugs, or a freebie with one of the hookers. Stuff that went with the life. The kind of street thugs and sex workers he used were long on schemes but short on work ethic and brains.

After a late lunch, he took a long nap. Since his business mostly happened at night he found a two or three-hour snooze helped keep him sharp during working hours.

After his siesta he headed over to the warehouse.

When Morano arrived, the sliding entry door was locked, but he could hear the whine of a treadmill inside. Which was good, because Morano's spotter was paid to be there every day, except Sunday, from three PM until Morano either called to say he wasn't coming or showed up to work out. Morano pressed his thumb against the security scanner and the door slid open.

The current flunky called himself a personal trainer, but Morano wasn't interested in being trained. He never bothered to learn any of the guys' names, just called them all Fitness. This Fitness was an actor wanna be—short, dyed blond flat top, unnaturally white teeth, and a diamond stud in his left ear. Wearing black Lycra shorts under cut-off, gray Nike sweats, he was running madly on the elliptical machine—full out, full bore, at full resistance. Sweat dripped down his face in streams. Morano thought the guy looked like he'd been running for hours and could go for another two or three without taking a break.

As soon as he noticed Morano, Fitness jumped off the machine. "Like to join me in some cardio today, Mr. Morano? It's very important for your heart."

Morano cut him off before he had to hear any more. "Last time I'm gonna tell you. Sissy's go for that cardio crap; I'm here to lift. Big iron. You're here to spot me and to make sure nothing happens while I do. Now shut up and load the bar."

Morano had never needed a spotter, but in prison he'd watched a lifer bench press 615 pounds. Close to a world record for a guy that size and a lot of weight, for sure, but the dude had lifted that much hundreds of times.

The guy sat on the bench focusing, huffing air in and out fast, doing the things you had to do to get your mind and body ready to lift a huge weight. He'd tightened his weight belt, rolled back on the bench, squirmed under the bar, huffed out some more air, and pushed the Olympic bar up off the black metal stand.

Morano was taking abuse from a guard when the guy screamed. It was a sound Morano hoped to never make himself. The guy's pectoral muscle had torn off his breastbone and rolled all the way up his chest into his deltoid. Morano hadn't heard pain like that since he'd gut-shot a wild boar.

The bar crashed down, crushing the guy between it and the bench. He'd have died if a couple of prisoners hadn't snatched the weight off him.

Prison docs patched up the guy's broken ribs and dealt with his collapsed lung. The prisoners guessed the guy had a congenital defect or small tear of some kind. Sort of a 'when it's your time, it's your time' thing.

It was nothing to Morano, just meant there was another guy on the wing he didn't have to worry about. And it meant he never lifted heavy without a spotter again.

Fitness loaded the bar up with two forty-five-pound plates on each side. With the bar, but without the safety collars which Morano never used, it weighed about 225 pounds—his beginning weight.

Morano eased himself back on the bench and slid under the bar with the weight belt loosely buckled around his waist Pushing the bar off the stand, checking to see that Fitness was paying attention, Morano did a quick twenty reps to warm up. Then, he slid out from under the bar, waved at Fitness, and sipped ice water from a bottle sitting on the floor next to the bench. He'd barely broken a sweat.

Fitness added a forty-five-pound plate to each end of the bar, moving things up to just over 300 pounds. For the next half hour Morano moved up in slow sets of six repetitions, gradually adding weight to the bar and alternately quenching his thirst with ice water or a protein drink.

By the end of his routine, everything around him was drenched in sweat, even though between sets Fitness's job—in addition to making sure that the ice water and protein drink containers were never empty—was to wipe the sweat off everything, especially the bar and the bench. Morano didn't want to die because a bar slipped.

Chalking up his hands, Morano snugged up his weight belt and did a burnout set of twenty-five reps with five-hundred pounds. By the time he was finished with the last rep, Fitness had replaced the ice water and protein drink with a six pack of beer. Morano twisted off a cap, chugged the beer down in one swallow and growled, "Best beer of the day."

33

From the big green recliner, sore leg elevated on an ice bag, Pay eyed Chase's clothes. Black and gray cashmere pullover, bespoke overcoat, charcoal designer jeans, and leather soled Italian loafers that reflected the streetlight streaming in the second-floor window. "Little fancy for a night out with Sam?" Pay took a gulp from his drink. "Too bad I won't be able to do Sam duty for a while. Could be another month or two. Maybe three." Pay patted his bad leg and smiled like a little kid who'd just discovered a dozen homemade chocolate chip cookies in his lunch box.

Chase groaned. "You've been milking the hell out of that thing. Two days after I fucked up my leg worse than that they shot me up with cortisone and shoved me into a Lakers' game against Kobe. Went fifteen for twenty."

"Could be I want to act like the boss and let you do the scut work for a change."

"Forgot to tell you, Sam called and said he was going to go walkabout on his own for a while."

"What did his wife say? She's the one who hired us."

"She said, and I quote: 'There's no talking to the old goat when he gets like this'—anyway, he's got his own guns now."

"He had a lesson at the range. Matt said he is fully qualified and ready to go." Pay pushed himself up in the chair and groaned. "With his military background it only took him an hour or so to get comfortable again."

"It's not like he's had any trouble since we started watching him. The guns should be enough."

"Matt says he bought a folding Buck tactical knife for backup. I think maybe he's getting his manhood back."

"From the look in his eye, I think he's hoping the guys who took him will try again."

"I ever tell you my favorite fighting old man story?"

"Not that I remember."

"Couple of slimeballs case a bar in New York City. Notice an old man—gotta be pushing ninety—who closes up the place about three or four almost every morning. Guy's always carrying at least one, sometimes two or three, of those gray cash bags retailers use to make after-hour deposits. Every night he walks, alone, three blocks to the bank's night drop."

"So, the dudes wait until one night when he's got some really full bags and jump him. Right?"

"Yep. Pulled a couple of pistols, rolled stockings over their faces—the whole deal. Poked the old man in the back with the guns. Next thing they know, both of 'em were in intensive care beat all to hell. Black eyes, concussions, broken ribs, broken noses, one broken jaw, and about a dozen missing teeth."

"Sounds like they picked the wrong old man."

"Fools jumped Jack Dempsey, one of the greatest heavyweight boxers in history."

Chase grinned. "Karma can be a bitch, can't it?"

"Dempsey said it was the most fun he'd had in a long time. Here's to anyone who jumps Sam having an even worse experience." Pay took another slug from his drink and settled back into the big green chair. "Anything on that stuff we got from Mary Ellen's and Richard's?"

"We've only had them a few hours. Jon D hasn't found anything yet on the hard drive. So far, the thumb drives are just Mary Ellen dancing. But there are hundreds of hours of video. Amy's working on them, but it's going to take a while."

"So, nothing for now."

"Just one thing."

"Yeah?"

"Last thing Sam said to me before he went off on his own was he didn't want a bodyguard who had to be rescued by his pet dog."

34

Wednesday morning, Pay called Richard. "Listen, here's the deal. The most important client qualification is trainability. If you can't follow instructions, get to places on time with the cash, the gun, the ammo…then nothing else matters."

"Okay."

"There's one other thing: our clients have to have been seriously, viciously wronged. If they haven't, I don't need 'em or want 'em. We won't help some guy whose neighbor made a pass at his wife. If you can't take care of that on your own, you don't need me. You need a sex change."

Pay thought Richard had proved he was trainable. So far, he'd followed instructions. On the range he was even hitting center mass on the target some of the time.

"I think I've done well."

"You have. Now here's the rest. My team and I will teach you to protect yourself. To defend your friends. We will show you how to hurt your enemies physically, morally, emotionally, and financially. If we don't succeed, we may die. This is not a charity. We don't work for free. Your first payment to us is ten grand. After that, the fees vary depending on the costs we incur."

"That's ten thousand dollars," Richard gasped.

"I'm not finished. If we are successful, every dime will be returned to you. I will pay you back from the funds we take from your enemies, assuming they have anything of value. In this case, if we aren't successful, the finances won't matter because you and I'll probably be dead."

"Dead?" Pay could hear the quiver in Richard's voice.

"We know enough from the police reports and your apartment to be sure that whoever beat Mary Ellen was extremely violent."

"Ten grand is a lot of money."

"Proves to both of us you are seriously committed. Gives you extra motivation. The balance of the money we take from your enemies will be divided in two. My team keeps half; the remaining funds go to charity. Usually it goes to an organization that benefits victims of violent crimes. But sometimes, we give it to other worthy organizations. You get a say in that decision."

"So, it costs me nothing?"

"Get the money together. This afternoon I'll have an associate meet you to pick it up. If you do it right, revenge won't cost you a dime. It won't make you a dime. It will make you a man." And he hung up.

Richard tried to figure out what to do. He wanted Pay's help. He needed his help. But ten thousand dollars? That was almost all the money he had.

35

"**R**ichard?"

"Yes."

"My name is Brooke, I work with Pay. Meet me at Crogan's in Oakland today at three PM. Bring the retainer and we can discuss the next steps."

■ ■ ■

Located in Oakland's upscale Montclair District, Crogan's was the kind of place where professional men drank, and where women came to meet them. Strong drinks, good basic food: Burgers. Omelets. Steak sandwiches.

At three, the bar area was empty and quiet. It was too late for lunch and too early for the after-work crowd. Richard was sitting on a stool at the bar sipping Chardonnay when a stunning redhead slid onto the stool beside him and smiled at the bartender. "Joe, I'll have what he's having."

Joe set a Cakebread Cellars Chardonnay on a white napkin in front of her, and then moved to the far end of the bar.

"Richard, I'm Brooke." She extended her hand. "Do you have something for me?"

Richard pulled a slim white envelope from his backpack and handed it to her.

Brooke glanced inside and her gaze hardened. "You'll need to take that back. No checks."

"I was worried you wouldn't take a check. But I'm afraid to walk around with ten thousand in cash."

Brooke's eyes softened with understanding. "After we're done, I'll go with you to the bank."

"Okay."

"Why don't you just let the cops handle this?"

"I've called them every day. All they ever say is stay out of it. 'This is police business.'"

"Is that the only reason you want help?"

"I'm afraid the guy who hurt us might come back and I won't know what to do."

"I'm betting there's more."

Richard closed his eyes, sighed, and ran his hands up his face, over his closed eyes. Elbows on the bar, face in his hands, he mumbled, "I'm not really sure. If this had ever happened to me before, I think I would have just let the police handle it." He raised his head and turned to Brooke, lips tight and eyes narrowed. "Now I feel like I need to do something myself."

Brooke nodded. "Let me tell you what happens next, Richard. If you were enrolling in a recreational martial arts class taught by a nice man with a black belt and a clean white uniform, this next phase would be called something politically correct like 'Self-Defense Training.'"

"That sounds good."

"But that's not what you are going to get. By now, I'm sure you've figured out we do things differently."

"That's very clear to me."

"We don't believe in self-defense. We believe in violent self-justice."

"What if I can't do it by myself?"

"Tomorrow you start your Revenge School training. The school is run by the Revenge Team. When clients need help, the team does whatever is necessary to help them succeed."

"Will I get hurt?"

"Yes."

"How badly?"

"Bruises, stitches, and broken bones mostly. I lost three teeth."

"You?"

"I was one of Pay's early clients. Before they got things smoothed out."

"Was it worth it?

"I'm not afraid anymore."

Brooke handed Richard an envelope filled with papers. "This is for you to read tonight."

"What should I do to get ready?"

"Please come to your first class wearing typical street clothes. I strongly recommend you take a couple of aspirin before you arrive and bring more with you. Do you have any questions?"

"I understand how the money works. And that I could get hurt. Which scares the crap out of me. Other than that, I'm not sure what to ask."

"We believe there are two kinds of bad guys. Most bad guys simply find it easier to be a bad guy than it is to be a good guy."

"Most?"

"The other bad guys are just plain evil."

"What do you do about them?"

"The prescription for both types is the same: instant, painful justice. Something you can't get from the police."

"Why not? Isn't justice their job?"

"Yes, but there are too many bad guys and too few cops. Plus, the police are restricted by rules that both protect us and hurt us at the same time. Rules we don't adhere to."

"I'm not sure what you mean."

"Say someone mugs you—steals your wallet, roughs you up a bit… You could probably pick him out in a line-up. But you don't know anything about him. The police will take a report, but they don't have the resources to chase all over town trying to track down an unidentified minor-league mugger."

"What about DNA and all that stuff?"

"CSI's take lots of time and big money. Time and money that has to be carefully budgeted. Violent crimes against rich or important people are the ones that get the most attention. The cops will work hard on Mary Ellen's case because it is a serious one, but they've got lots of cases. And they don't care as much as you do."

"So what do you guys do?"

"We teach people like you how to get even. Let's go back to our mugger example. With what you know right now the smart move would be to give up your wallet, take your lumps, and then call the cops."

"Hey! That's exactly what I did when a guy stole my backpack last year."

"What happened? Did they catch the guy?"

"No."

"That happens a lot."

"I saw the jerk in my neighborhood last week at Starbucks. I recognized him but he didn't seem to recognize me."

"That's because you aren't a threat to him."

"It really makes me mad that I can't do anything about it. He stole my Rolex and my Mac."

"You could call the cops, but unless you know where he lives or works, they can't do much."

"That's disappointing."

"Maybe we can work things out so you have a chance to get even."

"Really?"

"What you did was the smart move, back then. Once you've been in our program for a little while, you will have other options. Our clients wouldn't just call the cops and hope for justice. Last year you were a walking victim."

"And I'm tired of it."

"You were probably nicely dressed and not paying any attention to your surroundings. I've seen enough of you to know you're a gadget freak, so you were probably wearing those really expensive noise canceling headphones. Thief smiled and made you take 'em off, didn't he?"

"He grinned at me like I was nothing, and said, 'Give me the headphones, the backpack, and your Rolex, little man.' Boy, I really wanted to cream him. But I knew he'd beat me to a pulp if I tried."

"Were you carrying pepper spray or a knife?"

"Not where I could get to them."

"You were the perfect victim, then. Ten seconds work on you, five minutes with a fence, and your stuff becomes instant cash."

"He's still wearing my Rolex. I'd like to get it back. What could I do to get it back?"

"Nothing right now. But a few days with us and you'll never be that victim again. Even an eighty-year-old grandma who's completed our physical aggression course could do more than you did. First, she would mace the baddie with a good dose of Alaska Grizzly Bear Strength pepper spray. After he was blind and on the ground, at minimum, she'd have kicked him in the throat or the balls."

"At minimum?!"

"Fighting back tends to make you pissed off. Your hormones make you do surprising things. She might have cut him up a little bit to make sure he got the message and was easy to identify. From the cops' point of view it would be justifiable self-defense. From our point of view, it would be Karmic Justice. Grandma might call the cops; they could take it from there pretty easily. Assuming, of course, that she didn't finish things off herself."

"Finish things herself? That sounds awfully harsh."

"Guy stole from her, and he might have done worse. What would you do?"

"I'm not sure."

"You don't have to be. You just have to know that when we're done with you, you will have a number of new, aggressive options available."

"So, about the guy who stole my backpack…?"

"I'll talk to Pay and see if we can make him part of your lesson plan."

36

"**L**ocated Rock Duncan. Can't believe they let him out."
From the background noise, Pay guessed Chase was calling from his Ducati. "Nobody pressed any charges. Couldn't keep him."

"Duncan stops by Enrico's Café in North Beach before he goes to work. Gets there about six-thirty, has a couple of Johnny Walker Blacks with dinner, then walks over to Centerfolds. Even if things are busy he has plenty of time to make his eight PM shift."

"So he'll have time to talk to us?" asked Pay.

"I think we have a better chance of getting some answers at Enrico's than we do surprising him at work. Too many distractions and too much noise at Centerfolds."

"Wanna go tonight?"

"He's scheduled to work, so we're probably on. Enrico's hostess said she'll call me if he comes in."

"You sure she'll recognize him?"

"Guy goes there all the time. Plus, he's a big, muscular, sort of tubby guy with his arm in a sling. Not many of those around."

■ ■ ■

Pay picked up his cell and checked the caller ID. "Hi, Chase."

"Duncan's at Enrico's. If we get there in about half-an-hour, he'll be finishing his main course."

"I'll be across the street in twenty."

■ ■ ■

Approaching Enrico's, Pay waved at Chase and pointed to the left side of the café's patio. Chase jogged across Broadway moving nimbly through the traffic. Limping, Pay moved in on the sidewalk from the right. It was an efficient pincer movement designed to convince a target that running was not an option.

Rock must have felt pretty safe. The fool had picked a chair that faced the rear wall. Chase slid around the small table, pulled out a chair and sat while Pay stood, just slightly behind and to Chase's right, resting his weight on his good leg and wearing his most intimidating scowl. They'd done this routine countless times. Experience had proven that Chase's 'good guy,' backed up by Pay's smoldering, violence-barely-contained 'bad guy' worked best.

"I'm Chase. I assume you know my angry friend." Indicating Pay with his eyes.

Rock glanced up at Pay. "Don't know him. Know his club. One of these days I'm gonna knock the crap out of him."

"Shut the hell up." Chase shook his head in dismay. "You should be happy I didn't decide to meet you at home and let him spend twenty minutes pounding you like a tetherball."

"I got friends."

"Both of us are out of your league. And your friends' league, too." Chase reached out with a soft, almost languid touch. Half his giant right-hand forced Duncan's left hand flat on the table; the other half forced the bouncer's thumb away from his palm, over the back of his hand toward his little finger. The maneuver was simple and effective. It was a move even a martial arts expert wouldn't expect because it couldn't be taught or done by anyone without giant hands and NBA strength.

Duncan went white. Sweat poured from his forehead and he stopped breathing.

Chase let up a bit, and Duncan gulped in a breath.

"Hurts like a mother, doesn't it?" Chase nodded at Pay. "I'm every bit as sadistic as he is. But ever so much subtler."

Duncan sort of nodded and tried to pull his hand back. Smiling sadly, Chase twisted the thumb, almost gently. Duncan whimpered, sagging in the chair.

Pay watched him wilt. "You were right; you can see the manhood just leak out of them. Hard to believe all you have to do is grab his thumb and a tough guy completely collapses. I'd never have believed it if I didn't see it for myself."

Of course, he'd seen it dozens of times, but the words cemented the deal. Guys were a lot more talkative when they believed they no longer had any control. "Works so much better than when I punch 'em in the throat, jam my thumb in their eye, and squeeze their balls in my fist."

"That's because about half the time you kill them, and the other half they have trouble talking with destroyed vocal chords."

Pay glared at Duncan. "Need to know everything you can tell me about Destiny."

"Ho' shorted me."

"Let's not speak ill of the nearly dead." Chase gave Duncan's thumb a gentle tweak.

"Nearly what?" The pained, shaken look on Duncan's face would have been hard to fake.

Pay snorted. "Don't worry about the cops. They've cleared you. That broken shoulder's your alibi. Worry about us."

Chase increased the pressure on Duncan's thumb. Pay smiled when Duncan groaned.

"Somebody beat her real bad 'bout an hour after I busted you up Friday night. Couldn't have been you, but you guys were fighting about something. I need to know what."

"I set her up with a big spender and she didn't want to pay me my cut."

"Who's the big spender?"

"Destiny called him Mikey. Good looking. Expensive clothes. Throwing Benjamins around for special treatment."

Pay moved from his spot just behind Chase and sat in the chair beside Duncan, working hard not to grimace as he bent his knee. Extending his baton with a quiet click, he slid it discretely down his leg and under the table, where it gently stroked Duncan's shin. "I'm sure there's more. Lots more."

Duncan swallowed. He looked around furtively, as if expecting his friends might magically appear out of the potted fern by the grand piano.

Chase leaned into Duncan's thumb.

Pay's baton whacked his shin.

"Damn it. Okay." Duncan muttered through clenched teeth, "I pay security to make videos of some of the customers. But that's gonna cost you."

Chase twisted.

Pay bounced the baton off Duncan's shin.

Duncan blanched.

Pressing his free hand on Duncan's broken shoulder, Pay squeezed gently. "Guy's like us don't pay assholes like you. When we're done, all three of us will walk over and get copies."

"We done then?" wheezed Duncan.

"We're done when you've told us everything."

"That is everything." Duncan glanced at his thumb and jerked his shin backwards.

"That crap work with your normal marks, asshole?" Chase snorted.

Duncan shifted nervously in his seat, as Pay's baton tapped gently as a reminder.

The server walked towards them and Pay waved him off, mouthing, "Check please." He looked Duncan directly in the eyes. "It'll be over soon. As soon as we know why you're having video made of the customers."

Duncan eyes darted sideways. "I can't tell you."

Chase glanced at Duncan's hand, sighed, and then looked at Pay. "Some guys never learn. Your turn or mine?"

Pay grinned. "Yours."

"Wait. Wait. Please wait."

Pay's grin became an ear-to-ear smile. "Less than fifteen minutes and this guy's whimpering like a hamster in a pit bull cage."

"There's a guy."

"Describe him," Pay demanded.

"Big guy. Goatee. I've only seen him once."

"What's he pay you?" asked Pay.

"Guy pays me two hundred bucks for video of any high roller I can get doin' stuff with a girl. And a hundred for any Middle Eastern guys. That night all I had was the high roller with Destiny, but I never got that video to him because you busted me up. Don't really remember much else. I was pretty high. That's the only reason you could take me down."

Pay and Chase both laughed. "You high now?" asked Chase.

"No," Rock whispered.

"Listen, tough guy. I just took you down with my thumb. Broke you down like a little girl. Turned you into a stinky, flop-sweaty mess. Guess if you'd been high I could have done it with my pinky. Think about that before you decide to come after us looking to get even."

Pay broke in, "We're getting off track here. We need to find this big guy. Where's he hang? What's he look like? What's his name? We know you know him."

Rock's head looked like one of those bobble-head dolls. It swiveled from Pay to Chase and back again. He wanted to know where the pain was going to come from and how to avoid it. "Big guy. Fat. Six-foot…maybe six-one. Weighs about 450."

"He sends a delivery guy by. Only came himself once. And it's not just Centerfolds. He's offering cash and has video installed all over town."

"How'd you figure that out?"

"Nudie bar business is pretty small. Dancers, bouncers— everyone moves around."

"Anybody else know him?"

"Navarro, but I ain't seen him in weeks."

"What's the head guy look like?"

"Shaved bald, mid-thirties, gray and black goatee. His flunky usually picks up the videos, drops off some cash. If the dude is a real roller and I can get a name, address, or a phone number, I get a bonus."

Pay slammed the baton down on Duncan's instep, stopping just short of breaking bones. Simultaneously, Chase leaned over and pulled Duncan's face into his shoulder. A well-rehearsed man-hug that prevented anyone from seeing the pain on Duncan's face. It also smothered any screams.

Chase whispered in Duncan's ear, "Idiot. Guy isn't going to drop around a strip club hoping the right victim has shown up and maybe you can get his phone number. Fat guy gave you some way to get in touch with him. You give me that, and any videos from the club. If you're lucky, neither one of us sees you again."

Duncan moaned the number.

To keep the waiter from getting in the way, Pay pulled a wad of cash from Duncan's shirt pocket and carried it up to the bar where their server was waiting on a drink order. "It's all yours. Keep the change."

Bill paid, the three of them walked down Broadway toward Centerfolds. Pay limping on Duncan's right side; Chase supporting the left. Duncan moved like he couldn't walk without their help. After the crushing blow to the top of his foot, he was probably right. Pay and Chase had carefully crafted their system. When they needed to take an uncooperative person out of a bar or a party, the baton to the foot worked perfectly. If the baton was used discretely, most bystanders assumed they were just a couple of good guys helping a friend who'd had too much to drink.

The trio stumbled in the front entrance of Centerfolds. Duncan waved at the hostess. "These guys are with me. They'll only be here a minute."

Pay pushed aside the entry curtain and they walked down a short, dark entry hall.

"See that window up there?" Duncan pointed to a square, mirrored glass sliding window on the second floor. "That's security. If the regular night guy is here, he'll toss down an envelope."

The music wound down slightly between songs. Duncan hissed, "Tommy, you up there?"

"Course I am. Who'd you expect? Charlie Sheen? He's in the shower room."

"Need my stuff."

"Been waiting for you to come by. You owe me fifty."

"Yeah, yeah. I'll hit you at the end of shift."

A tatted hand slid out the window, the butt of a cigarette wedged between the second and third fingers, a sealed white envelope pinched between thumb and forefinger. "Catch."

Chase snatched it out of the air and ripped it open. "More flash drives."

Pay turned to Duncan. "That's it for now. We find out you didn't tell us something, I'm going to visit you at home without my friend. You don't want that. Trust me. He's the one who controls my leash."

They left Duncan teetering on his bad foot and headed back to HQ.

Total time in club, less than sixty seconds.

37

After their visit with Duncan, Pay headed to SFO and took an evening flight to LAX. A past client wanted to open a Revenge School branch in SoCal. Pay wasn't sure how he felt about expanding, but he was interested in hearing about any ways the Revenge Team could help more people.

Brooke, Chase, and Jon D, spent that night and all the next day going through Mary Ellen's stuff and the thumb drives from Centerfolds.

■ ■ ■

That evening, Pay called Brooke from LAX. "Got anything new on Richard's case?"

"Phone number Duncan gave us is a prepaid burner, so there's no lead there. We did find out she's only been dancing for a few months and hates it. Everything points to her dancing career being a financial necessity, nothing more. Her father died about six months ago in a car wreck. Her mother's been dead for years. Jon D dug into her financials: Dad was sending her about four grand every month. When he died, her cash flow dried up. There doesn't appear to have been any life insurance, because for the last couple of months her bank statements show an average daily balance of about two hundred bucks."

"She into something worse than dancing?"

"It's hard to tell. There's no evidence she's working as a call girl or for an escort service."

"Any of the thumb drives have anything?" Pay asked.

"We're only part way through. I'll put together an edited version of the highlights for you when you get back."

"Okay."

"Most are of girls dancing for a series of guys wearing high-end watches, titanium rings, and designer clothes. All the men were flashing lots of cash."

"Men like that typical for a place like Centerfolds?" asked Pay.

"Like I'd know? You think I'm pole dancing when I'm not here?"

Pay knew he'd stepped in it. "Thought there was, maybe…a possibility that you'd know someone who was a dancer. Or, maybe Chase or Amy had voiced an opinion."

"Chase said, and I quote: 'I've never been to a regular strip club. The NBA guys went to very high-end places with private rooms, special security, and very expensive women.'"

"I've got some experience with places like Centerfolds."

"Why doesn't that surprise me?"

Pay decided to ignore her sarcasm. "Doesn't look like a place that should be that flush. My guess is, it's a twenty-buck lap dance joint. Any 'Joe six-pack' guys on the video?"

"Yes. There's a bunch of short two to three minutes videos of normal guys."

"Anything else?"

"One of the drives is only Middle Eastern-looking men."

"Does Mary Ellen dance in any of those?"

"Not so far."

"Probably not related then."

"Likely not. But Chase and I both think there's something hinky going on there. We just can't tell what from the video."

"Maybe I should visit Duncan again? I might enjoy that. I'm not real fond of guys who beat women."

38

Early Friday morning, Pay and Chase met to go over the videos and discuss the team's potential expansion into Los Angeles. Chase nodded. "Ready to get started?"

"Sure." Pay settled into his recliner while Chase connected a laptop to the plasma.

"Drives from Mary Ellen's and Richards don't seem to be anything. We're still working on them. This is the most interesting one and it came from Centerfolds."

The video opened with a title that read; 'Myron Baker 415-555-1732. 500 California St. Suite 3500-B2.'

"Figured out how they got his info?"

"After a while he goes to the toilet and leaves his coat hanging on a hook in the booth. She finds his wallet, takes a business card, but doesn't touch the credit cards or cash."

The video started with Duncan pushing aside a curtain covering the entrance to a private dancing booth. A well-dressed mid-forties male followed him in, glancing at the burgundy velour walls and dingy red vinyl bench.

Minutes later, Mary Ellen enters; dark hair curled behind her neck and over one shoulder, the end just barely covering her right breast.

In the background, techno pop blared as the DJ exhorted the audience to "spread the love around and be sure to tip our beautiful dancers!" Thankfully, the recorder was rigged so when anyone in the booth spoke, the music faded out. Mary Ellen turned on a thousand-watt smile, aiming it at Baker. "Hi, my name's Destiny. What's yours?"

"Mike. Nice to meet you, Destiny."

Pay hit the pause button. "Started lying from the very beginning. Any idea why?"

"Nope."

On the video Destiny was helping Baker out of his overcoat. She mugged and swooned while stroking her cheek with a sleeve. "Hugo Boss cashmere. Oooh, my."

Pay shot Chase a questioning glance.

"Brooke says the coat is worth at least two grand."

Destiny smiled some more. "Mike, most guys who walk in the door want to chill. Sit back, watch the girls dance, but Rock tells me you're different."

"Tonight, I just want to party."

"Well, Mike, how about you put some money in the motor and we get started."

Baker pulled cash from his wallet. "Here's two-hundred bucks. I gave Bozo the doorman plenty to cover him and the booth. He's out getting drinks. I hope you like martinis."

Mary Ellen's back was to Baker so he didn't see her frown at the mention of martinis. "Boy, Mikey, you know how to get my attention. So, hon, what's got you so hot tonight?"

"My girlfriend's husband is waiting for me outside. And I hear he's one mean son-of-a-bitch."

"Oops!"

"Tell me about it. The only thing saving me is he's a devout Muslim."

"Leaves him between a rock and a hard place, doesn't it?"

"It's a sin for him to come in here."

"So how can I help?"

"Let's party. I'm hoping he'll get tired of standing out there in the cold and leave."

"You came to the right girl. Relaxing, drinking, and entertaining handsome men is what I'm all about."

The music wound down and the announcer wound up, to a decibel level just slightly louder than the space shuttle blasting off. "Let's hear it for Tiffany on the main stage and Brittany in the lounge room. Look at those moves. What a show! And believe it or not, gentlemen, we're just getting started. Throw some money on that stage. It's time to reward our beautiful ladies."

Mary Ellen was dancing slowly, still mostly clothed, when a male voice caused the music to mute. It was Rock. "I'm here with your Belvedere."

"Come on in."

"Here's your bottle."

Destiny grabbed the bottle and squealed, "Belvy! My favorite! I'll go get glasses." She darted through the curtain.

Baker handed Rock some cash. "Here's your hundred. I need your help with something else. When you were outside, did you see a guy in a turban hanging around?"

"I just hustled out to get your supplies."

"Trust me, there's a guy out there. He's Middle Eastern, about five-foot-ten, 150, maybe 160 pounds. Last time I saw him he was wearing a light green turban and a tan jacket. I want you to watch him and tell me when he leaves. Got it?"

Destiny entered with an ice bucket, shaker, olives, and glasses. Shoving Rock out the curtained doorway, Destiny crooked her finger at Baker. "It's Silver Bullet time! Party Time, Mikey! Party Time!"

Pay glanced at Chase. "I think we better talk to Rock about Mr. Baker. Anything else happen?"

Chase pushed the fast forward button. "She dances some, they talk a little, and both drink a bunch of martinis. You can't tell at this speed, but she's pouring herself mostly water and him one-hundred percent vodka." He pushed play and the video returned to normal speed.

Baker was loosening up. "Destiny darlin'," he slurred. Pay smiled. "Guy's on his way to stinking drunk."

"Yes, Mikey."

"Coul' you check wi' Rock an' see if the husband is still hangin' round?"

"Sure, hon. Rock is usually right out front. Just give me a minute." She picked up her skirt, buttoned her blouse, and slid out through the curtain. A few minutes later she reappeared. "I couldn't find Rock. He's probably doing rounds."

"Listen, honey. I'd love to stay here and party with you all night." Baker was still upright, but barely.

"I'd luv that, too. You're my man."

"But I'm starting to run out of cash."

Mary Ellen smiled her biggest smile; a smile that promised any man un-imagined bliss. "How about we hit the ATM?"

"In a minute. But...I'm wondering?"

"Yes, angel?"

"When it's time to go, if the husband is still hanging around, does this place have a back exit?"

"We have a side door."

"That won't work. I saw it when I was in the john. The door just opens out about twenty-feet from the main door. I'd be walking right into the guy."

"The dancers have kind of a secret exit."

"Yeah?"

"Sometimes we get creeps in here. The kind of guys who follow a girl around the club pawing at her and won't leave her alone, even when the bouncers tell him to back off. Last week a jerk jumped me coming out of the ladies room and nearly scared me to death. When something like that happens, girls sneak out the back."

"Can you get me out that way?"

"I'm not sure. The door's in the dancers' dressing room all the way at the back, hidden in one of the changing stalls."

"That shouldn't be so hard."

"No guys are allowed in the dressing room. Ever. The girls are very picky about that."

"Huh? Everyone's already seen 'em naked."

"Mikey, honey, the dressing room is the only place where we're safe from grabby bouncers and freebie-wanting owners. Even dealers and husbands can't go in there."

"Damn."

"Let me think about it a little, baby. Maybe I can figure out a way. Let's hit the ATM." Mary Ellen turned up the wattage on her smile. "Then I'll make us another marti or two."

"Okay. Hard to imagine anything better than sharing another martini with a charming, beautiful woman like you."

Chase skipped the video ahead. "Nothing much happens for a while, but near the end it gets kind of interesting."

"Honey?" Baker was stinking drunk and stumbling over even simple words.

"Yes, Mikey."

"I gotta go."

"Can't you stay a little while longer, Mikey? Puhleeeze?"

"Darling, I'm just about outta cash."

Pay looked at Chase. "Bet she drops him like a hot rock."

But he was wrong. "You're such a great guy. And you're pretty high. Stay here and hang out for a while. You'll feel better."

"Really gotta go, but not out the front door. I'm afraid of that guy."

"Maybe I can bribe the girls into letting you use the private exit. Gonna cost, though."

"How much you think?"

"It's still pretty early. Probably only three...four girls in there right now. I'd guess fifty bucks a girl. So, it'll probably take a hundred fifty, two hundred."

"Here's my last hundred."

"Sweety, that won't be enough."

"It's all I got."

"Let's hit the ATM again."

Pay grinned at Chase. "She's really working him. Think it'll actually cost her anything to sneak him out the back door?"

"I bet the other girls will settle for the last of the Belvedere."

"We maxed it out last time, babe."

Destiny giggled. Even drinking watered-down martinis, she was looking tipsy. "Oh yeah. I forgot."

"Need to get out of here."

"Maybe I can get the girls to go for a hundred and the rest of the vodka?"

"Okay. Please help me get out of here. I'm way too drunk to deal with that husband."

"He sure does want to sneak out the back door, doesn't he?" said Chase.

"Any idea why?"

"I've watched it all. Other than the husband, there isn't a clue."

"Guess we're just going to have to ask him."

"Be a good idea to talk to Rock again, too."

"Sounds like a plan to me."

39

Nine-thirty Friday morning, Richard parked near the address Brooke had given him. A mirrored front door opened onto a vestibule with two doors. The left one read 'Classes.' The right one was locked.

The door to the classes opened on a good-sized gym full of exercise equipment. There were boxing bags and weight lifting machines. Midway down the left wall was a selection of what looked like theater props: a residential front door, a car chassis, and a small kitchen. On the right wall was a rack of mannequins and three skeletons. A locked glass case displayed knives, pistols, rifles, and other weapons Richard didn't recognize.

Everything at the rear of the room was padded except the ceiling. A pit bull rested on the padded floor next to a German shepherd with a guide dog harness. In a folding chair beside the shepherd sat a middle-aged woman wearing dark glasses and shapeless gray sweats with the Revenge School logo on the chest. She was so small her feet didn't touch the floor.

The woman looked in his direction. "I'm Peggy, today's instructor. What's your name and why are you here?"

"Richard. And I'm here because Brooke and Pay told me to come."

"Welcome, Richard. It is a pleasure to meet you."

"Where are Pay and Brooke, and the rest of the students?"

"Pay and Brooke don't teach the beginner's classes."

"Why not?"

"Beginning students generally believe that big guys like Pay can easily take care of themselves. They have a hard time believing Pay would ever have trouble handling a problem."

"I guess I can see that. What about Brooke?"

"She's in charge of some of the later classes."

"Then, why you?"

"I'm a little person. I'm middle-aged. I'm a woman. And I'm legally blind. Students figure if I can use our techniques to protect myself, then they can probably use them, too."

"Okay. Where's the rest of the class?"

"We don't start until ten, so they'll be here in about twenty minutes. We wanted you here a little early."

"Why?"

"Because you are a client, not just a student. Your training will be more intensive and customized, and, depending on your own personal reaction time and skills, your experience could be more painful."

"Boy, that doesn't sound so good."

"The way I understand it, you've got some major personal challenges to overcome."

"Well, I'm not a small, legally blind, middle-aged female."

"Yes, but you've been robbed by someone you can identify and have done nothing about it."

Richard dropped his eyes and focused on his shoes. "That's true."

"But someone you know was nearly beaten to death in your home and you want to do something about that. In order to do that, we're going to have to toughen and smarten you up."

"I think I'm smart enough."

"You are probably book or business smart, but not smart in the way you need to be to protect yourself. First, we're going to teach you how to get even with the backpack thief. That won't be a problem."

"What will be a problem?"

"The risk goes up when you start dealing with violent criminals, like the one who beat up your friend. Our risk goes up, too. It's going to be a while before you are ready to take him on."

The front door swung open and a young, very slight Asian girl entered carrying a gym bag, a fistful of keys protruding from the fingers of her free hand. Her torn Levi's and dark blue sweatshirt could have come from the kid's section of Goodwill.

Four adults wearing loose clothes followed her in. Richard thought they all looked like he felt: determined, but anxious and a little scared.

The girl tossed the keys into a bowl by the door. "Hi, Peggy, who's the guy?"

"Richard, meet my assistant Amy, and the rest of your class. Our lesson will begin in about five minutes, but before we start I'd like to brief you on the rules and what to expect. We are all here for different reasons. Your personal motivations are private, so whatever brought you here is no one else's business. We strongly encourage you not to ask. People can and will share if they want to."

Richard looked around and immediately wondered what had brought the other students to this place.

Peggy picked up a hunting knife and slung it across the room where it stuck quivering in a target embedded in the wall. "You are all here because you have a strong desire to be able to protect yourself. Most of you have been wronged or fear you will be. That is all you need to know about each other."

Richard realized the cute blonde girl across the room was staring at him. He turned away and concentrated on Peggy.

Amy picked up the lecture. "Peggy is legally blind. You should have figured this out without me telling you. The dark glasses, white cane, and dog are all clues. Awareness of your surroundings is important. You will learn to watch for signs of danger and take action before you become a victim. It is important you understand our philosophy. In order to protect yourself, you need to be able to react quickly when surprised, angry, upset, scared, or injured. You can't learn to fight from lectures; you learn to win fights by fighting. We will trick you. We will torment you. We will surprise you. Fights aren't fair, and if you are to survive, we can't be either."

"Amy, has everyone signed their waivers?"

"All the paperwork is complete."

"And everyone understands that they will get hurt during this program?"

The group murmured a quiet, "Yes."

A plump brunette woman stuck her hand up. "How badly can we get hurt?"

"Hopefully nothing worse than strains and bruises. At worst, broken bones or loose teeth. So pay attention. The first step in self-defense is avoiding fights. But even with careful preparation, you can't always avoid them. And sometimes you will want to win one that you could have avoided. All fights quickly dissolve into chaos with weapons, screams, blood, and pain. You've got to learn to control your reactions in order to protect yourself. And you've got to learn to harness your inner animal to survive."

Peggy stood. "Okay, group, it's time for your first lesson. Richard, you have thirty seconds to hit me as hard as you can. If you don't hurt me in less than thirty seconds, Amy will tase you."

"But…you're blind. And a woman."

"Don't worry about me. I can take care of myself. Worry about you."

"Where do you want me to hit you?"

"Wherever you think it will do the most damage."

"Are you sure?"

"Yes, I'm sure. Twenty seconds."

"But I'll hurt you."

"It's a fight. That's the idea. One of us will surely get hurt. Your primary concern needs to be protecting yourself. Fifteen seconds." Richard stumbled into a slow circle around Peggy. It had to be some kind of a trick. They couldn't really want him to hit a blind woman.

Peggy put down her cane. Her hands were empty.

The dogs perked to attention, as Amy approached from his right waving a Taser.

Taking a shallow breath, he balled up his fist and rushed Peggy. Screams exploded from the ceiling. The German shepherd charged at Richard, with the pit bull right on its ass.

Peggy reached in her pocket and pulled out a can of pepper spray, zapping Richard's face. The shepherd crashed into his back, slamming his face into the padded floor. Tears streamed from his eyes. Blood dripped from his nose. Richard fought to stand, but with the Shepherd on his back and the pit bull tearing at his pants' cuffs, he couldn't get his feet back under him.

Peggy grabbed his hair and yanked, twisting his head up off the floor. "Finish him, Max! Finish him!"

The shepherd's teeth snapped at Richard's neck.

Richard forgot where he was—he forgot who he was. Blind rage, jump-started by massive doses of adrenaline took over. Inside him, a voice screamed, "Roll! Roll! Roll! Kill the dog. Kill it now!" Peggy danced in front of him. "KILL HIM, KILL HIM, KILL HIM!"

Richard threw a vicious elbow shot at the dog's throat. Missed. Shit. As he rolled right, the voice in his head screamed, "LEFT ARM UP! UP!" He rammed it over his head and swept Peggy off her feet, slamming her to the floor. Ha! Got the dwarf bitch!

And…Amy tasered him.

He kicked, cried, moaned, and sobbed, raging against the electricity and his own hormones. There was a loud whistle and the dogs retreated.

Peggy pushed a button on a handheld remote and the screams immediately stopped. "Class that was the end of our first lesson. You need to know that my pepper spray canister was diluted and the Taser was set on low. Richard has experienced no permanent damage. Please take a fifteen-minute break outside. When Richard's recovered, we'll discuss what we learned."

■ ■ ■

Peggy sat quietly on a bench near Richard—close enough to be reassuring, but not so close as to be threatening. And far enough away that she could protect herself if he attacked.

The next few days were going to be critical if Richard was going to make the transition from 'Richard, The Emasculated' to 'Rich' a man who could take care of himself.

Peggy rolled a bicycle water bottle across the floor toward him. "Richard, drink that. Panic and adrenaline make your thirsty." Richard struggled to his feet and lurched at her, launching a massive right hook which missed by inches. The next thing he knew, he was tottering on his knees, crying.

"Thirst is only one of the side-effects you are going to experience. Extreme stress and adrenaline really mess you up. Your emotions will be in disarray for days, and tunnel vision is common. For the next couple of days, you're not going be able to see anything that isn't right in front of you. But all that's temporary. And it's not the worst part."

Richard sank to the floor, sobbing. "God damn it! As soon as I can see again, I'm going to beat the crap out of you and that freak with the Taser. What the hell is the matter with you people? You could have killed me!"

"Yes, we could have. And whoever beat your friend Mary Ellen, would have. If you'd attacked him like you just attacked me, he'd have slammed a knife in your heart and left for lunch."

■ ■ ■

A few minutes later the shocked group returned. "Welcome back, class. Richard, what'd you learn?"

"That a Taser hurts like hell."

"Imagine if it had been set on high. Anything else?"

"I wanted to kill you."

"First thing you did after you recovered a bit was attack me again."

"I thought I was going to die. There was like…a switch in my brain. It screamed at me to 'kill, kill, kill!' It completely took over. Then, I knocked you down. Don't even know how. Still don't. But that felt good. Damn good. I just wished I'd hurt you more. And I would have. But somehow I knew I had to get the dogs first."

The man sitting next to Richard—a chubby, pony-tailed guy named Gavin, who wore a T-shirt that read, 'Vegan for Life'—moved his chair away.

"Do you still want to hurt me?"

"God help me, yes."

Amy stepped in from the corner of the room. "That's a hard thing. Richard is not the person he was minutes ago. He knows new truths. He is no longer the nice, friendly, civilized young man he believed he was. When you are about to die, cruel, violent, merciless acts are automatic. Your brain is hardwired to kill so that it can live. The realization that your brain will force you to be someone you deplore is terrifying. Knowing you are capable of killing someone will shake you to depths you cannot imagine. The flood of hormones, rage, and indiscriminate, vicious violence will never leave you. Once you've gone there, you can never go back to the person you were before. You will do, say, and think things that you would have never believed possible."

Peggy patted Richard on the shoulder. "Our goal is to teach you quickly how to win a fight. We've spent years studying different styles of fighting. Krav Maga, shootfighting, karate, wrestling—the team has researched them all. And learned that none of them is right for you because it takes years to get good at any of them."

The cute blonde girl frowned. "Then, what do we do?"

"We're going to teach you simple stuff that causes great pain and doesn't require years of practice."

Amy handed each student a piece of paper. "Here's what you are going to learn."

Richard read:

> Ways to damage throat & eyes with things you carry: fists, pens, keys, combs.
> Head butting.
> Eye gouging.
> Biting.
> Hair pulling.
> Fish hooking (inserting your fingers in someone's mouth and ripping their cheeks).
> Three Stooges (inserting your fingers in an opponent's nose and pulling hard).
> Groin attacks (punching, kicking, twisting, and pulling).
> Joint dislocation.
> Elbow strikes.
> Throat strikes.
> Kneeing and kicking of head.
> Stomping (head, groin, legs, kidneys, and feet).

"If you are in a fight, whether it is one you start or one someone else starts, you only have one goal. Inflicting great pain while experiencing minimal damage to yourself."

Amy waved her list. "Looks easy on paper. What's not easy for normal people is realizing you must strike first and cause painful damage immediately."

Gavin raised his hand. "I thought this was a self-defense class."

Peggy looked at him and smiled. "It is."

"Then, I've got a question."

"The answer is no."

"You haven't even heard my question."

"I've taught this class a thousand times. And in every one people think: 'That's sick, throwing the first punch and causing great pain…there has to be another way.' Unfortunately, there isn't. Not unless you want to continue to live in fear."

"That wasn't my question."

"Been here a thousand times, Gavin. It all boils down to the same question. But, please, go ahead."

"What if she's a little old lady?"

"Little, legally blind woman took Richard down."

"Yeah, but that was a setup."

"No, it wasn't. That was as close to a real fight as we could get without causing Richard permanent physical damage."

Richard rubbed the painful spot where the Taser had hit.

"I can't do that. It's against everything I stand for. I thought you'd teach me how to defend myself without hurting anyone."

"I understand. Amy, give him his money back."

"I didn't say I wanted to quit."

"Yes, Gavin, you did."

"I don't want to be afraid. But, I also don't want anything to do with causing pain or violence."

"It's the real world, Gavin. Ideology is wonderful. But what are you going to do the next time someone attacks you?"

"Run like hell, I guess."

"Then, I'd suggest you sign up for track school. You can stay if you want. But the offer of a full refund ends after today's class."

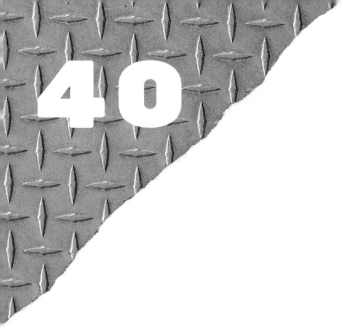

Chase chose Friday evening to invite guys from Brooke's club to his home. He'd gone back once after his first visit and a few of the members were starting to get comfortable with him. About twenty guys showed up for a little basketball followed by scotch, imported beer, quality Cubans, and idle sports chatter.

Later, Chase told Pay by the end of the evening he'd felt like he was hosting "The Best Damn Sports Show Period, Senior Division." The guys who showed up early to play were mostly late twenties or early thirties, tall and thin. Former college players, they were well connected and now successful investment bankers and entrepreneurs.

By nine PM most of the guys had left. But two of the older guys, Ted and George, were still hanging around. Neither had come to play.

Middle aged, balding, running to soft, and six feet only in their dreams, they looked like twins. Except George's thinning hair was going gray, while Ted's dark black combover and goatee suggested regular appointments with a stylist who had an intimate knowledge of hair coloring. Both wore new designer sweats and never touched a ball.

Chase poured them some Johnny Walker Blue. "You guys look like you got something on your minds. Might as well come out and say it."

Ted glanced at George. "Maybe you should start."

"You mentioned after you retired you started doing detective work."

"NBA players are targets for all kinds of schemes. Gold-diggers. Girls who say 'yes,' then scream rape. Blackmail."

Ted butted in. "Surely you don't need the money."

"Don't need it. But more money means more toys. And I enjoy helping guys out. They trust me because they know I've been where they are; that I can't be bought. And that I'll be discreet."

"Ever work with anyone other than NBA players?" asked Ted.

"Sure. Couple movie stars." Chase chuckled. "Lots and lots of pro football players. Those dudes are always in trouble. What kind of trouble you boys got yourself into?"

George looked at the floor, shaking his head slowly, fingers pinching his forehead. "It is not something easy to put into words." He tugged at an ear, groaned, and stared at the wall where a Leroy Neiman original showed Chase dunking on Tim Duncan. "Ah, shit. Ted and I are caught up in something." Grimacing, he stared at his unblemished Nike Air Jordan's and whispered, "Stuff we thought only happened to people on TV."

Ted shook his head in frustration. "C'mon George. Stop beating around the bush."

Chase grinned. "I'll bet bush is what got you fine gentleman in trouble in the first place. So, let me guess. You picked up a cute little girl, or two, one night. Everything went great—right up until you got the phone call asking you to drop a big bag of cash out back by your office dumpster."

"They want four million dollars. From each of us." George wilted in his chair.

For a professional investigator like Chase it was almost embarrassing. He didn't even have to ask any questions. The story tumbled out, confirming everything Brooke had suspected with some new twists. Video of them having sex with a beautiful woman. A synthesized male voice on the phone threatens to tell the new wife. The last divorce cost tens of millions, the new wife's brother is a hot shot divorce attorney; and there's no pre-nup.

George had even told the girl he loved her.

41

Pay gave Richard his cold, never-blinking stare. "You're doing okay in class."

"I feel better about my ability to protect myself."

"Still scared?"

"Yes, but not as much as before."

"Had any run-ins with people in your neighborhood? North Beach has some pretty aggressive street people."

"On my way to the Hyatt, I walked past Centerfolds. One of the doormen tried to sort of push me inside."

"Law says they can't touch you."

"I know. It looks friendly when they put their arm around your shoulder. But what they are really doing is using their size and strength to force you into the club."

"What'd you do?"

"I used to cross the street to avoid them. Last night I pretended I was you and used the hand sweep Peggy taught us to get him off me."

"Didn't have to head-butt him or jab a finger in his eye, huh?" Pay grinned.

"No. But I was ready if I had to. And I'm pretty sure he knew it."

"Confidence and being ready helps a lot."

"I didn't do much. But I got the feeling in a weird way he respected me."

"How'd it feel?"

"It felt good. And it felt kind of bad. I got really focused and intense. Half an hour or so later I got real tired. It shouldn't feel like that, should it?"

"It doesn't for me. I find the clean burning fury of justifiable rage to be one of the best feelings in the world."

"Really?"

"Yes."

42

After his meeting with Richard, Pay called Chase. "You track down Myron Baker?"

"Spent some time on Google and LinkedIn. Guy's a single, successful businessman. Does something to do with developing and manufacturing batteries for electric cars. His Facebook is mostly business stuff and lots of party pics. Reading between the lines, he's just a guy who screws around."

"Like to talk to him face-to-face."

"I called the number on the video. It's his cell. The voicemail says he's in Europe on business. When I called his office, his admin said he'll be back in about a week."

"So, doesn't look like he connects with the Mary Ellen thing?"

"Nah. Just looks like a player who got stalked by a pissed off husband. I can follow up when he gets back."

"That asshole Rock can probably tell us what we need to know. Let's grab him again. My turn this time."

Pay hung up and headed out to meet Sam Hong for a late lunch. Even though the team wasn't following Sam around anymore, Pay wanted to check in. He liked the guy and wanted to make sure he was safe.

Pay decided to walk the six or so blocks to the café instead of taking a taxi. His injured leg was feeling pretty good and he had plenty of time.

Sam ordered the senior breakfast: small cheese omelet, hash browns, one slice of sourdough toast, and coffee. "When you walk most of the night you tend to sleep late."

The waitress knew Pay and brought him his usual: double cheeseburger, green salad with thousand, and a pitcher of iced tea. "Any trouble?"

"I still haven't been able to find my old boss."

"Couple thousand bucks could take him a long way."

"Yes. But I'm going to keep looking. I'd like to help him if I can."

"Other than that, everything okay?"

Sam smiled. There was a glint in his eye. "I think a man followed me the other night."

"Yeah?"

"He stayed pretty far away. But he was the right size to be one of the men who kidnapped me."

"You thinking about getting even?"

"Maybe."

"I was you, I'd want to fuck the bastards up. You want me to hang around?"

"How's the leg?"

"Almost a hundred percent. If you're worried about it, Chase could handle it."

"I've got the guns, pepper spray, and a knife. And I'm doing okay at the range. My military training is coming back faster than I thought."

"I could loan you Blade for a while."

"Jesus, Pay, beast like that will scare everyone away."

"Thought that was the idea."

"I'm not so sure anymore."

43

The Revenge School students found that class was full of surprises. Clearly, they couldn't actually break the instructor's bones. And no one was willing to be tasered or maced for practice.

But Chase was something of a demented inventor. Along with Jon D, he'd built a whole bunch of specialty equipment which was very effective. So effective, the team could have made a living just selling pieces to police departments and the military.

The Taser and the pepper spray turned out to be the worst surprises of the class. But there were others that kept the students from getting too comfortable. Punching bags that, when hit hard, randomly screamed or spurted red stuff that looked like blood. The artificial hands the class used to practice breaking fingers could suddenly zap them with an electric charge.

Richard hated the heavy bag. Sometimes you hit it and it swung and swayed. Then you'd haul off and slam it with everything you had only to find out that it was suddenly completely immobile. A couple of students had broken knuckles. But if you didn't hit it hard enough, it screamed, "Is that all you got? Losers die first." Or worse. Much worse.

Equipment was reprogrammed without any warning to provide new surprises. Richard found out the hard way. He'd kicked the crap out of the heavy bag, which triggered a huge, foam-covered pole that came crashing down from the ceiling. It knocked him 'ass over bruised elbows' into the mat.

Once he was back on his feet, blood spewing from his nose, Richard took a screaming sidekick at the pole and sprained his ankle. Peggy taped him up, handed him water, a few over the counter anti-inflammatories, and then shoved him back on the mat.

Richard thought she was crazy. "I can hardly walk. I think I broke something."

"Do you feel grating or grinding in your ankle?"

"No."

"Are you in so much pain that your vision is seriously distorted? Does the pain from standing on it make you want to puke?"

"No."

"Are you dizzy?"

"Uh, no."

"Is your bleeding serious?"

Richard pointed at the blood dripping from his nose.

Peggy shook her head in disgust. "I'm almost blind, so I'm going to pretend I didn't see you pointing at your stupid nose. Nobody ever died of a bloody nose."

Richard looked at the floor which was spotted with his blood.

"Do you think a crook is going to say, 'Oh poor guy, he's hurt? I better finish mugging him another day.'"

"Well, uh…no."

"Then get out of my face and back on the mat, or I'll have Amy Taser you again. Lordy, just when I thought maybe you were growing a spine."

The students had cuts on their hands, blood stains on their clothes, and bruises on their butts—a couple had even lost teeth. Gavin the Vegan had dropped out saying he just couldn't hurt someone. But the next day he was back sporting a broken nose and two black eyes. His mind had changed after he'd been mugged at his ATM.

Everyone was learning; and in the one-on-one bouts you could see visible improvement. If asked, they would have all said they were less afraid than when they began.

44

After class, Richard was in the men's room, washing off blood, when his cell rang. "Mr. Johnson, this is Alyssa with SF General; Mary Ellen momentarily regained consciousness and asked for you."

"I'll be right there. Is she still in the same room?"

"When they upgraded her condition from critical to serious, they moved her out of intensive care. Now she's in room four thirty-one A. She's weak, disoriented…mostly asleep."

"I'll be there shortly." Richard hung up and dialed Pay. "The hospital called. Mary Ellen regained consciousness. She asked for me."

"I'll go, too. She's the best witness we've got. Meet you there in about twenty." With a click he was gone.

■ ■ ■

As Pay walked toward Mary Ellen's room, he watched a nurse remove a name tag from its holder beside the door. She folded the tag and tossed it in a wastebasket. "If you're here to see Mr. Silva he's been moved to the second floor."

"No. I'm here to see Mary Ellen."

"As I told the other gentleman, we just gave her a sedative. So she'll likely be out of it for hours." She gave Pay a thorough once over, taking in the worn motorcycle boots, scarred knuckles, and vivid forearm bruises. "Please don't upset her. She's better, but she's still weak and badly hurt."

Pay wished Chase were around. When it came to charming women in the 'caring' professions—nurses, teachers, and the like—Chase was better than Pay. Even in shorts and a T-shirt, Chase came off as a high-end detective caring for his clients. Even dressed in a suit and wearing his best smile, they always put Pay in the thug category.

But Chase was at HQ. So Pay did his best to look sincere and non-threatening as he handed the nurse a card. The one that read only: 24-hour emergency number. No names, nothing to track back to him or the team. "Hard to know looking at me, but I'm one of the good guys. A real bad guy beat her. If anyone causes trouble, I'll protect her."

The nurse looked Pay in the eye, slid the card into her pocket with a small nod and a tight, not entirely convinced smile.

Pay was used to the aftermath of violence, but even he thought Mary Ellen looked ghastly. If he hadn't known from the stuff he found in her apartment that she was twenty-three, he would have guessed she was more along the lines of a teenager getting her driver's license.

Richard was holding her hand; he didn't look good either.

Mary Ellen's skin was gray-white where you could see it through the bandages. The only spots of color were bruises, scabs, and staples the doctors used to close the cut above her right eyebrow. And the bright yellow fluid in her catheter tube.

Richard looked like he'd lost too many Revenge School fights.

"How's she doing?"

"The nurse says she's weak but stable."

"She talk at all?"

"She's been unconscious since I got here. Nurse says the drugs they gave her will keep her out for a while."

"You should talk to her."

"Pay, she's unconscious. What's the point?" Richard shook his head and stared out the window.

"Guess you've never been in the hospital after a beating, huh?"

Richard looked at Pay like he was crazy.

"'Course you haven't. I've been beaten silly a bunch of times. Friendly voices really help. My mom. Brooke. Chase. Sometimes the nurses or the docs. You have to have a reason to get well."

"What should I say to her?" Richard knew it would be up to him. Pay wasn't Mary Ellen's friend; they'd never even met.

"Tell her the docs say she's gonna be okay. That you're here because you care and want her to get better. Try telling her you want to help find the guy who beat her. But watch the pulse meter. You don't want her to get agitated. There's no hurry. We've got time."

"Can you stay with me for a while?"

"Sure. You want me to wait in the hall? Give you some privacy?" Pay reached toward the small of his back and pulled out a paperback. "I've got a good Jack Reacher. You can have it when I'm done."

"I'd rather you stay."

"Okay."

Pay pulled up a chair, moved the reading light alongside, and rested his feet on the bed frame. Pulling his iPhone out of his pocket, he stuffed in the ear buds and settled down to read.

45

For three hours, Richard talked quietly in Mary Ellen's unconscious ear. Pay wasn't paying much attention, but when she mouthed the word 'water,' he put down his book, moved to her bedside, and showed Richard how to feed her ice chips. She quietly sucked on the ice, eyes closed. Then nodded, before silently drifting off.

An hour or two later Pay, finished with the novel, was sleeping quietly. Richard was about one-hundred pages into the book when Mary Ellen squirmed. "Throat hurts."

Richard moved to the bed, as Pay roused himself. "Hi, Mary Ellen. It's me, Richard."

"Throat hurts." Mary Ellen swallowed.

Pay leaned over the bed. "You're going to be fine. Docs say you are doing great and will have a full recovery. You were seriously hurt, girl. Emergency had to put a tube down your throat. Good news is Richard saved your life. Bad news is your gonna have a sore throat for a couple of days."

Mary Ellen swallowed and winced. Her eye's flicked to Richard. "Wha' you doin' here?"

"I like you and I want to help."

Mary Ellen's face twitched into a small 'oh-my-God-my-face-hurts' smile. "Thas' nice." Her eyes drifted shut and then slowly reopened.

Richard smiled back. "Your nurse says the drugs are going to keep you out of it. If you could answer just one question for us, it would really help. Who did this to you?"

"Back tomorro'?"

"Sure, I'll come every day."

"Good." She took a slow breath. "Don't kno'. Big, fat guy. Huge, fat guy." Her eyelids drooped and, with that, she was out.

Richard leaned over, kissing her lightly on the forehead. "I'll be back in the morning."

Pay waved Richard down the hall to the deserted visitors lounge. "We need to know more about this fat guy."

"Sounds like the guy who beat me up."

"Chase and I talked to a bouncer from Centerfolds. He's got some kind of scam going with a big, fat guy."

"Mary Ellen wouldn't be into anything crooked."

"I don't have any reason to believe she is. But a couple of days ago, you didn't know she was a stripper."

"So what's next?"

"You keep working hard at class. Chase and I will hunt down this fat guy."

46

E arly the next morning, Richard stopped by the hospital. The doctors said moments after Richard left the previous night, Mary Ellen had experienced a severe anxiety attack. They'd given her intravenous Valium to slow down her heartbeat. When that wasn't enough, they'd induced a coma. The nurse said she might sleep for the next few days.

Richard left flowers, chocolate, and a card. On his way out the door he wrote on the dry erase board: 'Richard was here at nine AM and will be back this afternoon.' Then he headed to his Revenge School class.

■ ■ ■

After the morning class, Pay pulled Richard aside. "How's Mary Ellen?"

"The doctors said she had a really bad spell. Her pulse went out of control, so they put her in a coma. But even unconscious, she looks better. Her skin isn't that sickly gray anymore, and there's a little tinge of pink to her cheeks."

"Sounds like we got a couple things to take care of."

"Sorry, Pay, it was a long night. I'm not sure what you're talking about."

"This afternoon Chase and I are working on finding the fat man."

"What are you going to do?"

"Beat the living crap out of a lying turd from Centerfolds. So far, he's our only clue."

"Can I help?"

"Nope. This one's right in my wheel house."

"Okay. What's the second thing?"

"Peggy tells me a while back some guy ripped you off."

"Yeah. I see him around my neighborhood once in a while."

"Can you prove he stole from you?"

"I sure can. The guy still wears the Rolex my parents gave me for graduation. It's engraved with my name."

"Want it back?"

Richard's face lit up. "Heck yeah! That jerk stole my laptop, the watch, and my backpack."

"Ready to get it back by yourself?"

The smile turned to a frown. Richard's gaze bored a hole in the floor. "I don't know. Do you think I'm ready?"

"Readier than you were. You're going to have to stand up to him. Take back your stuff. Things get out of hand, we'll keep you from getting hurt too bad."

Richard chewed on his lip. "Not counting the watch, he stole about twenty-five hundred dollars-worth of my stuff. I want to get even, but standing up to him…? I don't know."

"Aw, he's just a street punk. You can't stand up to him, you're not gonna have a chance against whoever beat Mary Ellen."

"Damn."

"Sucks, don't it? What you gonna do?"

"About Mary Ellen?"

"Today you visit Mary Ellen. And start thinking about how you can figure out where the mugger lives or works."

"Once I find him, I'll need your help."

"Sure. That's what I do."

"What do you think I should do first?"

"He's your thief. To get even you need a plan."

"Well, all I really want to do is punch him in the gut and get my watch back."

"Okay. Anything else?"

"Not really."

"Seems like you're letting him off a little easy."

"Maybe."

"He humiliated you?"

"Uh, yeah." Richard couldn't look Pay in the eye.

"And he's probably stealing from other people in your neighborhood?"

"There are a lot of people who seem to be scared of him."

"So, you really just want your watch back?"

Finally, Richard made eye contact. Pay could tell he was torn between what he really wanted to do and what he thought was socially acceptable to say. "Getting even is a new concept for me. I'm pretty sure I'd be happy just to get my watch back. But, I'd like to know what you'd do."

"Hard for me to imagine someone ripping me off like that. But I guess if someone did, I'd break 'em up. If I couldn't get my stuff back, I'd want the cash equivalent, plus extra for my trouble. More than cash, I'd want my pride. And

I'd want to be damned sure he'd never steal anything from me again. In fact, I'd want him so damn scared he left town."

"You can do that?"

"It's what I do."

"But what can I do?"

"First, you find him. Then, we find out where he keeps his cash or assets. Then we steal your stuff back and you beat as much living hell out of him as you want."

"Are you going to hold him while I hit him?"

"Hell no. This isn't torture. You're going to have to do that yourself."

"But you'll help me?"

"Yeah. But Chase and I won't be men for you. You gotta man up on your own."

47

The emergency hotline number rang. Pay hadn't given that card to anyone in a long time, so it was probably about Mary Ellen. "Emergency Hotline."

"The nurse at SF General gave me this number. She said you were helping my sister, Mary Ellen."

"Not sure what you're talking about." Pay wasn't going to give anything away until he was sure about the caller's identity.

"I want to know what's happening and how I can help."

"With what?"

"Okay. You need some proof. You've got Mary Ellen's background information, right?"

The choice of words and the attitude—short, aggressive, not polite but not rude either—made the caller sound like she had a military background. In his mind, Pay could picture her. Late twenties to early thirties. Caucasian. Fit and muscular, but not thin. Non-smoker.

"You know her father died in a car wreck, her mother's been dead for years, and she's got a big sister who's ten years older, right?"

So far, she was right on. "Tell me more."

"Her father's name was Robert Samuels; mother, Mary Jane Samuels. Most of her life Mary Ellen lived in Portland, Oregon. Now she's a med student and an, um…exotic dancer."

"If you say so."

"I'm her sister. Barbara Jane Samuels. Special Forces, just back from Iraq."

■ ■ ■

Pay decided to meet Barbara Jane in the hospital cafeteria. She told him to watch for a short haired brunette, five foot nine, who looked military.

Scavenging a discarded newspaper from a chair near the coffee machine, Pay started with the Business section. He was in the middle of an article about Google, when he felt a tap on his shoulder. "You must be Pay."

Pay glanced up from the paper and saw a mid-thirties brunette, khaki slacks, worn running shoes, light blue crewneck T-shirt. The body could only be described as world class military—hard and lean.

"I'm Barbara Jane." She smiled warmly and extended her hand. "You can call me Barb."

Pay decided it would be a good time to break out his best grin.

The one that Brooke said made him look boyishly delicious.

Barb handed Pay a set of dog tags. "That do it, or do I need to slam you to the ground and slit your throat with my K-Bar?"

In his mind, Pay compared the woman in front of him with the pictures they'd found when they searched Mary Ellen's place. "Let's go see your sister."

48

Mary Ellen lay there, still in a coma, while Pay explained the situation. Then made his excuses and left to meet Chase. They'd planned a surprise visit to Rock Duncan.

■ ■ ■

Duncan opened his front door, saw Pay's police baton, and blanched. His left arm, the one not in a sling, reached behind his back.

Chase laughed.

Pay's baton smashed down on Duncan's collarbone. The same one he'd crushed just days before. Rock screamed like he'd stuck his hand in a blender. The gun he'd been going for crashed to the floor.

Chase winced. He'd heard enough collarbones destroyed to last a lifetime.

Duncan collapsed. Pay kicked him in the gut and Duncan puked on a stack of Hustlers piled on the floor.

"I hate weasels that beat on women. Even more than I hate being lied to. Told Chase he was too nice to you. My turn now."

Duncan moaned and rolled toward the gun. Pay stomped on his wrist. For just a second, breaking bones were the only sound in the room. Rock screamed, and Pay jammed a small couch pillow in his mouth. "One more move and I'll break both your arms at the shoulder. You'll have to hire your momma to wipe your ass."

Blubbering, Duncan rolled into a fetal position.

Chase smiled. He liked it when scum got what they had coming to them. "You think you can handle this, big man? I'll search the place while you finish with him."

"Yeah, I got it." Pay scowled at Rock who was crawling away. He stepped on

Duncan's ass and pulled the pillow out of his mouth. "We watched the videos and know there's more than you told us. So here's how it goes. I'm not gonna play guessing games with a turd like you. You got thirty seconds to capture my interest. Tell me a good story, a story I believe, and that's it. Neither one of us wants to know what happens if you lie like a fool. Got it?"

Rock murmured something Pay took for 'yes.'

"We know you're hiding something. We know it has to do with the dancers, wealthy men, and the fat guy." Pay bounced the baton lightly on Duncan's forehead. "You got thirty."

"Man, I don't know nothing."

"Twenty-five." Pay picked up a dish towel off the floor.

"I don't know anything I didn't already tell you." Duncan was starting to quiver.

Pay read the towel's label. "'One-hundred percent polyester.' Guess it'll do for a gag. You got twenty. Hey, Chase, can you find me a big cotton towel back there? I'm gonna need something bigger than this to mop up the blood. Fifteen."

"Okay. Okay. Listen."

"I'm listening. Ain't hearing anything but crap. Ten."

"I told you a guy pays me to give him leads on rich guys who come to the club."

"Five."

"I'm talking!"

"Better tell me something you didn't tell me already."

"Fat man pays for video of rich, married guys getting it on with our girls. And Middle Eastern guys. Pays double if I get some kind of contact info."

"What's he do with that stuff?"

"Fucker doesn't tell me."

"Finally, something I believe."

"Rich guys would be good targets for blackmail."

"Can't blackmail a guy for getting a lap dance. Tell me about the Middle Eastern guys."

"Can't be blackmailing them. Towel heads we get at the club can barely cover the entry fee. None of them ever tips the girls. Dancers hate them."

"Destiny into anything else?"

"You mean like hooking?"

"What the hell you think I mean?"

"The other girls call her 'The Virgin.'"

"Need more about who pays you." Pay pointed his baton at Duncan's shoulder and he started to cry.

"Fat man sends flunkies with cash."

"Describe 'em."

"They're just punks, and they change all the time. The latest one is about five-foot-two, young, mixed race Asian and black. He has dyed, bright-red hair. Wears hip-hop clothes with pants hanging below his ass. Bright yellow tattoo of two skeletons fucking on his left forearm."

"Even a dumb shit like you would have tried to climb the food chain. Where'd you follow them to?"

"Always lost them in North Beach."

"Where?"

"They all jumped the rope at one of the dance clubs on Broadway. Last two I lost in The Black Cat."

Jaw tense, Pay ground his teeth. "Tell me about the head guy."

"Told you. Saw him once. Just a huge, big, fat guy."

Pay scowled. "Need more than that." He smashed his baton through an end table's leg and it collapsed on Duncan's head.

Blood burst from a cut above his eye and his mouth shifted into high gear as he tried to prevent more damage. "Guy's fat, but he's got lots of muscle. Black and gray goatee. Shaved bald. Swarthy skin. Might be Italian or something."

"Heard that before."

"I got nothing else."

"Tell me about the rich guy Destiny danced for."

"Guy blew into the club like he was the President. But he looked sort of scared. He says, 'Hey, big man. I'm kinda in a hurry. Here's a hundred. Take care of the entry stuff.'"

"So you grabbed the cash."

"I followed him down the hall, gave him the standard high roller spiel the fat man taught me."

"I need to hear it. Word for word."

Rock took a big breath and went into his routine, like a second grader at the Christmas play: "I'll be glad to take care of everything, sir. Just tell me what you need. And if you are in a hurry, let me set you up with Destiny. Real pretty brunette. Friendliest girl in the house, if you know what I mean. She's onstage right now. But I can have her with you in a booth in about ten minutes. First dance is on me. You can't lose with Destiny."

"Then he gives me two hundred bucks, tells me to get him a VIP booth and a drink. I'm thinking, two hundred bucks! I tell him my name and that I'll get him anything he needs. But we don't serve alcohol anywhere on the premises. Our license doesn't allow it.'

"He looks at me like I'm crazy, and says, 'How's this place different than any other old topless club?'"

I says, "'It's just like topless, sir. Except the girls are nude. And because we don't serve alcohol, the girls can be younger. A bunch of them just turned eighteen.'

"Dude laughs in my face and says, 'So, Rock. Here's what I think. The normal shmuck can't buy a drink here. But I don't think management gives a damn about me drinking here. Just like they don't care about the semi-pro hookers or jailbait or drugs in the dressing room or janitors working without green cards.'

"He gives me that look. You know, the one rich assholes give to guys like me. 'You got two hundred bucks of my money. Get me a drink. In fact, get me a sealed bottle of Belvedere. I'm going to be a while. And if Destiny doesn't like vodka martinis, get me a girl who does. There's another hundred in it for you if you're back in less than ten minutes.'"

"Then what?" Pay tapped the baton in his palm. He was getting impatient.

"Headed out to get his booze, that's what. Wanted as much of the guy's money as I could get. Needed to keep him happy."

"Yeah?"

"I'm on my way out for the booze and this little dude in a turban stops me."

"Ah crap." Pay's eyelid twitched, and Rock's pulse skipped a beat.

"Guy comes on real polite says, 'Excuse me, sir. I need your help.' I tell him, 'Buddy, I'm in a hurry.' He says, 'I'll pay you.' I told him I was listening and kept walking. He hustles along beside me, wants me to watch the guy I just set up with Destiny. So I say, what's in it for me? And he says a hundred. And I say, why don't you just go in and watch the guy yourself?"

"What's he say?" Pay's impatience shone in his eyes. He wanted to beat the crap out of Duncan, but knew if he did he wouldn't get any more information.

"Guy says something like, 'I cannot. My religion forbids strip clubs,' and I say, 'sucks for you.' Then he says, 'Will you do it?' And I tell him, 'Here's what I'm gonna do. I'm gonna go to that liquor store and buy a bottle. Then I'm going back to the club. After that, if you're still around, you got sixty seconds to tell me your story. And it better be good, 'cause nobody pays anybody a hundred bucks just to spy on a guy in a strip club.' Turned out he thought the big spender was banging his wife."

Pay figured he'd gotten what he was going to get out of Rock. "Chase, you find anything?"

"About eighteen hundred dollars, mostly twenties, small bag of white powder, four prescription bottles filled with Oxycontin—one for Ms. M. Wong, one for Mr. S. Alioto, one for P. Spitzer, and one with good, old Duncan's name. Plus three bottles of injectable Anadrol with his name on them. Looks like Mr. Duncan didn't come by those muscles naturally."

"So minor drug beef at best?" asked Pay.

"Yeah. It's barely gonna be worth the cops' time."

"Any suspicious thumb drives?"

Duncan twitched; his eyes got wide.

"Based on shithead's body language, answer's yes on that one."

"I'll look some more."

Pay unfurled his baton. "Aw, just give me a second here." Pushing himself up off the dining room chair, he took a step toward Duncan, who screamed, "Envelope taped behind the dresser! Envelope taped behind the dresser!"

Pay stroked Duncan's forehead with the baton. "Got it. Now, shut up while I decide what to do with you."

"Can't you just…" Duncan stuttered. "I mean…" The shakes of adrenaline-pumping fear overtook his voice. "I gave you everything you wanted; can't you just leave me alone?"

"I got three options. Option one, kill you."

Duncan went limp, tears running down his face. He knew he was staring at his own death.

"Seems kinda extreme, though. Option two, call the cops; minor drug beef should keep you out of my hair for a while. Or, I could just let you go."

"Just let me go. Please. Please. Please don't call the cops, the drugs will take me down. I've got two strikes."

"Chase, okay if I let this shithead go?"

"Hell no. At least break his legs or something. I don't need him out walking around trying to get even."

"Bring me the Oxycontin and a glass of water, okay?"

"Sure, just as soon as I get this envelope loose."

Pay helped Duncan off the floor, got him comfortable in a recliner, and lightly poked his broken shoulder with the baton.

"You pulled a gun on us. I can't let that go."

Duncan whimpered and rolled into a sideways fetal position, protecting his damaged arm.

Pay shook out a couple of Oxys and handed them to Duncan. "Here's the deal. The Oxys should take the edge off. When you can manage it, sling up and get to work. Nine, maybe ten PM a high roller's gonna drop in. You text the number and tell them you've got a new sucker. A real hot one. When's the pickup guy usually come?"

"'Round midnight."

"Tell him you got a number and a name. And the mark is complaining his wife's a bitch. Got it?"

"What name am I gonna tell him?"

"High roller will show up with the info you need."

"But if I lie to the fat guy, he'll kill me."

"Not even close to your biggest problem. You got two more jobs. Number one: Make sure there's no video of the high roller. None. If the pickup man asks, you tell him it was a technical problem. Number two: Tomorrow you use that eighteen hundred to pack up and leave town. Got it?"

"Got it."

Pay nodded at Chase and flicked his eyes at the door. "Time to get out of here."

Rock sagged with relief, and Pay whipped the baton down twice on his shooting hand.

Bones cracked. Rock bellowed.

Pay bent over and whispered in his ear, "You ever point a gun at me again, I'll cut off both your hands and stuff 'em down a garbage disposal. Then I'll cauterize the stubs with a blow torch before I turn you over to the cops."

■ ■ ■

Chase pulled the Bugatti's door closed. "I'm not real happy leaving him alone and mobile. Aren't you worried about him double crossing us?"

"Hoping he will. But don't really think he can."

"What exactly can't he do?"

"All he's got is a text message number for the guy we want. He doesn't know much about us. 'Bout the worst he can do in the next couple of hours is use his one good hand to send the fat man a text saying a big, handsome, strong, white guy and his skinny black Tonto are causing trouble."

"He could get a couple of friends and wait for us to show up tonight."

Pay snorted. "Shit. You worried about the friends of a pissant second-rate hood like that? What happened, you miss a couple of testosterone injections?"

"Just your faithful Tonto watching out for your ass, Mr. Ranger. And mine. Your leg is better, but without your pet dog, Duncan and a couple of friends with machetes might make you break a sweat."

"But you, me, and Blade?"

"Good point."

"Print up a card for a dummy high roller. Make sure the phone numbers got caller ID and tracking. Add an email address. Our stooge can pass them around tonight. Maybe we'll get lucky and the fat man or one of his gophers will contact us."

Chase nodded. "So, who are you thinking of having play the high roller?"

"I figured one of those two guys from Brooke's club. Ted and…what's his name?"

"George."

"George the one who told the stripper he loved her?" Pay laughed.

"That was George. What an idiot."

"Let's use him. Fool like that deserves it."

"I'll tell him to be at Centerfolds tonight and that he needs to spread around a grand or two and the cards. And I'll make sure he gets there no later than nine-thirty and gone by ten."

"You need to be there tonight when the gopher arrives. Gonna have to tail him."

"How come I've gotta do the night scut work?"

"Cause I'm the boss and you're my faithful Tonto."

49

Early the next morning, Richard found Pay at the team's HQ. "Just got back from the hospital. Mary Ellen's doing better. She's no longer in a coma, but still on lots of drugs. She can't remember anything about the beating except a bald, fat man with a salt-and-pepper beard."

"The bouncer at Centerfolds described the same guy. Last night we set up a trap, but it didn't work out."

"What can I do to help?"

"We're spread a little thin. Might need you to do some surveillance."

"I'm ready. I've got my pepper spray and my cell."

"Bring your gun, too." Pay was surprised at Richard's eagerness. "No questions? Not scared?"

"Of course I'm scared. I'm not nuts. But I'm starting to think I'm more likely to get hurt in class than I am by some low-level guy on the street."

"Probably right about that."

"Why?"

"This afternoon's class is how to win a gunfight when you only have a knife. Everybody gets hurt."

"It can't be that bad. You don't use real knives and bullets, do you?"

Pay laughed. "I'll see you this afternoon."

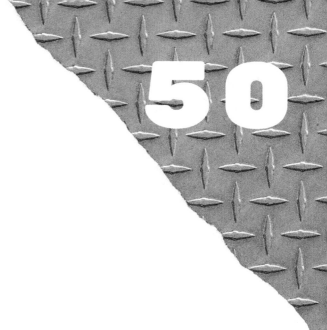

50

Barbara Jane and Pay walked back from a quick lunch at Gott's in the Ferry Building. Pay finished off a chocolate gelato cone, while Barb scooped tiny bites from a cup of strawberry sorbet.

Pay hadn't yet made up his mind how, or if, Barbara Jane should be involved in helping to find whoever'd beaten Mary Ellen and Richard. He knew he needed to test her somehow, but if she had the skills implied by her Special Forces pedigree, the team could use her. "Might be a good idea for you to meet Richard."

"Okay. When?"

"How about this afternoon's class?"

"I'm on R&R for two weeks. And I'm not leaving until this thing with my sister is finished."

"Today's lesson is knives versus guns. Wanna help? We usually need an extra or two. People get pretty beat up."

"Do I have to play client self-defense?"

Pay tilted his head and squinted at her. "I'm not sure what you mean."

"Do I have to let the students win? Because they're paying clients?"

Pay snorted out a laugh. "Hell, no. Not in my world. In my world, skill, viciousness, and the ability to use them, are the only things that count."

"Sounds fun." Barb grinned. "Knife fight with a bunch of newbies. Are there prizes?"

"Winners get something. Losers get nothing. Just like real life."

"So why'd you change your name to Pay?"

"Change?"

"Oh, come on. You don't expect me to believe your mother named you Pay, do you?"

"Honest to God, name's Pay. Says so on my birth certificate. Not that mom was any too happy about it."

"If I ever have children, I think I'll have the final say on names."

"Mom probably thought she would, too. But in my family things were different. You know how after Christmas or Thanksgiving dinner people play dominoes, cribbage, or something?"

"Mary Ellen and I used to play fish for M&Ms."

"In my family the adults played poker. Games could be damn serious. Great grandpa Thomas on my mother's side owned a poker parlor and billiard hall back in the day. Mom was a pretty good player, and my dad's dad was a card counter. Sometimes they played five, ten, twenty bucks—which back then was pretty big money."

"You were named at a family poker game?"

"Pretty much. No limit Texas Hold 'Em. Mom wanted to name me William like my dad and his dad and his dad's dad. But my grandpa was dead set against it. Said the world didn't need another William Back. Everyone called Grandpa 'Bill Back' and he hated it."

"So?"

"So, Mom was holding pocket aces. Being the short stack, she had to be aggressive or she was gonna get bet out. She went all in. Flop turned over two kings. Next card was nothing. She figured two pair, kings over aces was a winner, but grandpa had more chips and overbid her."

"What did she do?"

"She could have called short, but she was so sure she had a winner she offered up her gold watch."

"And?"

"Grandpa knew it meant a lot to Mom. Her grandmother'd given it to her. Gramps wouldn't take the watch, he wanted naming rights."

"What happened?"

"He'd been playing big slick, ace-king. Last card was a king. Mom had a full house, aces over kings, but that last card gave Gramps four kings. He cleaned her out."

"What did your dad have to say about that?"

"They tell me dad said it was better than having another damn Bill."

51

Richard pulled a bottle of aspirin from his gym bag and swallowed down two with Gatorade from his water bottle. He'd survived the morning class undamaged but was worried about the afternoon. So far, all Pay's threats had come true.

Making sure his pepper spray was close at hand, Richard set his iPhone so the alarm would go off fifteen minutes before class. Folding his sweatshirt to use as a pillow, he lay on the mats at the back of the room. Richard didn't know whether it was the increase in physical activity or his body needing rest to repair the bruises, cuts, and sprains, but since he'd started at the Revenge School, he'd needed a lot more sleep.

Nodding off, he dreamed about Mary Ellen and tropical beaches.

■ ■ ■

Richard woke to a warm, wet tongue on his cheek. At first, he thought he was dreaming, but then Blade nipped his ear.

Pay stood laughing about ten-feet away. "Was going to wake you myself but saw the pepper spray and figured Blade had a better chance of not getting blasted."

Richard yawned and stretched as the class straggled in and Pay got things rolling. "First I'd like to introduce a new student." He pointed at Barbara Jane. "She's a little late in the curriculum, but with her background we think she'll get up to speed pretty quick. So, bad guy's real close to you. Say, ten-feet or so. What's better, knife or gun?"

"Only an idiot brings a knife to a gunfight." Richard snorted.

"Great, I was looking for a volunteer." Pay held up a holster and something that looked like a rubber band gun. "This is a training pistol. It fires high-impact rubber band ammo as fast as you can pull the trigger."

Then he pulled an eight-inch hunting knife from a sheath. "This is an electro-shock training knife." Pay pushed a button on the hilt and the blade crackled with electricity. It looked like a lightning storm had erupted in his hand. "Can't cut you with it. The blade's aluminum. Delivers a shock powered by a nine-volt battery. At max, it's like getting hit with a cattle prod. I've set it on low, but still delivers a jolt."

Richard stared at the pulsing blade. "I was already Tasered once. Shouldn't it be somebody else's turn?"

Pay looked at the other class members. "Any volunteers?" No one raised their hand.

"Here's the deal. I'm going to stand about twelve to fifteen-feet away from Richard. Give him a little more chance than a guy might in the real world. And, also unlike the real world, he knows I'm coming, and that I'm going to knife him. Amy's going to blow a whistle and the fight is on."

Pay pulled chest armor over his head and picked up a helmet with a full faceshield. "These high-power rubber bands hurt like a mother, and if you take one in the eye it's going to be a while before you can see out of that eye again."

"Ready?"

Richard shook his head.

"Doesn't matter. Bad guy would never ask anyway." Pay flipped the face shield down and nodded at Amy. The whistle blew. Richard stepped back, reaching for the pistol. Pay charged in low, slashing at Richard's legs.

They crashed together and slammed to the floor. The pistol flew from Richard's hand, skipping across the mats. He grabbed his crotch and shrieked, "What the hell happened?" His inner thigh felt like it was on fire. Plus, he was sure he had a least a dozen cracked ribs.

Pay pulled Richard to his feet. "Takes most professionals about a second to draw a weapon, aim, and fire. Plus another half a second or so to decide to shoot. Average person can cover ten feet in less than a second. 'Course, I'm a little faster than average.

"While you were drawing, I was busy crashing into you, cutting your femoral artery. And, if I'd hit you full strength, breaking a whole bunch of your ribs. If this was real, you'd have bled out in seconds." Pay held up the knife. "This is a slashing tool not a sticking tool. There are five lethal spots. Two carotids." He touched locations on the left and right side of his neck. "Two femorals." He drew the training knife along the inside of his thighs.

"Fifth is a chest cut. That one's not for beginners." Pay pointed the knife at his chest, just below the breastbone. "Push in. Slash left or right." He wiggled the blade. "Knife disconnects a whole lot of vital stuff, including things you need to breathe. And, if you are good, or really lucky, maybe the bottom of the heart."

Chase moved from his spot at the edge of the mat to the front of the class. "Fucking knives scare the shit out of me. One good slash, even a lucky one, will buy you enough time to run like hell."

Richard pushed himself up off the floor and crawled over to a bench. "So what good is a gun, then?"

"Not much if you let the bad guy get too close."

"So what are you supposed to do? I can't imagine a guy with a knife is going to line up thirty or forty-feet away and let you know he's coming."

"Only the stupid ones. Them, you shoot to kill."

"What about the other ones?" asked Richard. "I mean, not every guy with a knife is an idiot."

"That's what today's class is about." Pay motioned to Chase who bent over and grabbed Richard's still fully loaded training gun. In the real world, Richard would have died without having gotten off a shot.

Chase smiled at the class. "Now you're going to learn why this is my favorite class."

Pay took his place about ten-feet away. Richard noticed Pay was closer to Chase than he'd been when Richard was the student.

Amy blew the whistle. Pay charged. Chase took two quick steps to the right followed by one step back and started shooting. Pay yelped when rubber bands hit his left shoulder and bicep.

The armor only covered his chest.

He crashed to the mat, scrambling into a wild leg kick. Chase jumped over Pay's sweeping legs and shot him twice more in the back, hitting body armor. But when he landed, Pay's reverse leg kick upended him, and Pay's knife strafed Chase's carotid. The class heard the sizzle as the knife made contact. Chase swore and both men collapsed in a heaving pile. "Thought you set that thing on low, you bastard."

Pay shoved Chase off him and rolled to his knees. Chase collapsed in the corner.

The class looked back in stunned silence.

"What'd you learn?" Pay rubbed at a welt on his left deltoid.

Chase struggled to a chair. "You learned: don't shoot first, move first. And your first move has to be sideways. That's vital." He rubbed the scorch mark on the side of his neck. "I also learned I have to go even farther sideways than I did. Bastard got me with that reverse leg sweep."

Richard pulled the training gun from Chase's hand. "But Chase, he couldn't have cut you or swept your leg. Everything happened awfully fast, but I'm pretty sure you shot him at least three times before he got you with the knife."

Pay'd removed his armor and was counting welts from the high-powered rubber ammo. Two were oozing blood, a third was a mottled red already turning black-and-blue. "Got me five times. And I know you're thinking—if they'd been bullets I'd be dead. Maybe. Maybe not. But which shot was the kill shot? You can't count on the first shot, or the second shot, or the third shot killing a guy. Lots of good men have died because they shot a guy once or twice and assumed he was dead. But the bad guy was some drugged-up dude and a couple of bullets didn't stop him. Plenty of guys survive seven, eight, nine—even ten bullets."

Chase scanned the group. "I can see some of you guys don't believe it. So here's the real deal. I've got a good friend, a Special Forces macho man. Real tough guy. He's on night maneuvers in some Central American country, under fire, scared as shit, running like hell from one trench to another; he stumbles in the dark and figures he's tripped on a rock. He runs another fifty-yards, shoots two bad guys, and broad jumps over a wall into a trench full of friendlies. Once he's reloaded and got his breath back, he realizes his ankle is soaking wet. He figures he must have stepped in a puddle. Thirty minutes later, when he pulls out his flashlight to help fix a broken radio, he discovers he's been shot in the calf."

Pay nodded. "Under stress, it's easy for even a pro to shoot once and figure everything's over. This is real life, not the movies. One bullet won't stop a guy in his tracks. If you hit him—and that is a huge if—you might kill him. Probably won't. Adrenaline, testosterone, fear, anger, and drugs can keep a guy going a lot longer than you think. So, if you shoot, shoot to kill. Then shoot and shoot and shoot again. And move, sideways and back, sideways and back, until you run out of ammo. Then reload and keep shooting. And the minute you have a chance, run like hell."

■ ■ ■

Amy divided the group in two, handing training knives to half the class and rubber band automatics to the rest. "Listen up, here's how this drill works. Everyone alternates turns with the gun or the knife. After every match we rotate. Lose five times and you're out. If you win five matches, you get dinner with the instructors tonight at Morton's. Our treat. Just like real life, the losers get nothing. Winners are the first to score a major slash, slice one of the vital spots, or shoot the knife wielder four times. Fight starts when the whistle blows." With that, she blew the whistle.

Richard sliced a sizzling track across vegan boy's carotid before he'd had a chance to blink. Turning to Chase, he smiled. "I think I understand why this is your favorite class."

■ ■ ■

The winners' dinner might have been the shortest, quietest celebration in

Morton's history. Predictably, Barbara Jane had come in third behind Pay and Chase, who'd done the drill hundreds of times.

The other students were too exhausted and beat up to really celebrate.

Pay was glad Brooke had reserved a private room as most of the conversations, if you could call them that, involved comparing the severity of their wounds. The students numbed their aches with liquid painkillers dispensed by Morton's excellent bar staff. And while everyone had a good time, it was readily apparent they needed an early evening.

52

The next morning, Pay found Richard at the team's HQ. Richard winced as he stretched out his ailing body. "I don't know how you guys do surveillance half the night and then come to work in the morning."

"Now you know why I'm addicted to espresso. Anything happen after I left?"

"After dinner at Morton's last night I figured out where the dude who stole my things lives."

"Got a plan to get even?"

"Chase and I talked about it a little last night. Can you tell me what you think?"

"Sure."

"I saw him getting coffee in North Beach and followed him home. Found out his name's Ray MacDonald. He shares a flat on the second floor of a three-story walk-up. It's not a very nice place. And before you ask, I took my pepper spray and had Brooke meet me there."

"Good. What'd you find?"

"I snuck up the back stairs and peeked through a couple of windows. The place was a sty—pizza boxes and beer cans were lying around everywhere. One of the windows was open and I could hear snoring."

"What else?"

"About midnight, we followed him to work. He's managing the velvet rope at one of those hot, after-hours clubs south of Market. Brooke says people give him tips to jump the line."

"Look like he takes in much cash?" asked Pay.

"Brooke couldn't tell. She says he's taking advantage of guys leaving the club."

"What'd she see?"

"Nothing specific, but she says something is not right. About three AM one of the guys from her club showed up. Brooke's sure my mugger was sending signals to someone that the dude was a ripe one."

"So, what do you want to do?"

"I want to go to his house and beat the crap out of him. Then I'm going to zip tie him to a chair and take everything he's got."

"That's a good start, but once the adrenaline gets going I bet you'll come up with something better."

▪ ▪ ▪

Pay and Richard were sitting in the front window at North Beach Restaurant. Richard drinking a decaf Chai Tea latte; Pay having a light beer. They were going to break into MacDonald's flat as soon as they were sure it was empty.

"How'd you get into this business?"

"Long story."

"Doesn't look like we're pressed for time."

"For years I worked a regular job. Used to play mostly by the book. Did things to help my friends out when I could."

Richard nodded.

"The people who knew me then would say, 'Never make the big man mad.'"

"There's a lot of territory from working a regular job to leading the Revenge Team."

Pay decided to give him the PG version. The one where he didn't admit to killing three mobsters. That was a story only Chase and Brooke were allowed to know.

"I didn't start out to be some modern-day Robin Hood. Just got tired of rude jerks. One night at the grocery, an asshole gets in the express lane with an overflowing cart. This clown's holding up a whole bunch of tired people who are just trying to get stuff they need. There's a sick-looking guy in sweats and slippers buying Pepto, and a cute young mom in a Britney Spears T-shirt with a quart of milk. I really felt bad for the husband getting tampons, diapers, and Kaopectate."

"What'd you do?"

"Everyone was too timid to call this guy out. I'd had a bad day and was already grumpy. Just wanted to get home with my beer and pizza. So, I said— and very pleasantly, I thought— 'The check stand for the math deficient is number eleven. Move your stuff there. Now.' Then I gave him a little help. Folks insisted I go right to the front of the line."

"So, from check stand expediter to vigilante?" Richard paused.

"Took a while."

"What did it take besides time?"

"Figuring out it felt better to stand up and do something instead of just stand by and watch."

"I'm really looking forward to that."

"You're getting there."

"My progress seems really slow. Is there anything I can do to speed it up?"

"Only thing that speeds it up is motivation."

"Like Mary Ellen."

"Yes. Now, random acts of violent personal enforcement make me feel good." Pay took a sip from his espresso. "Then this freak raped my friend." The bartender set down a fresh espresso. Pay nodded his thanks. "Richard, meet Brooke's fiancé Denny."

Denny nodded and turned back toward the bar. "What happened?"

"Peggy's sleazy little maggot ex-boyfriend started creeping around. Little SOB looked like a muscular ET. Started with petty stuff. Stealing the mail. Filthy graffiti. The kind of mischief a skunk in the middle of the night does to a nearly blind, little person.

"She ignored the bastard. Because the damage he did was as insignificant as he was. But, as anyone who's ever been robbed can tell you, it's not the stolen fifty bucks or the property damage, it's the violation. Once someone's broken into your car's trunk or lobbed rocks through your bedroom window, it takes way too long for you to feel safe again. If they've raped you, you will never be the same."

"Never?" asked Richard.

"Never."

"But you'd already started helping people?"

"Was right at the beginning of the career. I was working my last real job writing advertising. Having what I used to think was a stressful day. I'd turned off my cell so I could meet a deadline." Pay closed his eyes, shook his head slightly, and sighed. "Just before lunch, the receptionist runs in. She's shakin' and talkin' so fast all her words are running together.

"'Pay-I-know-you-are-working-on-deadline-and-said-not-to-be-disturbed-but-you-gotta-take-this-call.' She stops to take a breath and, BAM, she's right back at it again. 'It's somebody named Koa. Says he's your friend. He's scream-in' and cryin' and I can't understand him. But he keeps saying he's gotta talk to you and his sister is hurt and bleeding all over.'

"So I grab the phone and Koa says, 'Oh Jesus, there's blood. It's everywhere. All over the floor. Peggy's right in the middle of it. Oh God.'

"He'd already called 9-1-1." Pay chuckled. "Good thing I only worked two blocks away. Even back then I hated runnin'. Now that's Chase's job."

Richard signaled Denny for another chai.

"Place was a gory mess. Peggy was moaning and writhing. I grabbed the first towel I could find and pressed the gash on her head. When the ambulance left, I realized most of the blood was from her head, but the rest came from between her legs."

Richard gulped his chai and held his breath.

"Peggy's been my friend since grade school. Anyway...got her in the ambulance. Did what you'd do. Made up my mind to kill the son of a bitch. Called her sister and had her cover the hospital. Then called the cops. Panic doesn't begin to describe it. I completely lost it."

Pay crunched the ice in his empty water glass. "What a cluster fuck. It took the cops hours to get there. Since Peggy was already at the hospital, and the bad guy was gone, they had to concentrate their resources on more urgent situations. Peggy being blind didn't help. She couldn't identify her assailant because she couldn't see him, and he hadn't said anything. Just beat the crap out of her and raped her. When the police finally arrived, they did a report. Said they'd give it to the DA who'd decide whether or not to take things any further. Suggested I visit the county sheriff and help her get a restraining order.

"Peggy deserved justice and I was gonna get it, damn it. I ripped down to the county sheriff's office and got the only speeding ticket I've ever had. First restraining order was rejected by the judge without us ever seeing him. I figured we'd done it wrong, so I did it again. The judge turned down the second request, too. Never even talked to her. Just sent a note that said there wasn't enough evidence. Wasted two days filling out forms, re-filling out forms, and standing in a line that never moved."

"Wow. That's hard to believe."

"Ever been to the Sheriff's?"

"No, never."

"Think of the DMV from hell, with metal detectors and armed employees added in for fun."

"Is it really that bad?"

"I started out pissed off. By the end of the second day, I'd chewed my fingers until they bled. I'd screamed at armed men. Only thing kept me from strangling a cop was I knew I couldn't help Peggy from jail."

"People at the Sheriff's office want the system to work. They help you with the paperwork and stuff. We filled out forms, waited, filled out more forms, and waited some more. In the end, nothing got done."

Richard shook his head. "It's hard for me to imagine they didn't want to help."

"They wanted to help. Just couldn't."

"Is it always like that?" asked Richard.

"The system can, maybe, get you legal justice. If the criminal was an idiot who left behind a zillion clues it's easier."

"It must have been awfully frustrating."

"Yeah. No one else was going to take care of that freak. It was gonna have to be me. And I knew I didn't know how. That night, I decided I wasn't going to settle for getting even. I wasn't just going to walk up to him outside a bar and belt him a couple of times. I was gonna make that silly, sick bastard afraid. Afraid to go to bed. Afraid to walk down a dark street."

"Fortunately, the little creep had money. I stole every dime and gave it to Peggy for therapy, a new house with a state-of-the art security system, and a nice long vacation."

"But stealing from him wasn't enough. I got him disowned. I got him fired. It only took two months to turn that little fool into a mess of bruises and bandages. With my bare hands and my high school Louisville Slugger I broke his bones. And for the first time since that little slime ball hurt Peggy, I felt good. Peggy felt safe. The only hard evidence was the baseball bat, and that I cut it into little pieces and used it to grill a steak. It was the best steak I ever had."

"Couple weeks later I set up RevengeSchool.com to help people get even. And a while later I found some videos by a guy named Larry Wick. He teaches the cops and military practical self-defense techniques. Says martial arts are a great sport. Good for exercise and a calm mind, but useless for self-defense because they take too long to learn. His 'Split Second Survival' videos gave me some of the ideas behind our training."

Pay was finishing his double espresso when Richard's head jerked back and his eyes grew wide. "See that guy coming out the front door? That's MacDonald."

"Medium-sized guy with long, black hair? Needs a shave?"

"He looks like one huge scary nightmare to me."

"Good thing you and Brooke didn't take him on. He's packing. Two. One shoulder; one ankle."

Richard gulped a ragged breath. "Oh shit. The fat man just came out the door right behind him. Does he have guns, too?" Flop sweat broke out on his face.

"Shit."

Richard trembled. "What?"

"That fat man is one dangerous motherfucker. Vinnie Morano. He's like me."

"Like you?"

"He doesn't need a gun."

■ ■ ■

"We need back up." Pay pulled out his cell. "Chase, the fat man is Morano. Richard and I need you up at North Beach Restaurant, now."

"Morano, like Vinnie Morano? Fuck."

"When can you be here?"

"Fifteen."

"Richard will be waiting for you."

Pay hung up and turned to Richard. "You keep watch. If Morano shows up, text me. I'll bail out and meet you guys back here."

"What if it's just the mugger?"

"Once Chase gets here, come meet me."

"Then what do we do?"

"Depends what I find inside. Have your zip ties and duct tape ready."

For ten anxious minutes Richard squirmed and waited. He tried the deep breathing technique he'd learned in yoga class, but he couldn't focus. His heart pulsed and his mind kept flashing to Morano killing them all.

So he sat, nervously scanning the street, a text message to Pay cued up and ready to send.

Chase dropped into the chair alongside him, fear blowing out the whites of his eyes. "Should have killed Morano a long time ago. Where's Pay?"

Richard pointed down the street. "That's my mugger. Pay said if he came back alone, I should follow him in. You watch our backs. If Morano shows, send him a text. We will meet back here."

Richard closed his eyes, examined his soul, and asked it if he really wanted to get even. Something inside him said 'yes.' Heart racing, pepper spray in hand, Richard raced across the street toward MacDonald.

The bastard recognized him, smirked, and ignored him like he was no threat at all. Richard followed, staying about fifteen-feet behind. When Mac-Donald stuck his key in the door Richard slunk past him, shoulder rubbing the far wall.

Richard knew getting in front of MacDonald would make him even more relaxed. Not that the bastard looked the slightest bit concerned. The team had taught him people were afraid of being attacked from behind, but almost no one was scared of someone who'd started behind them and then moved in front.

When the lock clicked open, Richard reversed course and ran full speed into MacDonald, slamming him through the open door into Pay's waiting arms.

Pay tossed MacDonald to the floor, laughing. "Pay back's gonna be a bitch."

The creep rolled away, and Pay kicked him in the kidney. "Keep moving and you'll be pissing blood for a month." He tossed rubber gloves like the ones he was wearing to Richard.

"Time for you to prove we got the right punk."

Richard jammed his knee into Ray's back and wrenched his right arm up between his shoulder blades. Pain flickered across MacDonald's face as he twisted to relieve the pressure.

Richard rammed MacDonald's arm farther up his back. "I'll rip this arm off. You stole from me. Today I'm getting even." Richard threw his body weight into the joint lock. MacDonald screamed. "I'm taking back my Rolex. And enough of whatever the hell else you got, for me to be even." Removing the watch, Richard tossed it to Pay.

"Says here, 'Congratulations, Richard! Love, Mom & Dad.'"

"It better." Richard kicked a pile of discarded pizza boxes off a kitchen chair and zip tied MacDonald to it, wrapping duct tape over the ties. "Why do I have to use both?"

"Tell you later. Just do it."

MacDonald looked like he was going to scream. Richard grabbed a filthy sock from the floor and jammed it in his mouth. "Shut up!"

"What you wanna do?" asked Pay.

"Take enough to get even for my time and trouble."

"And?"

"This guy didn't hurt me. He just stole my stuff."

"And has some scam going with drunks outside his club."

"That is not my problem."

"True."

"So, I'm just going to take enough stuff to get even."

"Just take what you want and split?"

"That's what I planned on."

"Before you got here I found a safe. It unlocks with a finger print scanner, but there's a regular dial, too. Probably got some cash. Maybe drugs."

"Let's flush the drugs and take the cash, I guess?" Richard asked.

"Leave the drugs for the cops."

"Okay." Richard tugged a folded hunting knife from his pants pocket and a Taser from its belt holster and sat them both on a side table. Jerking MacDonald's chin up and back with his gloved hand, he glared into his eyes. "Listen, I'm not the same stupid, scared little boy you stole from. The big guy thinks I should steal you blind, beat the crap out of you, then cut off a few critical body parts and leave a bleeding carcass for 9-1-1 to find. And I'm pretty sure if he thinks I don't have the guts, he'll do it for me."

"Nah, you can do it all by yourself."

Richard's maniacal look had MacDonald on edge. Richard softened his gaze. "You didn't hurt me. I won't hurt you." He paused and took a long slow breath.

"Much."

Richard slammed his fist into MacDonald's nose. Blood dripped down his chin. Richard stroked MacDonald's cheek, pressing his left thumb against MacDonald's right eyeball, he glared into the open one. "Here's the deal. I see you again, I break all your fingers and toes. Then, I cut them off and cauterize them with a blow torch. Not because I'm worried about you bleeding to death. I'd use the torch because it hurts a thousand times worse than just cutting off an appendage. But you'll really hate it when I use the torch on what's left of your dick after I cut that off." Grabbing the knife from the table he plunged it into MacDonald's crotch, slicing a ragged hole in his jeans. The knife quivered, its razor-sharp edge rubbing against the mugger's femoral artery. "Then, I castrate you."

MacDonald pissed his pants.

Richard pulled the sock from MacDonald's mouth. "I need the combo for the safe."

Quivering, MacDonald whispered, "Can't do it."

Richard pulled the knife from the chair and stroked the edge slowly along MacDonald's forearm shaving off a swath of dense black hair. "Thank God for the gloves."

MacDonald shook his head and frowned. "Huh?"

Richard smashed MacDonald's hand flat and grinned. "The gloves will make cutting off your finger a lot more sanitary. Now, you going to tell me which one to cut off or should I just do all five fingers on your right hand?"

MacDonald screamed, "Combos on a note under my socks. Under my socks!"

Releasing MacDonald's hand, Richard ruffled his hair. "If I were you, as soon as I recovered, I'd move. Maybe to Bakersfield."

"Recovered?" mumbled MacDonald.

And Richard Tasered him. Right in the balls.

Pay was so startled, for a second he stopped breathing. "Looks like you're a better student than I thought."

▪ ▪ ▪

They left MacDonald in the chair, whimpering.

In his safe, they found over twenty grand. Richard knew he wouldn't get to keep the cash, but he figured he'd get enough for a new Mac and cover some of the costs of helping Mary Ellen. The rest would go to the team, and charity.

They walked out the door with Richard's Rolex, the cash, several flash drives, and nineteen computer CDs they found in the safe.

More important to Richard, he left with his pride. "Why are we taking the drives and the CDs?"

"Morano's never into anything good. Whatever is on them, taking them could make things better for a lot of people."

Pay hit the speed dial on his cell and called Chase. "We'll clear the building in about thirty seconds. Scumbag is gagged and tied to a chair. He's in no danger unless his friends kill him before the cops get here."

"Could that happen?"

"Morano's not gonna be happy."

"Until you called, I thought Morano was doing life in Pelican Bay."

"Me, too. Something bad is going on. Richard's punk had a lot of cash on hand."

"While I was watching your backs, I used my cell to create a message with synthesized voices. I'll send it to the cops from a burner phone, then ditch it."

"Good."

"Pay, won't the cops come after us?" Richard's voice quaked with adrenaline.

"Nope."

"Why?"

"Between our gloves and being careful, we didn't leave any real obvious evidence behind."

"He saw our faces and he knows my name. Plus, I'm sure he knows where I live."

"Be an idiot to come after you, though. He knows you can take care of yourself now. And he knows you've got me."

"Won't he just give the cops my name?"

"Morano won't let him. He'll want the cops gone ASAP."

"So that means we're home free?"

"Only if the cops put Morano away for a long time."

"Huh?"

"If the thumb drives or the CDs are for a big score, Morano's gonna want 'em back. And that's not gonna be good news."

53

Pay, Richard, and Barbara Jane headed to the hospital to see if they could learn more from Mary Ellen.

Chase went back to HQ to explore the stuff they'd taken from Mac-Donald's safe. Knowing the CDs and thumb drives could hold hours of video, watching them was going to be a full-on marathon. He watched two of the discs beginning to end at quadruple speed. Both were high definition video with crystal clear audio taken in the VIP room of a club he didn't recognize. Recessed lighting, rich leather booths, designer furniture, exotic hardwoods, and a rotating selection of gorgeous women set the scene.

Whoever produced the videos had spared no expense. Multiple high-resolution cameras recorded every detail, from the moment a gentleman turned his car over to the valet until he left.

Beautiful women arrived every hour. As new ones appeared, unattached women were discreetly handed an envelope by one of the tuxedoed waiters. Moments later, they departed.

The remaining women sipped Cristal champagne, while men took slugs from large tumblers of Glenfiddich single malt.

The crowd was unique in its age composition. The women were all between twenty and thirty and looked to be doing okay, financially. When they didn't leave with a man, their choice of rides were a Lexus SC 430 hardtop convertible, or one of the medium-sized Mercedes. The men were all older and wealthy. Most were overweight, balding, and seemed to fall in the mid-to-late 50s. Without exception, the men drove high-end luxury cars. Chase saw Lamborghinis, Bugattis, Bentleys, a couple of classic Porsches, and two brand new Mercedes-Benz S65 AMG Roadsters. Their jewelry was designer platinum and gold. They didn't wear merely upscale watches, like Rolex, Baume & Mercier, and Longines; they preferred Vacheron Constantins and antique Patek Philippe's.

Chase hit Google and found one of the guys was wearing a Patek Philippe Sky Moon Tourbillion. It had sold at auction for a hundred and forty-nine million, which made it the most expensive wristwatch in the world.

Prior to entering the club, each gentleman had a quiet word with the doorman, who in many of the videos was the recently encouraged to relocate, Ray MacDonald. During the conversation each man slipped the doorman several bills. After he entered the club, MacDonald or one of his counterparts carefully fanned the bills—always hundreds—so they could be recorded by the security cameras.

At the end of the evening, gentlemen would tip generously and pay for everything, mostly with cash, but occasionally an American Express Centurion Card came into view. The sophisticated black cards were the delight of club owners around the world; they were available exclusively to the rich and had no spending limit of any kind.

Some men left alone. Some drove away with a beauty. Others left with one or more women in a club limousine. Later there were explicit videos of them having sex in opulent bedrooms.

Two hours after midnight, Chase quit. The last thing he did after shutting down the equipment was send Amy an email asking her to come in after the morning class and give him some help.

▪ ▪ ▪

The next morning, Chase was munching a bran muffin when Amy arrived with a huge, pink ice pack Ace-bandaged to her shoulder, and a massive black eye that seemed to swell as he watched. She looked like she'd gone a couple of rounds with Pay. "Either the class is getting better or you've lost a step."

She slumped into a chair. "Damn vegan dude nailed me this morning."

"How the hell did that happen?"

"Turns out he's a Buddhist. All his religious beliefs are about being grounded in the fundamental universal values of peace and love. He actually told me, 'We Buddhists believe there's tremendous power in non-violence. Violence comes from the hearts and minds of human beings.' Then he got mugged at the ATM. In his head he wanted to fight. But in his heart, he just couldn't cross the line."

"And?"

"It's my job to move him into our world. Pay said to push him until he either quit or hit back. I did all the usual stuff and got no response. I started calling him vile things I'd never ever say to anyone. Poofter. Asswipe. Limp Dick, salad-eating homo. I shoved him. Tripped him. Hit him when he wasn't looking. Spit in his lunch. I was starting to make myself sick."

"What finally did it?"

"I pelted him with raw eggs."

Chase burst out laughing. "That did it?"

"Apparently, he considered it egg abortion."

"World is full of all kinds." Chase shook his head. "Good thing you didn't wring a chicken's neck. Dude might have destroyed you. Doesn't the idiot know that store-bought eggs are infertile? What a goofball."

"Goofball with a good punch."

"Apparently."

"So, what do you need my help with?"

"We've got lots of video of a blackmail operation."

"What makes you think that?"

"The usual—rich, older men, gorgeous women, and lots of clandestine sex videos."

"So, what are we supposed to do?"

"Scan everything and ID the men if we can. Then warn them, if they don't already know, that they could be the target of a sophisticated blackmailer."

"Do we try and turn them into clients?"

"You know Pay. He doesn't believe in hard sell. If they want help, we'll help. I'm hoping they all decline."

Amy looked up, eyes wide. "That's not like you, Chase."

"Did Pay tell you we think the blackmailer is Morano?"

"Oh, Christ!"

"Oh, Christ, is fucking right." Chase dropped his eyes to the floor. He looked miserable…and scared.

"All that Morano stuff happened before I joined the team. Didn't he put you in intensive care?"

"Me and Pay."

"Why didn't he kill you? He must have known you'd kill him."

"Peggy shot him. Twice."

"But Peggy's blind!"

He shrugged. "What can I say? Sometimes God is on your side."

"Why isn't he dead?" Amy asked.

"Guess Peggy's not that good a shot."

"Or God wasn't that much on your side."

"Ouch."

"Chase, why didn't you get rid of him permanently? It's not like Pay or you to let something like that hang out there."

"By the time we got out of the hospital and found out Morano was still alive, he was back inside. Pay wanted to kill him. So did I. In fact, I never wanted to kill someone so badly in my life."

"Why didn't you?"

"You know how Pay is. He believes in personal vengeance. That's personal with a capital 'P.' There is no way he was going to pay some felon to off Morano."

"How'd he get out?"

"There's a rumor Morano flipped on somebody. All we know for sure is he's out. And he's hooked into these videos."

"Has Pay said anything about what he plans to do?"

"Just if anyone deserves killing, it's Morano. And Morano's not going to leave either of us walking upright for long. Not much scares the crap out of me. And I've never seen Pay scared. But Morano freaks us both out. There's no way I'm taking him on without help. And I don't think Pay will take him on mano a mano, either."

"I always thought Pay'd take on anyone one-on-one. Even Superman, if he was a crook."

"Me, too."

■ ■ ■

They watched video until the combo of Visine and Red Bull stopped working. Amy was out by midnight. Chase lasted till about two. Neither went home, electing to sleep on couches at HQ so they could get an early start.

The next morning, Chase contacted a friend at the newspaper who emailed over their file photos of wealthy San Francisco males over 50. He and Amy imported the photos into his Mac, then pulled stills from the videos and imported those, too. Chase loaded up his facial recognition software and they left for a late breakfast, knowing it would take hours for the program to complete its work.

After breakfast and a nap, Amy checked the system while Chase made coffee. "The search isn't finished but a few of the men have been identified."

Chase set a steaming cup of what looked like jet fuel in front of Amy and clicked a few keys on the keyboard. "So far, we've got names for five guys." He chuckled. "Of course, Ted and George are both there."

"What do we do now?" asked Amy.

"We start learning more about them."

Amy pulled out her cell. "If we want dirt on the wealthiest men in town you and I could spend all day poking around the internet. Brooke probably knows most of these guys by sight. She'll know where to dig first."

Brooke picked up on the first ring.

"We've ID'd some guys from the video. Could you come look over what we've found?"

"Sure. I'll be there in a little while."

■ ■ ■

Less than an hour later they had everything they needed. A few minutes on Google and a couple of calls to Brooke's friends was all it took. All of the men were über rich, recently divorced, and even more recently re-married to world-class trophy wives.

While Amy researched the potential victims, Brooke and Chase briefed Pay.

"Lotta horny rich guys. Get the right footage of them with someone other than their wives, it's a perfect blackmail setup." It never took Pay long to get to the point.

"Morano figures these guys went through an ugly divorce and won't want to go through another. And he's got all of them making Mr. Happy with someone who isn't their wife." Chase frowned. "They'll run the math and decide it's cheaper to pay him than it will be to go through another divorce and lose half their assets, again."

"Got it. Now what."

Brooke said, "You and Richard could interview employees at Centerfolds. One of them might know the location of the other places in the videos, or someone who's involved besides MacDonald."

"What are you two going to do?"

"Chase and I are going to visit the rich guys in the videos and see what they can tell us. If Morano is behind this, we might as well figure out a way to get paid for taking him down."

"Okay, but I want you, Barb, and Richard to interview as many people as you can at Centerfolds. Then hit the other strip clubs, and the after-hours place MacDonald worked. Before we talk to the other rich guys, I want to talk to Ted and George myself. They're probably scared nearly shitless now. And they know it's going to get worse. Pretty soon, they're going to worry that Chase alone isn't tough or violent enough for the job. They'll decide they need a brutal, sadistic thug. That's me."

■ ■ ■

Pay met Ted at the Transamerica Pyramid. Ted's office was on the next-to-the-top floor, so high up you had to change elevators to get there. During the day it granted views of the Pacific, the Bay, the City, and southern Marin, but this late on a summer evening the setting sun glittered off a base of fog, with only the Golden Gate Bridge towers and the peaks of a few skyscrapers breaking through the gray-white blanket.

Ted poured some obscure, forty-year-old single malt over one lonely ice cube sitting in an oversized Steuben crystal rocks glass and handed it to Pay.

He took a sip and sighed. He'd have preferred plain old Wild Turkey with lots of ice. "So you had sex with a woman who isn't your wife and now you're getting blackmailed."

Ted stammered. "It wasn't exactly like that."

"Aw, jeez, don't waste my time."

"Well, it started out pretty innocent. I was in this strip club."

"Yeah. Yeah. Let's pick it up a bit. I know about your trip to Centerfolds. I've seen the video. And more video of you at a luxury private club."

"Ah, Club Savory." The fond memory on Ted's face melted into one of fear.

"Get to the blackmail part."

"Okay. Okay. A few days after my first trip to the strip club, I got a call inviting me to a special event at Club Savory."

"Just you?"

"No. They said I could bring a friend. I took George so I wouldn't be alone."

"What did you and George do?"

"The club was surprisingly nice. It was luxurious and extremely classy, not at all like that sleazy strip bar. Club Savory has wonderful food and the best wine cellar I've ever seen." Ted started to drift off into some wine-enthused reverie. "And I've been to some of the best in the world, so I know.

"George and I went several times. The food, the décor—everything was perfect. But it was the women who made it really wonderful. They all wanted to talk with you and listen to you. All these beautiful girls. That's what made Club Savory worth every penny of the thousand-dollar cover charge."

"Then what?"

"A few weeks later, a gentleman with a refined British accent invited us to an exclusive event at the Brannon's penthouse."

Pay shook his head in dismay. "You got a call from somebody you didn't know and went to a party thrown by people you've never heard of?"

"They said it was an exclusive party for Club Savory's VIPs."

"That all?"

"The party was restricted to upscale gentlemen and there would be lots of beautiful women and girls in a relaxed, private atmosphere. They promised an experience California's liquor licensing laws prevented them from offering at the club."

"You went."

"George and I went together."

"Of course, you did." Pay sighed. He couldn't figure out what was worse— stupid rich men or stupid rich men, times two.

"There was this beautiful woman. Mei Ling. She couldn't leave me alone." For a brief second, Ted almost grew a backbone, and his voice slid into what Pay was sure he thought of as his 'Captain of Industry' voice. "Mei was one of the most wonderful nights of my life."

"Yeah. Sure. Right up until you found out everything was taped."

"The worst part was when I got the call."

"Tell me about it."

"This raspy voice growls: 'We got video of you in bed with Mei Ling. You'll get a copy in tomorrow's mail. It's going to cost you four million to get the original. Pay up, or we send it to your wife.'"

"How long they give you to pay?"

"Two weeks. I told them it would take me that long to get the funds together."

"They agreed?"

"I told them it would take me a month to pull together that much cash in small bills without my wife or accountants getting suspicious. They said I had two weeks."

It didn't take long for Ted to agree to Pay's terms. The team would shut down the blackmailer. In exchange, Ted would pay them fifty percent of the blackmail demand. Pay agreed to a quarter-million-dollar, refundable retainer, which Ted paid out in cash.

54

Early in his career, Pay had used guns a lot. As he'd gotten more experienced, he'd relied on them less and less. When he was younger, he'd loved the confidence a piece gave him. But over the years, he'd learned to rely on brains and a well-targeted blow from his collapsing baton. He'd seen too many innocent bystanders become collateral damage.

With Morano on the loose, Pay called Jon D and set up a meeting at Jon's machine shop in the Mission. "Everyone on the team needs to be better armed."

"Why?"

"Morano's back."

"Shit."

"Yeah."

"So get forty-fives for you and Chase, with thirty-eights for backup. Get thirty-eights and twenty-twos for the rest of the team. Whatcha need me for?"

"Was hoping for something with more firepower. Maybe something like we got Sam."

"There's a revolver version of the derringer, the Judge Magnum. Shoots forty-five Colt ammo, shotgun shells, and non-lethal ammo. It is perfect for killing Morano."

"Why?"

"Because the ribbed rubber grips don't take palm prints. If you use shotgun shells there's nothing for the CSI's to trace. I'll crosshatch the trigger to prevent fingerprints. Just shoot it and drop it."

"What about DNA?"

"DNA's overrated. First, you gotta leave skin or hair or something behind. Second, SFPD's lab is so overworked that only really high-profile stuff ever gets run. Right now, SFPD is five years behind."

"What about ammo?"

"Against Morano? I'd be carrying a forty-five and grenades." He laughed. "I'd load the Judge with shotgun shells. Cuts down the need for accuracy, which is always a bitch when the shit hits the fan."

▪ ▪ ▪

In addition to weapons for himself, Pay ordered Judge Revolvers and "Sam Hong" derringers for the entire team: Brooke, Peggy, Amy, Chase, Denny, Richard, and Barbara Jane were now perfectly armed.

Richard already had a thirty-eight, but Pay wasn't sure he was a good enough shot to use it effectively, and he didn't want Richard to run into Morano holding nothing but a can of pepper spray and a gun he wasn't proficient with.

55

Just after midnight, Pay was sitting in the big green chair thinking about Morano when he got a call. "Sam Hong's hurt," Brooke said.

"What happened?"

"I don't know for sure. His wife said the police called and Sam was admitted to Saint Francis Hospital. She asked if we could meet her there."

"I can be there in about twenty. You wanna go?"

"Yes. Pick me up, please."

■ ■ ■

As Brooke and Pay stepped off the elevator, two cops stepped on. Pay guessed they'd been talking to Sam or his wife.

They turned the corner into Sam's room, expecting to find a beaten old man at death's door, but found a drowsy Sam smiling loopily at his wife; a woman who was most definitely giving him hell.

"You dumb old goat. I told you this walking around thing was stupid, stupid, stupid. Stupid and dangerous!" Her voice got shriller and louder with every word, but her eyes glistened with tears and love.

Sam just sat there wearing a dazed smile, a bloody bandage wrapped around his head, and dark blue-black bruises on both arms. Pay looked at his giddy smile and wondered if he was high on painkillers or had sustained some sort of brain damage.

Sam's head turned in Pay's direction and his smile brightened. His voice came out as sort of a cross between a whisper and a chuckle. "Got 'em. God damn it. I got 'em."

Liu Hong shook her head, sighed, and slumped in the room's only guest chair.

Brooke went to comfort her, as Pay leaned over the bed. "Whatta ya mean you got 'em?"

"Those bastards jumped me again. They thought they were going to get a chance at a double dip."

"Looks like you put up a fight."

Sam's eyes brightened. "I blew 'em away."

Pay looked over his shoulder for the cops. "Good time to be quiet. Can't talk about stuff like that here."

Sam mumbled, "Not gonna matter. Trust me. It's not going to matter." His eye's fluttered and the drugs took him into oblivion.

Liu looked up at Pay. "He's got a concussion, broken ribs, and minor internal injuries. Doc says it's painful but he'll recover." Her skin was pale. "Police say he shot and killed two men. They said it appears to be self-defense."

56

Pay decided to call and see how Richard was doing after getting revenge on MacDonald. "How do you feel?"

"How do I feel about what?"

"Getting your Rolex back. Whatta ya think I mean? How 'bout those Lakers?"

"Honestly, I feel good. Except I've got a little guilt about Tasering MacDonald in the gonads."

"Understandable. I'd worry if you didn't."

"Why?"

"Because I don't feel guilt anymore. Worries me sometimes. Maybe I like the rough stuff too much."

"I'm pretty sure we did a good thing. We got the money, my watch…and I think I scared that shit pretty bad."

"Was a lot easier than taking on Morano's gonna be."

"Am I ready to start helping with Mary Ellen? I'd like to do more than surveillance and questioning strippers."

"Yeah, you're ready. We're meeting at the office in an hour. Be there."

"Really? Are you sure?"

"I was sure right after you Tasered MacDonald."

■ ■ ■

Pay pointed Richard to a seat alongside Brooke's at the team's Formica conference table. In addition to hosting business meetings, it served as the lunch table, Chase's chess table, and was occasionally pressed into service when Pay needed to sort bills. Which wasn't often. Minimal paperwork was one of the great benefits of an all cash, mostly underground business.

Richard thought the thing looked like it belonged in a Junior High lunch-room. It had long, skinny, uncomfortable benches on both sides, and was covered with stains. Some looked like blood. Brooke said it was from a lifetime of the team's spaghetti lunches and midnight pizzas, but Richard wasn't quite sure he believed her.

Blade rested quietly under the table.

"I don't feel like I've done anything to really help Mary Ellen yet."

Pay shrugged. "You weren't ready. At the beginning, finding us was the only thing you could do. And we've done lots of stuff you don't know about."

Brooke sipped from a glass of orange juice. "We've got standard procedures. First, we talk with the victim's regular Joe, good citizen contacts, friends, relatives, neighbors, and the like. We need to know what people are involved in before we start rubbing up against bad guys. It's vital to know if Mary Ellen is involved in something crooked."

"She wasn't involved in anything crooked, Brooke. There's just no way." Richard's eyes pleaded.

"Your heart is in the right place. But you don't know that for sure."

"We won't risk our lives until we're pretty sure. …And we're sure," Pay said, settling into a chair at the head of the table. "You ought to feel good; our money from MacDonald will go toward her medical bills. Should help with her deductible."

"I thought you were going to donate the money to a kid's charity?" said Richard.

Brooke smiled. "You can do whatever you want with yours. Ours will go as an anonymous donation to her medical bills."

"You guys aren't keeping anything?"

Pay looked up from the dark glasses he was cleaning on his T-shirt. "Nah. She needs it more than we do."

"Please donate mine, too."

"Why don't you use yours to help cover her living expenses? She's not going to be able to work for a while. Brooke can set it up so she doesn't know the funds came from you."

"Okay. So, what happens next?" asked Richard.

"Need to take care of Morano."

"What are we going to do?"

"At minimum, get him sent back to prison. I'd rather kill him. Chase is trying to find out where he's based. Maybe we can find a house or something where he's vulnerable."

Pay set a duffle bag on the table with a metallic thunk. "Paid a visit to Jon D. Got his input on the latest weapons. I got everything he recommended for all of us. Ammo, guns, and holsters are on the table. Anyone gets a shot at Morano, you all got the green light."

Brooke picked up a pistol.

Chase flipped open his revolver and checked the loads. "Should have killed him last time."

"Get everyone checked out on these. Brooke and Barb take care of Amy and Peggy. Chase, you set up Denny and Richard."

"Pay, honey, Richard isn't ready," said Brooke.

"Jesus Pay, are you losing your mind?" added Chase. "Rich's been a client for less than a month. Last week the vegan kid almost tore him a new one."

"Hey, I'm right here." Richard's face screwed up into what Pay thought might be his version of a scowl.

"Doesn't matter. Morano knows you're our weakest link. Can't have you running around out there like a bacon-coated nudist at a grizzly convention."

For the entire span of time Mary Ellen was in the hospital, Richard had visited two or three times a day. The doctors told him she was getting better. Her heart rate and blood pressure were stable. The lacerations, bruises, and broken bones were all on the mend. She could talk but wasn't talkative. Unfortunately, her memory was severely damaged, and no one knew if she'd ever remember the details of what happened that night.

Pay dropped by often but left most of the talking to Richard. So, it was a surprise when he got a late afternoon call from Mrs. Nako, the head nurse. "Mary Ellen wants you to come by and talk with her."

"I'll be by later this evening with Richard."

"She's asking to talk with you alone."

"Why?"

"I have no idea. I'm just her nurse. But she's lucid and says she remembers some things."

"Be there in a few."

"I'll let her know you're coming."

■ ■ ■

In less than half an hour, Pay sat down in Mary Ellen's room.

Mary Ellen looked up drowsily. "No Richard?" Her voice was raspy.

"I can get him here if you want."

She shook her head and mumbled, looking down where the blanket covered her chest, "No. I'd prefer to talk with you alone."

"Why?"

"Because some of my story is embarrassing and I'm not sure how he'd look at me after he heard it."

"You care what he thinks?" asked Pay.

"Um, I might."

"Tell me."

"This has to be in confidence. I'll tell Richard when I'm feeling better."

"I'll do what I can. Anything you know puts Richard and my team at risk." Pay let the statement hang.

"I understand. Before I get too tired, let me tell you what happened."

Pay pulled a notepad from his jeans pocket. "Lots of questions."

"Please, let me tell you what I remember my own way. If I've got the energy, I'll answer your questions at the end."

"Can save you some time. I've talked with Rock."

Mary Ellen gasped. Over her head the beep of the heart monitor quickened.

"Don't worry. He's never going to hurt you again."

"Did Richard help?"

"Wanted to, but this time it was one of my guys and me."

"Rock set me up with this rich guy in a private VIP both. It was a pretty typical thing." She couldn't look Pay in the eye.

"I know. Saw the video. Everything you did in that booth was recorded in high def."

"Has Richard seen it?" All of a sudden, Mary Ellen looked tired, small, and ashamed.

"No. But I wouldn't worry. You didn't do anything wrong."

"Maybe you better tell me what you know."

"Video shows you drinking with some guy named Myron Baker. He told you his name was Mike."

"I kinda remember something about a Mikey and martinis."

"Do you know anything about him? We don't think he was part of it."

"He was just another guy."

"That's what we think, too. It would also help to know why you were dancing for the fat man."

"What do you mean dancing for the fat man?"

Pay pulled out his phone and flicked through several mug shots. "Recognize any of these guys?"

Mary Ellen scrolled back through the photos until her quivering finger landed on Morano. "He's the guy. Isn't he?"

"Name's Morano. He's the guy who beat you. And we think Duncan works for him."

"Doesn't Duncan work for Centerfolds? I thought his job was to protect us dancers."

"He's also been helping the fat man spy on dancers and customers. We don't know if the owners of Centerfolds know anything about it."

"I figured out they were taking videos of some dancers, and I got some copies."

"Did he give you cash if you got info on the big spenders?"

"Yes. Usually a hundred bucks."

"What for?"

"Rock told me it was a tip for helping build the club's client list. That management used the information to get the big spenders to come back. They offered incentives, like free limo rides, special private rooms, and Cuban cigars. He invited me to some 'anything goes' private party, but I told him no."

Pay considered how much information Mary Ellen could take in her current condition. "Let's just say you were misled."

"Tell me. Please. I can take it."

Pay decided on part of the truth. "Looks like you were the first stage of a honey trap. We think the fat guy was using the information to bait and blackmail high rollers. At this point, we don't know if anyone in the club's management was involved or not."

Mary Ellen started to cry and the beep of the heart monitor over her head increased alarmingly.

Mrs. Nako appeared in the doorway immediately. Taking one look at Mary Ellen sobbing and the heart monitor, which read 150 BPM, and was climbing fast, she said, "Sorry, Pay, but you better go."

58

As soon as the elevator door opened on the team's second floor work area, Pay shouted for Brooke and Chase. If was anyone was around, he wanted to update them on his conversation with Mary Ellen.

In the main room, he discovered the conference table was stacked almost to overflowing with Zero Halliburton briefcases. On the corner of the table was a note stapled to a white envelope. Brooke's stylish script read, "This was delivered by messenger to your attention. There's no indication who sent it. Chase ran everything through the scanner and the sniffer."

Inside the envelope Pay found two sheets of paper. The first was drawn in a feminine hand. "Before he wound up in the hospital, which as far as I'm concerned is his own damn fault, Sam had just finished getting these ready to deliver to you. He'd probably have preferred to deliver them in person, but he won't get out of the hospital for a while and I'm scared having them around. He doesn't know I'm having them delivered. But given his last few days, I'm sure he would want you to have them now more than ever." It was signed, Liu Hong.

The second sheet was a distinctive combination of block printing and shaky script Pay recognized as Sam's. The note was short and to the point, like everything Sam and Pay did. It was probably one of the reasons Pay liked Sam so much.

"This is my gift to you and the Revenge Team. I don't want financial constraints to ever keep you from helping someone. There's more, should you need it."

It was signed: Sam.

Pay was pondering the briefcases when Brooke and Chase entered carrying pizza.

"Tony's combo," Chase said, cracking open a pair of Red Stripe beers while Brooke poured herself a white wine.

"We got a present from the Hong's." Pay nodded at the table and knocked back some beer. "Grab a case."

Locks clicked open. Pay whistled.

Chase broke into a big grin.

"Mine's full of hundreds," Brooke laughed.

"Sam's note says he wants to make sure we never turn anyone down for lack of cash."

Chase was counting cases. "Ten."

It took Brooke almost a minute to count the bundled bills in her attaché. "There's five-hundred thousand in this one."

"Holy shit," said Pay.

"We've got enough for Jon D's surgery," whispered Brooke.

"What surgery?" Pay frowned.

"He didn't want you to know because he knew we couldn't afford it. Doc says there's a new procedure that will eliminate his pain. He might even be able to walk without the canes. But his insurance won't cover it."

"How much does Doc say it will take?"

"Maybe a briefcase and a half."

"Put the cases in the safe and mark Jon D's name on two of them."

59

Pay called Liu Hong. "How's Sam."

"Darn fool's doing better than he deserves. I was surprised when they released him this morning."

"I'm guessing he's sitting right next to you."

"The old grump's in the other room watching Cheers reruns, whining about how he hurts and running me ragged asking for something to eat or something to drink, more pain pills, more ice, a pillow, and a blanket...name it. Now he wants me to rub his feet. He's wearing me out and he's only been home half an hour."

Pay heard Sam groaning in the background. "Honey, where's the remote?"

"How's the head? Docs said he had a concussion?"

"The head trauma specialist told me Sam had the fastest recovery he'd ever seen. They think it might have had something to do with all the walking."

"So, he's gonna be okay?"

"Right now, the biggest threat to his health is a few broken ribs, and me."

"Honey, I really need the remote." Sam's voice was getting stronger and more insistent.

"You would have thought they'd give consideration to how much work it will be for an old lady like me and kept him another month or two."

"Really need your help, please?"

Liu's voice raised a couple of decibels. "Give it a rest, Sam. I'll be there in a minute." Her voice returned to normal as she refocused her attention on the phone. "Doctors say I'll have to put up with him for the rest of his natural life. Which right now I'm hoping is going to be real short."

Pay laughed, "I thought Asian wives were supposed to be demur. Sort of fade into the background."

"My mom, sure. I'm American to the core, however. Born and raised in Oakland."

"Can I drop by and visit? I'd like to thank you both."

"Let me get him settled in and hire some help first." Pay heard more urgent noises in the background.

"Pay, I've got to go. Time for his meds," she mumbled. "I may have to give him a few extra tranquilizers."

Chase, Pay, and Barbara Jane were working out. Richard stood to one side, watching them go at it.

Pay was boxing. Working the double bag. Jab. Jab. Jab. Missed uppercut. Jab. Jab. BOOM. Right hook. Jab. Jab. Missed uppercut.

Every time Pay missed a punch, Chase screamed, "Morano just cut your throat."

Chase was kickboxing on an oversized heavy bag. Hard. Elbows. Knees. Fists. But even throwing perfect punches, he could barely get the huge bag to move.

Barbara Jane was running, side-stepping, jumping, skipping, and crawling through a complex razor wire obstacle course.

A bell rang and they rotated positions. The difference was unbelievable. On the double bag, Chase never missed. Combination after combination, his hands flew.

Across the room, Pay moved quickly through the first part of the course but slowed dramatically as he struggled to get his bulk under the lowest razor wire.

Barbara Jane didn't use her hands on the heavy bag, but her kicks were as violent as Chase's punches.

The bell rang again and Pay slammed the heavy bag. His punches weren't as fast or pretty as Chase's, and he couldn't get his feet high enough off the ground to execute a proper Muay Thai kick. Nor could he move fast enough to complete multi-kick combinations. But Richard felt the explosions from his kicks clear across the room.

Chase danced through the obstacle course as Barb's fists blurred the double bag.

Five minutes later, they switched again. By then, the mat where Pay stood was coated with sweat. Chest, face, and ears flushed red, while perspiration drenched his hair, streamed down his face, and dripped off his chest, pooling on the floor. He lumbered from bag to bag. Gulping water by the bottle. He looked exhausted.

By comparison, Chase was fresh. Of course, it would be hard to tell if his dark brown skin was flushed, but there was no sweat on his closely shaved scalp. He flowed from station to station, and his water remained untouched. Until Pay plodded over and drained it in one go.

Barbara Jane couldn't match Pay for power, or Chase for speed, but she bested them both on the razor wire.

Twenty minutes or so had gone by when they stopped, and Chase waved Richard into the room. Pay collapsed onto a folding chair at the edge of the mat. Chase jogged to the blender and began mixing a protein shake.

Richard sat beside Pay. "Don't you guys think we should be looking for Morano?"

Doubled over on the chair, face resting in his sweat-soaked Muay Thai gloves, gulping air, Pay grunted and pointed a gloved paw in the general direction of Chase and the refrigerator.

"Rich, that's his way of asking you to get him a Gatorade," Chased shouted over the blender.

"Pay looks beat."

"Shaddup," mumbled Pay through his gloves.

"We never miss more than two days of workouts. It's an absolute, ironclad rule. Helps keep us alive. Miss any more than a couple of days and you get slow and sloppy."

"Chase, you look pretty good."

"Thanks. But wait until tomorrow. Pay'll look great and I'll look like a shaved Shar-Pei."

"What happens tomorrow?"

"Tomorrow's heavy lifting. Deadlifts. Squats. Bench Press. Clean and Jerk. Snatch. Stuff like that."

"He won't be so pretty tomorrow." Pay groaned.

Chase handed Pay a tall glass filled with something that looked suspiciously like blended grass. "This'll make you feel better."

"Not as good as a quart of beer."

"C'mon, we talked about that. You said you wanted to drop a few pounds." Pay scowled.

Chase danced back until he was out of Pay's reach. "Not that you're fat. It's just that any extra weight'll slow you down. With Morano out there, we both have to be in top shape. And you can't rehydrate on alcohol. That can leave you dragging for days."

Pay stripped off his gloves and chugged the green glop. "Deal was if I drank that entire quart of blended cow cud, I got a beer, right?"

"One."

"Damn." Crouching down, he reached all the way to the back of the refrigerator. Hiding behind Chase's bottles of organic fruit juice and bottled spring water was a quart bottle of Stella. Pay smiled, twisted off the top, turned the bottle upside down, and Richard watched it disappear as fast as it came out.

Chase shook his head. "That's not exactly what we agreed on."

"Better than the six-pack I'd usually have."

61

Since taking down MacDonald, Richard had done nothing but help with surveillance, attend Revenge School classes, chug painkillers, and go "home" to the Hyatt. When a friend who knew a little bit about his situation asked him how long he was going to stay at the Hyatt, he told him, "I don't know. I'm not sure I'll ever be able to go home again."

But he was surprised to find that as his self-defense skills improved, his attitude changed. With his pepper spray, his pistol, and his new attitude on aggressive action, he was a completely different man than he'd been a few days ago.

And now he wanted to go home.

■ ■ ■

His first call was to Officer Delgado. "Hi, this is Richard Johnson. I'm the guy with the nearly dead girl in his bed."

"I remember."

"I want to go home.

"Okay. What are you calling me for? I told you a couple of days after the incident you were free to go home anytime."

But I imagine the place is a wreck."

"Likely. It was when I left."

"If it was your house, what would you do?"

"I'd call Aftermath, Inc."

"What do they do?"

"Make your house better than new in a few days. They put in new rugs, and paint. I've heard they'll even restock your fish tank."

"How much does something like that cost?"

"I really don't know. Richard?"

"Yes."

"Before you move back into the place—and if I'm ever asked, I'll never admit I said this—get a gun."

"What would you recommend?"

"You know anything about guns?" Delgado asked, like he expected the answer to be 'no.'

"A little." Despite his lessons with Matt at the range, Richard knew he still had a lot to learn.

"Get a tactical shotgun."

"A shotgun? Isn't that what the Mob uses?"

"Yeah. In the movies they used sawed-offs, which are illegal and not what I'm recommending. There are a bunch of good reasons a guy like you should consider a regular shotgun."

A guy like me. God, I hate that. "I'm listening."

"The most important thing a weapon does is kill people. The second most important thing a weapon does is scare the crap out of people without shooting it at all. Worst thing a weapon can do is kill the wrong person."

"Why's a shotgun better than a pistol?"

"Because every crook knows the sound a shotgun makes when you rack a load. When a crook hears you pump the rifle, they'll run like hell."

"I could scare somebody without shooting them?"

"Yeah. And you might hit what you're aiming at."

"But in the movies a shotgun seems like it'll kill anything that moves."

In the background, Richard heard someone yell, "Delgado, we gotta go. Move it!"

"If you load it with low penetration shot, the pellets will hurt or kill whoever they hit. But they won't go through the wall and kill your neighbor."

"I'll check into that."

"Tactical shotgun is what cops get for their families."

"Is that what you have?"

"Yes. But I've also got an alarm system, good locks, a Rottweiler, and a nine-millimeter Glock. Just the Rott would have prevented everything that happened to you, but I don't think the landlords going to like you having one in your flat."

Richard heard the voice grow more insistent. "Delgado!"

"Gotta go."

■ ■ ■

Richard took Delgado's advice to heart. His next call was to Pay. "I need a weapon for protection at home."

"No problem."

"I talked to a police officer who recommended a tactical shotgun. But I'd appreciate your opinion."

"I keep a Remington 870 shotgun under my bed."

"Why a Remington?"

"Seven shots without reloading. Shoots easy. You can buy used ones for a reasonable price. You want me to keep going?"

"No, I want to try one."

Pay told Richard to meet him in Oakland. When Richard pulled into the drive he found Pay standing alongside a black Chevy SUV parked next to a shipping container. The container looked like it had been sitting there for a dozen years. It had an almost abandoned look—rusty, dirty, and dented.

Pay opened the truck's tailgate and pulled out three protective carry bags. "I brought a selection, so you can try all the standard versions. The first one is a basic Remington pump action, like we discussed. It used to ride in an Oakland police car. Cops cut down the stock so it can be stored in the vertical rack without hitting the windshield. I also brought a typical automatic. It shoots bullets faster, without pumping, but doesn't give off that room-clearing, pump-action sound."

"What's this one?" Richard pointed at a matte black rifle with a pistol grip. It looked like something a SWAT team would use in a Die Hard movie.

"That's the one the Marines use, a Benelli M4. The Marine version comes in desert camo, mine's black synthetic. An excellent weapon, but Bennelli's are on the pricey side."

Pay handed Richard shooting glasses, ear cups, and the older police model. "The first thing you need to learn is a good safety practice. Never put your finger on the trigger until you are ready to shoot. It belongs flat, resting alongside the barrel until you are ready to pull the trigger." Pay demonstrated loading and unloading, using the trigger bypass button. Next, he pointed out the sights and safety. "Ready?"

"Wow. It looks so easy in the movies. But there sure is a lot to remember."

"Yeah, and if you don't practice, it is really easy to lock up under pressure."

Pay pulled open the front door of the shipping container, stepped inside, and nodded at Richard to follow. Closing the first set of doors he pushed open a set of inner doors.

Richard was amazed to find a gun range inside the container. "Is this safe? Aren't these things just made out of aluminum, or something?"

"This is a friend's private shooting facility. It's a full IPSEC-approved range. Lined with cement, sound controlled, and a bunch of other stuff. I've shot a fifty cal BMG in here."

Richard was beginning to find all the acronyms confusing. "Fifty cal BMG? IPSEC? What's all that mean?"

"To tell you the truth, I can never remember what IPSEC stands for. It's some kind of international standard for gun ranges. But a fifty cal BMG is the seven hundred-grain bullet used in a Browning machine gun. One huge bullet."

Pay sorted through a bunch of loose ammo sitting in a cardboard box behind one of the shooting benches and handed Richard a bronze cartridge bigger than a cigar. "You can rapid fire these in here pretty much all you want. Bullet just goes down range and gets funneled into a snail trap at the end."

"Snail trap?"

"You ever played miniature golf?"

"Of course."

"You know at the nineteenth hole there is always a place where you putt, and then gravity feeds the ball into a lock box? That's what happens here. Only louder and at much higher speeds. The range is a special shape. Natural forces funnel the bullets down to the end where they get fed into a vertical slot. Underneath the slot is a catcher that holds the spent bullets. Just like peewee golf."

Pay picked up the Remington, wedged it firmly against his shoulder, and welded his cheek to the stock. "You can shoot a shotgun two ways. One way is called shooting from the hip, which is misleading. You actually wedge the stock between your arm and your chest. Or, you can sight it like a rifle. That's the way most beginner's find accurate."

He handed the gun to Richard who pulled gently on the sliding section. When nothing happened, he looked at Pay, confusion written all over his face.

"Pump action shotgun is a man's weapon. You treat it firm, even hard. Be nice to it and the thing acts up. You need to use force, like this." He grabbed the gun and violently racked a round, and then pulled the gun into position. "The kick on this is a lot different than a pistol. If you don't weld your cheek to the stock and get everything firm, you're going to wind up with a bruised shoulder or a black eye."

He ejected the load, pointed the weapon down range, pulled the trigger, and then showed Richard the empty breach. "Your turn. But before you load, let's get the firing position right."

Richard thought it would be easy to hold the gun to his shoulder. But the place he wanted to put the stock wasn't where Pay said it belonged.

"Not there, here." Pay readjusted the butt for the third time.

Finally, Richard got the location correct. Then he found it was almost impossible to keep the butt of the gun in the right spot and get his eye lined up behind the site.

"Pull everything firm and tight into your shoulder, breathe deep, release your breath slowly, then pull the trigger." Richard followed his instructions to the letter, but nothing happened.

He pulled the trigger again. Still nothing. "Check the safety."

Richard pushed the safety with his thumb, re-welded his cheek, placed his index finger on the trigger, stared at the target and pulled. BOOM! The big gun rocked him. He opened his eyes and looked down range at the brown, corrugated target. Meeting his gaze was a big hole right where the heart would be.

Pay pulled the target in close. "The biggest hole is where the wadding hit the target, the small ones are the pellets. Definitely a kill shot."

They spent another forty-five minutes shooting ammunition of increasing power and weight. With each step up, things became louder and the guns kicked harder. One hundred rounds later, Richard was the proud, concerned owner of his own pump shotgun.

Pay read the anxiety in his face. "Something wrong?"

"I'm not sure I'm ready for this. Just a couple of weeks ago I was a card-carrying pacifist. Now I own a shotgun. I'm not sure who I am anymore."

"It's not like you're gonna go all Eliot Ness on me and wind up in a fire fight with the Mob. Right?" Pay laughed.

62

Pay, Chase, and Brooke discussed the best way to approach the men in the videos—all of whom were likely being blackmailed by Morano.

The team had two approaches. People like Richard they took on as Revenge Team students, teaching them the skills they needed to get even, and helping them as situations dictated. Others who were incapable of learning the necessary expertise, but who had a morally justifiable need, were charged a fee.

And thanks to Sam Hong, if someone wasn't able to pay but the team wanted to help them anyway, there was no charge.

Pay's decision was simple. "Way too many soft, old guys used to paying other people to do their dirty work. Never be able to teach 'em the stuff they'll need to do. They can pay. And we gotta take care of Morano anyway. Minimal increase in risk. Significant reward."

Knowing the victims would be unlikely to accept an unsolicited call but would take one from a wealthy counterpart, the team decided to make the initial contact indirectly. Ted and George reluctantly agreed to call the men in the videos and recommend the team as a solution for their mutual problem.

All the meetings followed a pretty standard pattern with only minor variations. First, Chase handed them graphic photos of dead people who had crossed Morano. "You are being ripped off by one of the most dangerous men ever released from Pelican Bay. We believe you have three alternatives. One, pay him—maybe several times. Two, live with the knowledge he might kill you at any moment. Or, three, hire us."

Then he got into the risk/reward scenario. "The solution to your problem is dangerous. There will be considerable risk to my associates. Your identity will be kept confidential. Your name will never appear in the news. If we go to court, you will never be called as a witness because there will be no paperwork or evidence of any kind that we were working together. Our fee is fifty percent of the amount you are being blackmailed, with twenty-five percent to be paid up front, in cash. The balance is due, also in cash, when we eliminate the blackmail operation."

All of the men squawked about the fee, but Chase didn't take the objections seriously. From birth, these men had been taught to complain about price. For them it was just a knee-jerk reaction. They knew there was no one else with the skills, ability, and desire to help them. At any price.

Ultimately, they all agreed to pay.

63

Mary Ellen's condition had been upgraded from critical to stable. The doctors were cutting back her painkillers and the nurse called to tell Richard that Mary Ellen had asked to see him.

In the elevator on the way to her room, Richard was rubbing red, inflamed wrists. "One of the things we learned today was how to escape zip ties. Getting loose hurts."

"Now you know why I had you duct tape over them at MacDonald's." Pay unconsciously rubbed his own wrists, remembering the day he'd mastered the skill.

"I'm surprised anyone uses those things. They are really pretty easy to get out of."

"Once you know how to get the right angle—wham, you're free. But it only works on the consumer version. The zip cuffs the cops use for riot control are damn hard to get out of."

Turning into Mary Ellen's room, they were greeted by a huge smile. Pay noticed that, for the first time, she was wearing make-up. A little lipstick, maybe some blush. Certainly, her cheeks had lost the ghastly white hospital cast. He figured Brooke had brought by some girl supplies.

Richard and Mary Ellen chattered away, ignoring Pay. After about ten minutes of chitchat, his impatience filled the room.

Richard finally noticed Pay's agitation. "You look like you have something on your mind."

"You don't need me for this. Can you catch up after I leave?"

"Sure, Pay. Richard and I will have plenty of time to talk later."

"Mary Ellen, we've got a pretty good idea what happened at the club. Is there anything else we should know?"

Mary Ellen nervously plucked at her sheets and snuck a glance at Richard.

"Don't worry. I know about the blackmail and I know you were dancing because you needed the money. You don't need to worry about what I think."

"What do you want to know?" Mary Ellen's earlier smile had been replaced by a small, scared voice.

"How sure are you this guy Baker isn't involved? Don't really know what happened from the time you left the booth until I took out Rock."

Mary Ellen sighed, took another deep breath and glanced away. Pay could tell she was listening for Richard's reaction. "I practically had to carry him out the girl's exit. He'd had eight or nine huge martinis."

"Looked like a drunken jerk."

"As men in the clubs go, he was okay. Not rude. Didn't make any grabs."

Richard frowned, and Mary Ellen winced. "I made about six hundred. Plus, I didn't really have to do anything. Just sit there and talk, look cute, mix drinks, and listen. I didn't even have to take my blouse off."

"Video shows you making your drinks mostly water. Must be hard to do with a guy watching you."

"The guys want you to party with them and it wears on you. For the customer it is just one wild night. For us girls it is night after night after night of wild nights. And those vodka calories in your stomach wind up on your butt."

"I was working the happy hour, early shift, and Baker was my last customer. I was about to leave when Rock went batshit."

"What did that fool want?" Richard asked.

"He starts telling me I owe him his cut. Then he grabbed my purse and started beating on me. The next thing I know, Pay showed up. Thank God."

She smiled at Pay. "Have I ever said thank you for that? Thank you very much." Her smile, ringed by two black eyes, warmed Pay's heart.

Pay grinned. "You're welcome."

"Why did you do it?"

"What?"

"Get involved. There were lots of people closer. And the club has bouncers who are paid to protect me."

"I hate bullies. Especially men who beat women. Can't let that slide."

Richard watched her yawn. "She needs to sleep. We can pick this up tomorrow."

64

ay hadn't had a real relationship with a woman since he'd become a vigilante. Sure, there'd been flirtations, brief romantic encounters, and a few women where he'd even hoped for more. But he couldn't ask a woman to be with him when she'd be the first one an enemy would try to hurt.

Pay was hoping Barbara Jane would be different. Clearly, she could take care of herself. Black belt, Delta, weapons experience. If she could live with what he was, maybe she could be a friend and partner. Not a soul mate, which he thought was the kiss of death. He didn't need to be fulfilled. But he wanted to share the important stuff in his life.

Given the potential that Morano could kill one or all of them, Pay decided she needed to know why he did what he did. Tonight, he planned on telling her the truth about how he'd gotten in the business, not the Disney rated version he'd told Richard.

With that in mind, he invited her over for a simple Italian dinner. Originally, he'd planned to cook, but he'd been too nervous. In the end, he had Il Fornaio deliver.

Pay was finishing his second Wild Turkey and opening a good bottle of Napa Valley Sauvignon Blanc for Barbara when she knocked on the door.

Barbara glanced around the room, taking in the black leather couch and the tiny Formica dinette wedged in the corner. In the bedroom, Blade sat quietly on his pad at the foot of Pay's king size bed.

For the first time ever, Pay was embarrassed about his home. He could afford a better place but had never seen the need. His apartment was secure, quiet, and convenient to both the team and work. But seeing it through a woman's eyes, he was pretty sure it was lacking.

"Love what you've done with the place," Barbara said, eyeing the fresh pink carnations in the center of the table.

"Mostly a place to sleep." Pay almost stuttered.

"I can see that."

Barbara Jane set her purse on an empty section of bookcase shelf—a spot Pay had dusted only moments before. She shrugged out of her coat and Pay hung it in the room's small coat closet.

"Before dinner, I've got a couple of things I want to tell you."

"That doesn't sound good," Barbara Jane frowned. "I've never had a conversation that started out with 'I've got something to tell you' that went well."

"Still." Pay grimaced.

"I'm starving. Can we please eat first? I prefer my bad news on a full stomach."

"I'd kinda like to get it out of the way."

"So, let's compromise. Tell me over dinner. But first pour me some wine." Barbara Jane smiled, pulled out a chair, and started serving the salad.

Pay groaned, helped himself to a slice of sourdough, and took another swig from his drink. "Listen, there's some stuff."

Barbara Jane gave him a disappointed look. "We need to set some ground rules. Only small talk until after the first course. You can wait until we've finished the salad and I've finished my wine."

Pay sat, chastened, and chewed his salad. Never one of his favorite parts of a meal, tonight it tasted like cardboard mixed with cigarette ashes. What seemed like twenty minutes later, Barbara Jane finished hers.

She must have chewed each bite fifteen times, thought Pay. While Barbara served the penne in spicy caviar-vodka sauce, Pay refilled her wine and his bourbon. "Now?"

"Maybe."

Pay sighed.

"Now would be fine," she said.

Shaking his head, he wiped his right hand over his eyes and down his face, pulling at his jaw. Then he took a deep breath, resting his chin in his hand, fingers covering his mouth.

"Before this thing with Morano goes any farther you need to know some stuff about me. We haven't known each other nearly long enough for me to tell you what you need to know. A lot of it is not good."

"Pay, there's nothing I need to know. I know the important things already."

"There's stuff I feel like I have to tell you."

She took a sip from her wine, forked the penne, and smiled her best smile. "Please start, I'm ready for anything. And relax, I know you've helped people and killed people who deserved it. Anything worse than that? You aren't having sex with Blade, are you?"

"No! Jeez. Hell no!"

She leaned over and kissed him on the cheek. "Why don't you tell me how you got started?"

"Okay, I guess. You sure you want to know?"

"Yes."

"Been doing this about fifteen years. It all started while I was in college. Be good to tell you, if we're going to take this anywhere."

"Where are you planning on taking it, big man?"

Apparently, she wasn't going to make this easy on him.

"Well, um. You know."

"No, Pay. I don't know."

"Ah, damn it. Can you just let me tell it? Please."

Barbara took a bite of penne and washed it down with the wine. "I'm going to sit here and enjoy my dinner. I won't say another word until you're done."

So Pay told her the whole story. The true one.

"Being a vigilante has been hard on my body. I've been shot, lost about half a dozen teeth, broken both arms, my leg, and both collarbones, luckily not at the same time. It all started with an ugly dude with a silenced forty-five. I'll never forget that day. A few hours before game time, I was sitting at home getting prepped for my last college football game. I was kinda wondering how high I'd go in the NFL draft when the doorbell rang."

Pay looked at Barbara as if asking for permission to continue.

She smiled.

"Opened the door and three guys in suits push their way in. I wasn't afraid of them. Hell, I was an All-American lineman. Absolutely in my prime. There was no way they could take me, but the one ugly guy had an automatic with a silencer. Little guy next to him had a mini-tape player. Third guy, almost as big as me, but fat, just stood there and grinned like a stooge.

"Smaller thug put his tape player down on my coffee table and pushed play. Mom's voice screamed out: 'Honey, they've got your dad and me. They say they'll let us go as long as you'—there was a slap, mom cried, dad swore— then nothing, except the sound of the ugly crook cocking his gun.

"It was the only time in my life I'd felt completely helpless. The guy said, 'Here's the deal. You don't have to throw the game. You guys can still win. Just make sure you don't cover the spread.' I gasped. 'You guys nuts? You must have taken too many shots to the head. I'm a lineman. Got no control over stuff like that.

"He jabbed the gun barrel into my chest, and said something like, 'Listen college boy, we've been doing this a while. We're not fools. Good weak side offensive tackle can be the key to the whole game. You miss five, maybe six important blocks. Superstar QB gets blindsided. Maybe gets a concussion. Late hit knocks him out of the game. Or a running back's knee gets tore up. We don't care. What or who. But we know you can do it. And you will.'"

"Then the big, fat stooge dialed my phone and handed the handset to me. I heard a guy I knew. Robert Dombroski, a rookie lineman with the Steelers. He tells me these guys are assholes. Last year they did the same thing to him. Took his mom and sister. Scared them to death. He threw a few bad blocks, so his team won by six instead of twenty. Nobody got hurt but the gamblers. By the time he got home, his mom and sister were back. Both were sluggish from drugs, but okay.

"Then the leader sneered. 'You got it? Win by less than eighteen. Mom and Dad come home. Next year you make a call. You'll never see us again. Screw up and your parent's funeral will have to be closed casket.'

"It was an awful game. Rain and mud turned to sleet then snow. I missed the blocks I needed to miss. We won the game, but I didn't play the whole thing. Midway through the fourth quarter with the game essentially over, I accidentally blew a block on the defensive end. Notre Dame's middle linebacker slipped through the hole and got creamed by our pulling guard and landed on my leg. Their outside backer speared my head and I woke up in the hospital, Mom and Dad at my bedside."

Barbara Jane shook her head and frowned. Her eyes were bright with small tears. "What happened?"

"Apparently, that's the first thing I asked," said Pay. "I mumbled, 'Wha' happened?' through the anesthetic cottonmouth. Mom cried and Dad hugged her. Once she was calm, he told me the creeps dropped them off, drugged, at my house. Heard on the news I was hurt.

"It was a couple of days before I learned the docs had put two permanent titanium plates and about a dozen stainless steel screws in my tibia and fibula. Months later I realized my NFL career was kaput.

"Took me almost a year to find Ugly Man and his friends. I made sure they learned the hard way what a large, pissed-off man can do when he is willing to fight dirty. I stole everything of value they had and used it to pay my medical bills. The rest I donated to charity. I used my own fists to make damn sure there would never be another tape. Ever.

"I was kind of proud and figured that was the end of it. It wasn't until later I realized I could replace the rush I got from football with the high that came from putting an asshole down."

"So, big guy, that's it? That's all you got?"

"Yep."

65

arly the next morning, Barb got a call. She grabbed Pay's T-shirt from the foot of the bed, pulled it over her head and stepped outside the bedroom, closing the door behind her. From the rhythm of the conversation, Pay believed it was serious. There was no choppy, angry back and forth. But there was no happy laughing, either.

Barb opened the door, holding her phone. "Mary Ellen's being released. We talked things over and agreed she wouldn't be safe at home alone, so I'm bringing her to my house."

Pay groaned, quietly. But not quietly enough.

"Listen, Pay. I can take care of myself. I know this guy is bad ass. In case you haven't noticed, I'm pretty bad ass, too."

"The last time I took on Morano, I lost."

"I've got a good security system, the Judge revolver, and a double barreled, eight gauge sawed off for clearing rooms. I even have some military ordinance."

"One of the team should be there as back up. Me or Chase. Even Blade."

"You and Chase need to be out finding and killing Morano."

"At least let Jon D put video surveillance on the entry points and give you panic buttons. If something happens we'll know right away."

"Okay. I'll take panic buttons, exterior surveillance cameras…and Blade."

66

Brooke placed dirty china in the dishwasher and finished cleaning up the debris from a brunch-hour meeting. Normally, the club didn't open until four PM, with most of her serious clients wanting attention between happy hour and eleven PM. But her best customer had requested her for a special meeting, and she'd reluctantly agreed.

Brooke didn't like to be in the club alone, and she didn't want to be at work. With the Morano situation still unresolved she wanted to be helping the team.

Straightening the fringe on a hand-tied silk Persian rug, she then plumped a leather bolster on a wing chair and walked the room to be sure it was ready for her next event that evening. Satisfied with the scene, she headed to the dressing room to change out of her Armani work uniform.

Relishing changing into sweats and tennies, she had just touched her index finger to the scanner on her locker when the dressing room door swished open. Surprised a coworker was there that early, she twisted to look over her shoulder…and Morano slammed her into the locker.

ay recognized Morano's growl from his nightmares. "I'm at your friend's club. Chicken-shit security for such a ritzy place. Say hello, honey."

Pay heard muffled female moans.

"Poor thing can't talk too well right now. She's all tied up." Morano's laughter was more menacing than his growl. "Meet me here. Now. With my videos. We handle our stuff one-on-one. You win, you get the videos and the girl."

"Love to, but only an idiot would let you dictate terms."

"Guess I forgot to mention, if you aren't here in ten minutes I'm gonna take Brookie somewhere and play with her. Once I'm done, couple of days from now—days that will be fun for me, but not so much for her—I'll kill her. After that, I start killing your friends. One at a time. Stab 'em in the back. Sniper 'em from blocks away. Beat 'em to death. Gonna start with that little turd Richard. After that, who knows? Last one before you scream will be Barbara Jane. By then I'll be ready for a little more fun."

Pay started to yell, but Morano was gone.

■ ■ ■

In his truck, racing towards the club, Pay called Chase. "Where are you?"

"Oakland police department. I have a friend who thinks he knows where to find Morano."

The irony almost made Pay puke. "Bastard has Brooke and is waiting for me at her club. Says if I don't meet him there, one-on-one, he's going to rape and torture her, then start killing team members."

"What do you want to do?"

"I'm going to put him to bed. Permanently."

"Wait for me. You need help."

"No time. Got to be there in ten."

"I'm fifteen minutes away."

"You carrying?"

"Judge loaded with shotgun shells."

"Jon D's got me fully loaded."

"Pay, I get any kind of shot, even a back shot, I'm killing that bastard."

"Good. Shoot early and often. Don't care if you hit me. Dude needs to die."

■ ■ ■

Morano charged Pay like a rhino in heat.

Pay'd seen a rhino charge. Five-thousand-pound bull was lying on its side dozing. Except for the tail swatting at flies, it looked dead. Fifty-feet away, behind a Jeep, a female rhino in heat passed by.

BAM!

Rhino goes from nearly dead to full speed humpmaster faster than a turbo-charged Ferrari. Rather than going around the Jeep it just steamrolled right over it, like a demented Abrams tank.

When Morano attacked, Pay wondered if he was the Jeep.

Pay jumped left and forward, hoping to get behind Morano for a kidney strike. Or better yet beside him, sidekick to the knee being the best way to take down a big man. Morano, thinking the same thing, lunged forward and to the right.

They crashed together like the former football linemen they were.

The club's most famous work of art, a Rembrandt, or something—like Pay gave a damn—smashed to the floor.

Pay and Morano were stuck together like two racked moose fighting for mating rights. They'd charged hard, slammed together, and now neither had the upper hand. The slightest shift in balance meant being crushed by the weight and power of the other.

Faces inches apart, Pay stared at blood vessels bursting in the whites of Morano's eyes. Sweat from Morano's hair dripped onto Pay's cheek; the garlic and onions on Morano's breath made Pay's eyes water.

Stalled, panting, they squirmed for leverage, seeking an opening—anything to get an edge.

Out the corner of his eye, Pay could see Brooke handcuffed to a chair.

Morano sucked in a breath and closed his eyes, and Pay readied for a charge. He didn't know if Morano had backup, but he prayed for Chase to arrive.

Then, his surgically repaired leg began to buckle.

Desperate, risking everything, he ripped his hand off Morano's pec, targeting a killing Adam's apple blow.

Morano dipped his chin, protecting his throat. Pay's hand slipped on Morano's sweat soaked cheek and his thumb slammed into Morano's eye.

Morano screamed. Pay took the split-second advantage, tossing Morano in the direction his body was already going, and reached for his gun. Chase appeared in the doorway directly behind Morano, pulled a pistol, and charged.

Pay retreated, dodging left and back.

Chase was barely ten-feet behind Morano but he couldn't shoot until Pay was clear of the line of fire. "Down! Down!"

Pay dropped to the floor and Chase pulled the trigger. BOOM! Blood sprayed and Morano staggered.

Chase's second shot missed, sending pellets sailing over Pay's head.

Pay prayed it was over.

But Morano was still coming.

Morano fired at Chase, who collapsed. He whirled and shot as Pay leapt behind a brown leather couch.

Bullets slammed into the sofa. Stuffing and crap flew everywhere.

Pay scrambled away. Morano screamed.

Pay exploded from a crouch and, barely aiming, pulled the Judge's trigger. Pain exploded from his shoulder and his thigh. Flop sweat ran from every pore. As he fell, the last sound Pay heard was Brooke's muffled screams.

68

What is that smell? Where the hell am I? Chase thought, wondering why his eyelids were too heavy to open. He was nice and warm. But that smell…. It was a hideous combination of industrial disinfectant, expensive perfume, and cafeteria food. Before the drugs took him away, his last thought was of Brooke and the hospital. *That's what that smell is.*

■ ■ ■

Richard sat on one side of the overflowing hospital bed, holding Chase's slack hand. Brooke was nodding off in the guest chair. Richard had never seen her look so awful. Her face was scratched and bruised. Her cobalt blue Armani skirt was a torn, bloody mess. Black alligator heels leaned against an overflowing wastebasket. As far as Richard knew, she'd been there all night.

"We have to do something about his bed."

Brooke roused herself. "What?"

"He's too tall. His feet are sticking out."

Brooke waved her hand in the air like she was surrounded by bugs. "Richard, I think the bed is the least of his problems."

"What the hell happened?" he asked.

"Honey, no one knows."

"How did Chase get here?"

"Pay was working on the blackmail thing. Morano broke into my club, knocked me out, and tied me up. I heard him threaten to rape me and kill the entire team. Pay and Chase got there as fast as they could."

"He took down both Chase and Pay?" Richard blinked and swallowed hard.

"Amy saw Morano peel out of the garage in a black pickup truck with a dark gray camper shell. She untied me and we followed the ambulance here."

"The police must know something."

"Blood spatter indicates three gunshot victims. But when they got there all they found was Chase."

"So, Pay got away? Why'd he leave you?"

"If Pay was okay he would never have left us behind."

"So, what then?"

"If he isn't dead, we have to assume Morano has him."

"Jesus."

"More like, Holy Fucking Christ," whispered Brooke.

▪ ▪ ▪

While Brooke and Richard waited at the hospital, the rest of the team worked to figure out where Morano could have taken Pay.

They knew Morano and Ray MacDonald were involved in the blackmail ring. And Morano sometimes hung at MacDonald's North Beach flat. But they were also reasonably sure Morano wouldn't go there. It would have been impossible to get Pay, unconscious and wounded, up the stairs and into the flat without someone noticing.

Jon D, Peggy, and Amy went from the hospital to headquarters for supplies. Then, they'd broken into MacDonald's apartment because it was the best lead they had. But their search, as originally expected, had come up empty.

They'd installed battery powered, internet surveillance cameras to watch the doors and windows. The cameras would send visual alerts to their mobile phones. Nobody figured MacDonald would come back, but if he did, Peggy was going to tie him naked to a chair and wave a Taser in the general direction of his balls. If that didn't work, they were going to rub a steak on his crotch and serve Blade his evening meal.

69

Pay came to slowly; he lay shivering, face down and bound on a cold concrete floor. There was barely enough light to see, and what he could make out wasn't exactly encouraging. Right in front of his face were the legs of a rocking chair, and a pair of big, worn, black, bloody leather boots.

Morano grunted, and Pay heard the skittering sound of buckshot hitting cement.

"Fucking Chase ought to know better than to shoot at a big guy with buckshot. Body armor got most of it. The rest is just buried in fat." There was another 'ping' and one of the boots slammed into Pay's chest.

His ribs throbbed. So did his shoulder and leg. Pay recognized the pain. He'd been shot before. And he knew the wound was the least of his problems. If it was serious he'd have bled out by now. Which meant Morano wanted him alive…at least for the moment.

"Hey, asshole. Welcome back." Morano's heel stomped down where the bullet had exited Pay's shoulder.

Pay groaned as he craned his neck to look up at Morano. "Can't say I'm glad to see you."

"If you'd kept out of it none of this would have happened."

"Guess I'm just a natural born trouble maker."

"I want my videos back."

"Where's Brooke?"

"Couldn't carry both of you."

"What happened to Chase?"

"Shot the shit out of him. Got no idea after that."

The first time he came to it had been light. The next time, after Morano threw a bucket of ice water on him, the sun had set.

Pay's shoulder hurt worse than his leg. His nose was broken. Again.

He probed his teeth, several were loose. Near as he could tell he was in a warehouse. A big open space that smelled like machine oil and sweat. Over his right shoulder, he could see an Olympic weight bench with about 300 pounds on the bar.

In front of him was a treadmill. The windows to his left were covered with filth or a film of some kind. Other than the lamp on the table Morano was clearly using for a desk, the only light came from dim fluorescents high up in the ceiling. A breeze filtered through holes and cracks where the metal walls had rotted away.

Pay's mind raced with thoughts. He's gonna want to trade. Me for the videos. And he's going to demand somebody from the team deliver them. Wonder who they'll send? My choice would be Chase, if he's still alive. But Morano will never go for that. Maybe Peggy? He'd figure there's not much to fear from a blind woman. But he'd be wrong. I'd be better off with Jon D. Other than Chase, he's got the most experience in a gunfight.

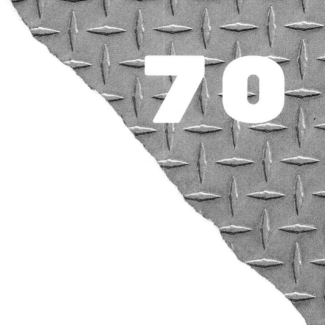

70

At the hospital, Richard and Brooke took turns working the phones. Cell phones were blocked in the room, so they rotated. One always stayed with Chase while the other went outside.

Thanks to her job, Brooke had the most extensive contact list, and the most friends in high places. So the bulk of the calling fell to her.

Richard only knew a few people who might be able to help.

His first call was to David Hunter at the Chronicle. "David, its Richard."

"Hey, how are you?"

"Okay. Remember that Pay guy I asked you about?"

"Sure, how did that go?"

"He turned out to be the real deal. Got us a great lead. We can't prove anything yet, but the guy we're interested in is a felon, Vincent Morano. We're trying desperately to get a lead on him. I've tried the usual stuff, like Google, Facebook, and LinkedIn. But, I'm coming up blank. I figured you might know some way to track a guy."

"I'll check into our records and see what we've got. But we don't keep much personal info on criminals. Does the guy own any property?"

"I don't know. Why?"

"It's surprising how stupid some of these crooks are. They use throwaway phones, drive cars with stolen license plates, and work hard to keep a low profile, but then buy a house or something else using their real name. Any realtor or title company can do a search and the owner's name pops up in seconds."

"Thanks, I'll check that out."

Richard hung up and hurried back to Brooke. "Know any realtors?"

"Several of the guys at the club own real estate firms."

Fifteen minutes later one of her contacts emailed them a list of every property in San Francisco, Marin, Alameda, and Contra Costa counties where the recorded owner was named Morano, V. Morano, Vincent Morano, or Vinnie Morano.

The bad news was there were over two-hundred properties. But lots of the properties could be eliminated. First, they got rid of all the mansions. If Morano could afford a multi-million-dollar piece of real estate—and with the apparent success of his blackmail ring, he could—there was no way that he'd be stupid enough to bring Pay and extreme violence to its doorstep. Then, they went on to eliminate anything that listed a 'Mrs.' as a co-owner.

Richard suggested Morano wouldn't have gone too far away, so they started with buildings he could drive to in about half an hour. Once they had a list of likely properties, Richard had Amy research them on the internet. Internet photos helped eliminate more. Others were dropped because they were for sale. Morano couldn't stash Pay at a place where a real estate agent could drop in without notice.

Then, they started calling the properties to see who answered. It took a few hours, but they ultimately narrowed the list down to a derelict building on the Richmond waterfront. Google Earth photos showed a neighborhood of dilapidated, mostly single-story metal buildings with rusty walls, surrounded by abandoned equipment.

71

Jon D took Morano's call.

"Want my videos. Send Richard, alone. Midnight. I'll give you a location later."

"I need to talk to Pay."

"Sure." Morano chuckled and kicked Pay's wounded shoulder. Pay swore. "That's all you're gonna get."

Jon D tried a different approach. "Richard is out of it. He's not one of us."

"Even better. Anybody but him shows, I'll send them back in a box. Along with Pay's important parts."

"Richard can't do it," Jon D lied. "He got hurt bad during training. Can barely walk."

"I don't give a good god damn. Get him a crutch or your fucking chair." Click.

Richard looked questioningly at Jon D. "What do you mean I'm not one of you?"

"Listen, Rich, you're a client. You didn't buy into this."

"But what about Pay?"

"We'll think of something."

"You haven't got much to work with. Chase is in the hospital, which leaves Brooke, a blind midget, an assistant self-defense trainer, BJ, who has to protect Mary Ellen, you, and Denny. And he's almost as new as I am."

"I'll work with what I got."

"Plus, Morano specifically asked for me. Why the hell did he ask for me?"

"I don't know and it's not your problem."

"Pay taught me to think like a man."

"So you're in?" Jon D sighed.

"Yes, God help me. Why did you tell him I couldn't walk?"

He looked Richard directly in the eye. "I've been doing this stuff since you were a baby. I suppose I thought you might man up. And if you did, I didn't want to send you in there with nothing but a box of videos and some fighting lessons."

72

Pay'd been drugged.

He remembered being on the floor in a pool of freezing water with his arms tied behind him but he'd been moved. Now, he was sitting upright, zip tied to a wooden chair.

The bullet wound in his shoulder oozed blood. It hurt like hell, because every time Morano turned away Pay yanked at his bindings. He pulled until Morano looked back or his vision began to fade. Pay wanted to be ready when the team arrived. He'd lost to Morano for the last damned time.

The bad news was, Pay was sure, Morano was looking away on purpose, just to see how long he could go without passing out or bleeding to death. The good news was the chair was starting to come apart.

Pay was thirsty as hell. Probably from the shock, but maybe from a lack of blood. He'd refused to beg when he needed to go to the bathroom, and Morano'd laughed like hell when he'd pissed his pants. Then he'd tossed another pail full of ice water on him, "To keep the smell down."

So, there he sat; freezing, woozy, scared, and pissed—in more ways than one. "Hey, Morano, you heard from the guys?"

"Trading you for the videos tonight."

"So, you gotta keep me alive a little longer."

"Funny, I thought it meant I'd get to kill you while your friends watched."

"Chase must be out of the hospital."

"What the hell's Chase gotta do with anything?"

"He's the only one who can make the trade."

"Talked to Jon D. Told him I wanted my stuff. He said Chase was unconscious and he didn't know where the videos were. Told him to sell that stupid shit to some other fool. He don't deliver, I'll send over a few of your spare parts."

"Brooke's going to deliver?"

"Nope."

"Jon D?"

"Hell no! I don't want that murdering bastard anywhere near me."

"Who'd they decide to send?"

"They didn't decide nothin. I told 'em to send that Richard guy. Anyone else shows up, I'm killing them and sending bits of both you and them back in a box."

■ ■ ■

Morano thought the biggest problem with being a mostly one-man operation was when things went to hell, you didn't have any expendable foot soldiers to soak up enemy bullets.

He called Fitness. No answer.

Next, was messenger boy—the kid with the skeleton tattoos. "Five hundred bucks for you and any of your friends if they can make it to my warehouse in less than an hour. A grand if they come armed."

"Ain't getting shot for you." Click.

He dialed from the encrypted line in the office. "It's me." Morano called his unknown master. "I need some help tonight. Three or four guys. Machine pistols."

"Remind me how you stay outside."

Morano knew he wasn't talking about staying out of Folsom or Pelican Bay, but staying out of whatever black ops dungeon Homeland Security would put him in if his operation ever became worth less than the potential exposure.

"I run anti-terrorist surveillance in titty bars watching for towel heads who use nudie bars to celebrate their impending death and a heavenly date with ninety virgins. You provided the seed money. After that, I fund things by blackmailing rich guys. A twist on the way the CIA used Air America to move cocaine and generate funds for their own covert activities."

"Anything to report?"

"Well, no towel heads in any of the clubs getting ready for their moment of bliss."

"What else keeps you a free man?"

"Maintain a low profile."

"Machine pistols aren't part of the deal."

"They want to keep this thing going?"

"I'll communicate your request." And the line went dead.

73

Richard checked his twelve gauge. With Jon D's help, he'd cut the barrel down to nine inches. If things went to hell and he couldn't take down Morano with the sawed off, both he and Pay would likely be dead.

Jon D was sitting on his scooter making some final adjustments to a cardboard box. He flipped the box over, showing Richard the plastic shotgun clips attached to the bottom.

"What you're going to do is fake a bad leg and ride my chair in holding this box of flash drives and DVDs in your lap. We'll dress things up with a flexible cast, and a cane to help sell it. It'll look like you're crippled but you'll still be able to run."

"These the real videos?

"No. Just bait to get Morano close to the chair."

"Won't he be pissed when he figures out they are fakes? And won't he find the shotgun when he picks up the box?"

"He better. I want him to find it. And I want him pissed off. This plan only works if he does something stupid. So we're going to give him lots of encouragement and opportunities to do exactly that."

"He seems pretty smart."

"Only thing you can ever know for sure in combat is your plans are going to go to hell when the fighting starts. So, you have plans, back-up plans, then 'oh, holy shit plans.' Holy shit plans are the ones that count."

"Okay." Richard felt sweat break out on his back.

"If things go the way I want them to, when he gets close, you shoot him with the shotgun. If we're lucky, you kill him and it's all over. Nothing against you, but with the adrenaline, fear and everything, chances aren't too good for that. You gotta make sure you take the first shot. He's got to see the first blast. After that, he's going to take the gun away from you. Won't be anything you can do about it. I want both his hands busy with this shotgun. It won't matter if he shoots anybody."

"It will matter to me."

"First round in this gun is lethal. Next three rounds are non-lethal loads. While he's messing around with a shotgun loaded with non-lethal crap, you shoot him with this." Jon D pulled out a spring-loaded derringer holster. "This will be up your sleeve. It's loaded with buckshot. Give him both barrels."

"What if he shoots me or Pay?"

"Probably will. But he'll figure out that the ammo's no good real quick. Then he'll toss the shotgun, probably after the second or third round. That's why I'm loading it with three non-lethal loads. After that it's full of dou-ble-aught buck. When things go all to hell, if you get another chance at the shotgun, grab it and start shooting. Morano won't care. He'll figure it's full of non-lethal crap."

"If he doesn't fall for the shotgun and you can't get him with the derringer, then your job is to get him as close as you can to the front of the chair."

Richard stopped his nervous pacing. "Hey Jon D? What happens if nothing works?"

"Morano knows you aren't stupid enough to go in unarmed. And he knows you're a newbie. Once he finds the shotgun, he'll figure you're defenseless. If he finds the derringer, he'll know for sure."

"Won't I be?"

"Not when I get done, son."

■ ■ ■

Not one of them believed there was a prayer's chance in hell Morano would let Pay live. He'd probably figure Richard for a scared coward.

He might even kill Pay while Richard watched, or, vice versa. Just because he could.

Everyone figured Morano thought Richard was the weak link. Richard knew they were right.

To him, the rescue was surreal. A couple weeks ago he'd been afraid of Centerfolds's bouncer. Now the job of taking on Morano had fallen to him. Morano. A professional killer. A guy who'd taken down Pay and put Chase in the hospital.

■ ■ ■

Brooke pushed Richard down in one of the recliners. "Are you ready for this?"

"As ready as I'm going to get." He could feel the fear burn his eyes.

"You don't have to. I'm sure we could come up with something else."

Jon D rolled into the room. "Not with the time we got left. Morano demanded him. It's going to be a bloody mess. Maybe Morano won't kill you. He'll need you to make sure we gave him all the videos, and he needs you to deliver his message back to us—something like leave him alone and we won't wind up like Pay."

Amy was crying. "I agree with Brooke. You don't have to go. No one will blame you."

Richard looked at them. "Pay said I'd be a scared little mouse until I learned to think different. He said I needed to learn to think and act brave. If I don't go, I turn back into the old Richard. I'll be that guy for the rest of my life. I can't do that."

Brooke said, "I think we need a better plan."

"I don't think there's anything you can teach me in the next couple of hours I don't already know. Unless there's a secret lesson you've been holding back."

Peggy tossed Richard a switchblade. "There are a couple of advanced knife techniques I haven't shown you."

Jon D scowled. "Morano gets his hands-on Richard, game's over. You could give him a hundred hidden switchblades; he'd still be dead."

"What scares me the most is going inside, alone, and not having any idea what I'm going to find."

"Maybe we could get a surveillance camera in there?" said Brooke.

"Camera and a microphone would be better," Jon D added.

Brooke smiled. "Maybe Sam Hong could help. Doesn't he invent stuff for the CIA?"

"Call him. Now," Jon D ordered.

Brooke dialed and put the phone on speaker. "Sam, we need some help."

"Bad guy's got Pay," said Jon D.

"How can I help?" Sam asked.

"We think the bad guy's got Pay in a warehouse. We need some surveillance inside."

"Tell me what's going on."

"Need real time audio and video."

"We need to send something in from outside. Something we can remote control. You know, like those drones the army uses. And we need it now." Jon D's voice was forceful, attempting to get the end game he wanted.

"How many stories?"

"We're only concerned about the first floor. Even Morano would have a hard time carrying someone as big as Pay up a flight of stairs."

"Might have what you need. A prototype robot I designed. It has a low-res camera, microphone, and does all kinds of neat things. It can't climb stairs, though."

"When can we get it?"

"It's sitting in the charger like it was waiting for your call."

▪ ▪ ▪

The robot was amazing. About the size of a volleyball, self-propelled, coated in a soft, rubberized material, it was nearly silent. Manipulated by a wireless joystick and painted a camouflage gray, it would be all but invisible in the warehouse.

Other than Richard, Amy was their best video game player. So she'd been assigned the job of controller. She'd go to the warehouse early, park out of sight, and maneuver the robot inside. Given the age and conditions of the buildings in the neighborhood they were hoping she could find a big enough gap or crack in one of the metal walls.

Once the robot was in, she'd locate Pay, Morano, and anyone else in the property. Then, she'd use the built-in cellular broadband to broadcast re-al-time audio and video to the team. Jon D and Brooke would be able to see it on the van's LCD. And Richard could see everything on the electric chair's monitor.

▪ ▪ ▪

It was getting close to midnight.

Jon D was still tweaking his electric chair. "Rich, you got more stones than anyone ever thought. And this is happening way too fast. A few days ago you were afraid of that maggot, MacDonald. But you can't go up against Morano even with a sawed off and a derringer. You aren't that good."

"What am I supposed to do?"

"Your job is to distract Morano. Remember that. Piss him off. Shoot him if you can. Once Amy's got the robot in, we'll know where he is—and if he's got any friends. Twenty seconds after you're in, depending on what I hear from the microphone in my chair, I'll crash the van through the front wall. Since you've got my chair, I'm going to have a hard time getting around," Jon D shook an aluminum crutch at Richard.

He lifted up the right one and pointed at a hole in the anti-skid tip. "'Course there are some advantages. I've built single round shotguns into these."

"Let's go over what I'm supposed to do again."

"You've got to distract Morano and create chaos."

"First option is the shotgun, right?"

Jon D nodded. "Second option is the derringer up your sleeve." He pointed at the front of the chair. "See those?" Underneath the box of videos he'd weld-ed razor sharp blades to the chair's handlebars.

"Yes."

"If you can get Morano in front of the chair, hit the horn button hard, and bail out. Things will go to hell real quick. If Morano's already discarded the shotgun, then grab it if you can and start shooting. Remember, after the fourth round it's full of kill loads. Make real sure no one on the team is in front of the chair."

"What happens then?"

"Hitting the horn button kicks in extra battery power. Chair will take off straight ahead. Fast. If it hits Morano, he'll go down. It also releases spring-loaded knives around the chair's base. Hopefully, the knives on the handle bars will impale him, or the ones on the base will get him when he falls."

"What if one of us gets hurt?"

"We'll have Doc in an ambulance waiting outside."

"What about Morano?"

Jon D pulled out a wicked looking Luger. "Unless he kills us all, this is his last night on Earth."

The team nodded agreement. They were a grim, scared bunch. Without Pay and Chase, leadership was falling on Jon D and Richard—a strange duo to save the day.

Once Morano got his videos back he was going to kill Pay, Richard, and anybody else who showed up. After that, if things went well, he'd take his time tracking down and killing the rest of the team. And getting to know Barbara Jane and Brooke would be loads of fun, if they lived through the fight.

The encrypted phone in the back office rang. "When are your guys getting here? They're late."

"Bosses say the deal was you could do what you want, beat a few hookers, con some strippers, blackmail some rich guys—whatever. But going to war with private citizens? They denied your request."

"You want to keep this thing going, right?"

"Yes, but—"

"But nothing. I need guys here. Now."

"Not going to happen."

"Then you lose out on a real sweet thing."

"Management is getting to the point where they don't care."

"They need to care. If I die, info goes to the press that won't make them look so good." The phone on the other end disconnected with a bang. Smiling, Morano set down his headset. They'd send help. It would be reluctant and late, but they'd send it.

■ ■ ■

When Morano went into the back office to answer the phone, Pay wriggled the zip ties binding his wrists so the little plastic blocks were aligned one on top of the other. The rope around his chest and upper arms restricted his movements, and with his legs zipped to the chair, he wasn't sure he could get enough leverage to break free. He pounded his wrists hard on his knee. First time, nothing. Second time nothing.

Blood oozed from his shoulder. His knee throbbed, and his hands went numb. Pay refocused, took a deep breath, slammed his hands down as hard as possible and the ties broke loose. It took thirty seconds—thirty seconds he didn't have—before feeling returned to his fingers and he could pull the knife from his boot.

He was still slicing through his bindings when Morano slammed the office door. Pay palmed the knife, arranged the ropes and ties so it looked like he was still bound, and feigned unconsciousness.

on D's chair lurched over the rough ground outside the warehouse. Richard, hobbled by the cast, was barely able to keep the thing right side up. He chuckled, partly to relieve the tension, but mostly so he wouldn't cry. It would be ironic as hell if he killed himself in a wheelchair accident before Morano could murder him.

The toy robot's surveillance images were helpful, but a very large area inside was still masked. The LCD panel on Jon D's chair did, however, show Pay tied to a chair in the center of the room.

Morano was standing near a desk, holding a rifle, and looking at a computer screen. Richard thought he might be monitoring the security cameras that dotted the building's eaves. He appeared to be alone which was a surprise, too much of a surprise. Richard swallowed hard, wondering what was hiding in areas that the robotic ball couldn't show him.

About fifty-feet from the warehouse door, Richard heard Jon D's voice in his earpiece. "Good news. Chase signed himself out. He'll be in back of the building in sixty seconds."

Chase's voice broke in, "Richard, don't worry about shooting me. Just point at Morano and blast away."

Richard whispered, "I'm twenty feet from the door. It's open."

Jon D jumped back in. "Richard, count to ten, then roll in. If Pay's okay, shoot and get the hell out of the way. Right after you roll in the door you better be shooting, because I'm coming in after you and I'm not stopping until I'm parked on Morano's ass."

Jon D turned to Brooke, who was watching the street behind them through night vision goggles.

"You ready?"

"A gray car just rolled past. Two guys in suits. Doesn't look like they stopped."

Jon D shook his head. "Doesn't matter if it's a hundred SWAT guys with a tank. We got no time left."

■ ■ ■

As he wheeled through the warehouse door, Richard's eyes widened with fear. He remembered Morano being big, but he wasn't prepared for the huge, grinning, half-naked man pointing a gun at his chest. A man the roboball made look a lot farther away.

Morano stood there shirtless, dim overhead lights illuminating his sweaty body. Like the girdle from hell, fat bulged out above, below, and on both sides of his body armor.

If it hadn't been a life or death situation, Richard would have laughed. With the armor in place, Morano looked like an armed, hairy, foul-smelling Michelin Man.

Morano glared. "You're even wimpier than I expected." He shook the Uzi in his left hand at Richard. "Cameras don't show anybody outside. Can't believe those chickenshits sent you alone."

Richard looked at Pay who gave him a small nod. From where he was, it looked like Pay's hands were secured with zip ties. No duct tape in sight.

Richard snuck a quaking hand under the box and yanked the shotgun loose. Shooting fast, barely aiming, the gun twisted in his sweaty grip and dislocated his wrist. The shot went high. Tossing the sawed off at Morano, he flung the case of videos in the air. Flash drives and shiny DVDs went flying.

A knife flashed in Pay's hands and he slashed at the ropes binding his feet.

Ignoring Richard, Morano lunged for the shotgun. It took him two tries because his gut and the armor got in the way.

Richard maneuvered the chair closer.

Morano racked the shotgun and aimed at Pay.

Still fifteen-feet away, Richard shrieked, pulled the derringer from his sleeve and let Morano have it with both barrels. Blood flew, Morano dropped the shotgun and crashed down on his back, legs flailing.

Slamming the horn button, Richard heard the knives locking into place around the chair's base. He bailed off and scrambled to his left. Away from the roar of the accelerating van. Away from Pay. Away from Morano. Away from the shotgun. Away from the door. Now, he was trapped in the corner—leg in a fake cast, wrist throbbing, holding an empty derringer.

A firestorm shot from the chair's headlights, spewing fire, like a flame-thrower. Now Richard knew what the oxygen tanks on the back of the chair were for.

The flames torched Morano's legs, he screamed and ran. Rolling on the cement floor, he smothered the fire and stopped screaming…right up until he realized he'd stopped directly in front of Pay.

Pay looked like an exhausted gold miner who'd discovered pay dirt. Kicking loose the remaining ropes, he pulled Morano off the ground and attacked with a series of brutal punches. Left. Right. Left. Right. Every single punch powered by madness and fear, and delivered with the overwhelming strength of muscles that had been perfectly trained for this moment.

Punches flew faster than Richard's eyes could follow. Through the flamethrower's glare, Richard watched sweat fly off Morano's body with every crushing blow. He was sure the cracking sounds were Morano's ribs exploding.

The demon wheelchair from hell spun, spewing flames, its horn honking madly. One of the chair's wheels caught the shotgun and spun it across the floor just as Jon D's van burst through the warehouse wall. Morano feinted towards the shotgun, and Pay dove for it. Morano staggered towards his assault rifle.

Pay fired. All three shots hit Morano. Two bounced off the armor leaving almost no damage behind. But the third hammered into Morano's left deltoid, paralyzing his arm. Realizing the gun was shooting non-lethal bullets, Pay tossed it aside and charged forward, knife first.

Morano grabbed the assault rifle and turned towards Pay.

Jon D stuck his shotgun crutch out the van window and waited for a shot, but at his angle, there was nothing he could do.

Running full speed, Richard leapt onto Morano's back. Grabbing his beard in his right hand and his ear with his left he kicked at Morano's balls, but his legs didn't come close to reaching around the enormous gut. He ripped at Morano's ear, then slid his forearm around his neck to get a more secure hold before stabbing his right thumb in Morano's eye; so hard, it was like he was digging for brain cells. Morano screamed and dropped the rifle as Pay crashed into them.

Richard shoved himself off, knowing if Morano and Pay both landed on him he'd be destroyed. The two big men rolled on the floor, roaring and swearing as the weakening flames from the wheelchair hissed over their heads.

Throwing a devastating back left elbow strike that hammered Pay's head into the cement floor, Morano struggled to his knees, lunging for the chair's handlebars.

In the van, Jon D jammed a joystick straight ahead and the chair leapt forward. Morano screamed when a handlebar knife sliced into his arm. Jon D jerked the remote control to the left, hoping to embed the knife even further; but Morano grabbed the bars, lifted the front wheels off the ground and wrestled the chair in a new direction. Jon D grinned, slamming the joystick hard forward and right. The rear wheels caught, the handlebars jerked, and a blade slashed Morano's thumb off at the base. He howled.

A siren blared, followed by hellacious twin explosions that filled the room with tear gas.

An amplified voice said, "It's over now. We're coming in. Once we leave, count slowly to fifty. Then leave. We don't need you, but we aren't leaving without Morano."

Somebody screamed in frustration. Richard wasn't sure if it was Pay or Chase.

The voice continued, "The first two rounds were tear gas. The next one's going to be a flash bang. If we need them, we have a couple of room cleansers—nifty little rocket propelled grenades that'll kill everything within a twenty-foot radius. Dead or alive, we're taking Morano."

Richard heard a metallic 'click.' He rolled flat, face down on the cement floor. Even with his palms pressed hard against his ears, the BOOM was deafening.

"We're coming in. If you guys aren't hugging the floor, the next one's going to be a room cleanser."

A million-candlepower spotlight hanging from the barrel of an assault rifle nosed its way into the room, held by a man, face covered with a gas mask. A second man followed wearing a gas mask and pushing a rusty wheelbarrow. He struggled to load a barely conscious, badly bleeding Morano into the barrow.

Just before he cleared the door, the man with the rifle tossed a smoking white canister into the room

76

Brooke was slapping Pay gently in the face. "Pay, wake up. Pay! Pay!"

"What happened?" Pay groaned and slumped back into unconsciousness.

Later, he came to, this time wearing an oxygen mask. It hurt to move, but by shifting his eyes he could see he was outside the warehouse, propped up against an ambulance tire. The back of the wheel well pressed into his neck and shoulders, and Brooke hovered over him.

"Wha' happened?" he gasped.

"Doc thinks the last round was knockout gas. You guys have been out twenty, maybe thirty minutes."

"Everybody okay?" Pay struggled to pull the mask off.

Brooke pushed his hands away. "Leave it on. It is helping counteract the gas. Everybody on the team is okay. Nobody was seriously hurt."

"Everybody?" Pay stopped wrestling with the mask and slumped back against the ambulance.

"Richard's banged up. Mostly bruises, but he may have cracked ribs. Chase is okay. Jon D's fine." She smiled with wet eyes. "I'm doing better than any of you. You guys took the brunt of the gas."

"Morano?"

"From the blood trail, it looks like he was badly hurt. Guys in suits rolled him out in a wheelbarrow. Outside, they shoved him into the back seat of a late model, light gray Lincoln Town Car and took off. Amy got the license plate."

"What now?" Pay coughed up mucus and gas. Tears poured from his swollen, bloodshot eyes.

"We go back to HQ. Peggy, Amy, Denny, Blade, BJ, and I are going to stand guard while you guys get some rest."

Pay's face twisted with alarm and he pushed himself to his feet. He ripped off the oxygen, took a deep breath, and a ragged, wrenching cough collapsed him to his knees.

Brooke placed the oxygen mask back over his nose and mouth. "Pay, there is nothing to be done right now." A stern look backed up her words. "Don't give this mess a sense of urgency it doesn't need. Morano's gone. The team's hurt. You all need to rest."

She signaled Doc. He loaded Richard, who was just now shaking himself awake, into the ambulance. The rest of the team climbed into the van, ready to head home.

As the van started rolling, Pay opened the door. "Wait." The team watched him limp back inside the warehouse.

Five minutes later he returned and handed Brooke a bloody white handkerchief with a lump in it. "We might need this, if we have to unlock his phone, or if he's got more of those high-tech safes," he said, slumping into the passenger seat.

Inside the bloody rag, Brooke found Morano's severed thumb.

77

It was almost an hour before Pay was awake and alert enough to talk. He limped to the espresso machine, got things going, and signaled for Brooke. "Can you get everyone together for a team meeting?"

"Everyone except Richard."

"He okay?"

"Pay, everyone's okay. Richard was closest to the knockout gas and he was the lightest, so it hit him the hardest. Doc said he'll be fine. He's in the shower, shaky, bruised, but okay. I imagine he'll be here any time now."

Pay nodded.

"Do you want me to get everyone else, or should I leave Amy, Peggy, Denny, and Barbara Jane on guard duty?"

"If they wanted us dead, they'd have killed us all at the warehouse." Pay knocked back his espresso and started another. He knew the entire team would be experiencing emotional raggedness, unstoppable crying, inappropriate laughter, tunnel vision, and physical rigidity right now—just a few of the side effects that came from extreme violence.

"I'll station Blade at the front entrance. It's the most vulnerable," said Brooke.

Jon D struggled into the room on his crutches. It was the first time in a long while that Pay had seen him without his chair.

"Damn chair's at the warehouse."

Pay nodded. Talking was too much work.

"If we meet at the lunch table, I can keep an eye on the security monitors. Nobody will be able to surprise us."

Brooke and Pay both agreed.

"I've reloaded everybody's weapons and piled a bunch of grenades in the center of the table. Anybody gets past the alarm system and Blade, they're going to find out what it was like to storm the beaches of Normandy on D-day."

Pay frowned at Jon D. "Would have been nice to know about the flame-thrower. I damn near got turned into a flare."

Jon D shrugged. "Figured you and Chase were smart enough to stay out of the way. Told Richard to bail out and get away from the chair. Calculated risk."

"Gonna have to get you that operation and fix your leg. Damn pain has seriously fucked up your thinking." Pay groaned and hopped on his one good leg toward the conference table. "Brooke, you better run this thing. My head's not clear."

"I'm not sure where to begin. Suggestions anyone?"

While the team was recovering, Brooke had been calling their contacts looking for information on the guys who rescued Morano.

Barbara Jane had been working the computers looking for the same. "I ran the Town Car plates and got a total dead end."

"Whatta ya mean a dead end?" asked Pay.

"I mean the car's registered to a corpse. According to the Department of Motor Vehicles, the owner is one Ronnie Lucas of Carmichael, a suburb of Sacramento. License tags and insurance are current, but Social Security confirms Mr. Lucas has been dead for ten years."

"Any ideas about Morano?" asked Brooke.

"We need to find the bastard and kill him," said Pay. The team nodded their agreement.

"Any ideas on how to find him?" Chase voiced what everyone was thinking.

"Oakland, Richmond, and Contra Costa County Sheriff's departments all got calls from assorted federal agencies," said Brooke. Mary Ellen sat beside her, arm around Barbara Jane like she might vanish any second. "Different organizations got calls from different groups. But what it came down to was—FBI, Homeland Security, and CIA—the message was the same: 'Do not respond to the reports of shooting at a Richmond warehouse. Homeland Security has taken action and the situation is now under control.'"

"So, dead end on the car. No way to track the guys who snatched Morano, and the only lead means going to the mat with the government." Pay sighed.

The phone rang and Chase picked up. "Okay. Yeah." He listened some more. "They're all here." He punched the speakerphone button. "Caller says he's got something we need to hear."

A voice none of them would ever forget met their ears. "Remember me from last night?" It was the voice from the shootout.

"Hard to forget," Pay responded.

"You were a little outgunned. Sucks when that happens, doesn't it?" The voice continued, "You know who I represent?"

"Got a pretty good idea," Pay replied.

"That's all you're going to get. Have you tracked down the car license plates?"

"Yeah. We know all about Mr. Lucas."

"Anything you do to track us will end the same way. Dead ends. Dead people. Morano's ours now."

"Bastard threatened to kill me and my friends."

"It's an unfortunate, unfair situation. But nothing you say will change that. And nothing you do will help you get Morano."

"We can't just leave him walking around out there."

"Odious as it is, Morano is useful to us. And he won't be walking around anymore, anywhere near San Francisco."

Pay looked to the team for support. "I don't think we can accept that."

"Personally, I like what you guys stand for. Might even consider asking to join your team someday. But, if it comes down to you or Morano, I know who my current employers would support."

"What do you want us to do?" asked Pay. "We got people we owe. People Morano hurt."

"Drop it. That's your only play." The phone clicked off.

Pay struggled to his feet. "We've got to search Morano's properties before those guys get a chance to sanitize them."

Brooke pulled a list of Morano's holdings from a file on the table. "Barbara Jane and I will take the warehouse. Richard and Chase can take his penthouse. Pay and Amy, take his Marina home."

Pay pulled his gun and a grenade off the table. "Go heavy."

There wasn't much in the warehouse. Morano's weight lifting stuff, a power-boat, and an almost empty office suite that included a desk, a secure phone, an empty filing cabinet, and a filthy toilet. Finding nothing useful, Brooke and Barbara Jane went to help Pay in the Marina.

Chase recognized the penthouse from the videos. Other than high-end furnishings, artwork, and state-of-the-art video recording equipment, they didn't find anything useful there, either.

In just over an hour, everyone was searching the Marina home, which turned out to be the treasure trove of Morano's life.

In addition to hundreds of thousands of dollars worth of art, jewelry, and furnishings, Mary Ellen discovered a huge, finger print-scanning safe cemented into the floor under a hand-loomed Indian rug

■ ■ ■

Once Richard returned with Mornano's severed thumb it took Chase just seconds to crack the safe. Inside were stacks of DVDs, boxes of flash drives, gold coins, and rubber banded piles of cash. And a single sheet of paper with three handwritten lines of numbers, letters, and punctuation marks. Each line was sixteen characters long.

Chase immediately recognized the list as passwords, which he used to hack Morano's computers. In addition to blackmail emails, he found a list of New York City strip clubs and a proposed rental agreement for a Manhattan penthouse.

By the end of the day, they had compiled an inventory of Morano's possessions. Warehouse, penthouse, and personal residence with furnishings: total value, approximately seven million. In addition, there was a quarter million in U.S. currency, half a million in Canadian twenty-dollar gold pieces, thumb drives, DVDs, artwork, and high-end computer systems. They destroyed the thumb drives and DVDs. With the help of Craigslist and eBay, they sold everything but the real estate.

Selling the properties turned out to be easy. Pay called a realtor and told him he wanted to put them on the market. Claiming to be a successful businessman relocating to Hong Kong, he requested that the necessary documents be sent to him for electronic signatures. As was typical for real estate transactions in California, no ID would be required until it came time to notarize the final closing documents.

For the escrow, Pay and the team picked SF Title, which was owned by one of their blackmail clients. SF Title requested Amy, who was a licensed notary, to provide remote signing services for the transaction.

She delivered the documents to HQ where Pay signed Morano's essentially illegible signature and Amy notarized everything.

If anyone asked, Amy could show she had followed the approved system for working with an individual not personally known to her. For ID they used a forged copy of Morano's driver's license. Pay used a pair of tongs to remove Morano's severed thumb from a bottle of embalming fluid. After carefully drying it he pressed it on the fingerprint ink pad, then rolled it lightly in the notary log's thumbprint spot.

When everything was done, twenty-eight days and fourteen hours after the fight at the warehouse, the team was ready to distribute the funds they'd earned. All told, the total came to just over fifteen million. With just over seven million coming from the sale of Morano's properties, and another eight million from their happy blackmail clients.

The first ten thousand went to pay back Richard's initial investment. An additional fifteen thousand went to compensate him for damage done to his apartment. One-hundred fifty thousand went to Mary Ellen to pay her medical bills and to compensate her for pain, suffering, and lost income.

That left fifteen million.

Per their agreement, Pay asked Richard what charity he'd like to donate his portion to; Richard decided to give three million to the University of San

Francisco medical school to create a scholarship for financially stressed medical students. Behind the scenes, unbeknownst to Richard, Brooke made sure Mary Ellen would be the first beneficiary of the scholarship.

Richard suggested they donate the remaining funds to a charity that provided services for children who'd been victims of violent crimes. And he asked that sufficient funds be reserved for him to open a new Revenge School in the city of his choice.

Pay smiled and the team agreed.

One million dollars was reserved to cover the operation for Jon D.

The balance of the funds were split using a previously agreed formula between Amy, Peggy, Brooke, Jon D, Denny, Chase, and Pay. The team agreed that Barbara Jane had more than earned a share. Pay didn't ask how anyone planned to use their money, but he was pretty sure that as soon as Morano was dead, Chase would be using his to buy a fractional ownership position in a Gulfstream executive jet.

■ ■ ■

One month to the day after the shootout, Pay and Chase got on a plane and left for New York City. In their carry on they had several thousand dollars in low-denomination bills, a list containing strip clubs, and one of Chinese restaurants.

In their checked luggage were enough weapons to start World War III.

A WORD FROM MYLES

I hope you enjoyed Revenge School. Writing it was great fun! The second book in the series is completed and will be released very soon.

Pay, Chase and Brooke will reappear in New York City, chasing Morano. And getting tangled up in an adventure based on a fascinating, real-life, human trafficking story. A sample taste of Revenge School New York City follows this. If you would like advance notice of its release, please send me an email at Myles@RevengeSchool.com.

Reviews are the single most important thing in a writer's life. I read and respond to every review I get. Nothing is more important to me than hearing from my readers. And I would very much appreciate it if you would write a short, honest review of Revenge School and post it on your favorite website(s). Honest reviews on websites like Amazon, GoodReads, and Facebook can be the difference between your favorite author writing another book or returning to the day job they were hoping to leave behind.

An honest review from you would mean the world to me. And it will help make me a better writer.

Even more important to me, than reviews, I want you to be safe.

As an author of revenge thrillers, I've done a lot of research on ways people can protect and defend themselves. While Karate, Krav Magra and Mixed Martial Arts are great exercise, all the martial arts take a long time to learn.

In writing the Revenge School series, I have discovered a few things that can increase your chances of winning a fight. These items don't require years of lessons to be effective. Some of them may be illegal in your state. Others can be carried on airplanes without TSA blinking an eye.

My list of practical, easy to use protective weapons grows as I do research for my books. The list is updated regularly.

If you would like a copy of the most up-to-date list email me at Myles@ RevengeSchool.com.

I respond to everyone who contacts me.

I will never spam you. And I won't sell your email.

In addition to the practical weapons list, there are a few more free things that you might enjoy.

Because I wanted to know what behavioral traits and beliefs make Pay become a vigilante hero, I commissioned a comprehensive, scientific, behavioral report on him. I found the computer-based assessment and the consultants analysis absolutely fascinating. I shared it with a few early readers who said it was entertaining and insightful. If you'd like to read a copy, send me an email.

And last, but not least, I hope—about once a year, I write a Revenge School short story. It might appear on various thriller websites and may ultimately be available in print. But first, it is emailed, free, to any Revenge School fan who has asked for it. If you are interested, email me: Myles@RevengeSchool.com.

I hope you enjoy every book in the Revenge School series. And as always, if you find any mistakes, they are mine, not one of the dozens of people who helped bring this book to you.

I look forward to hearing from you.

About the Author

Myles Knapp has been held at gunpoint by the Rio police, fought for his life against a hammer-wielding psycho, and lost more full-contact judo fights to Marines than he can count. As a reviewer, he's read over 5,000 thrillers and is determined to read another 5,000. His column, "Grit-Lit," appeared in major newspapers and websites including The San Jose Mercury, Oakland Tribune, Contra Costa Times, and BayAreaNewsGroup affiliates.

A marketing and sales professional, he has lived and worked in the United States, Asia, Europe, Australia, and New Zealand. When not busy writing his next Revenge School novel, Myles is reading, lifting heavy weights, and riding his motorcycle.

Acknowledgements

Without the encouragement, support, and love of my wife Brooke, this book would never have been written. Thanks, honey for giving me the courage and support to believe. Thanks to the writers, friends, and relatives who encouraged me, read the work, and ripped me when I needed it, even when my irritable nature and testosterone-driven personality made their knowledgeable suggestions dangerous to make (Corey Knapp, this is directed mostly at you). Steven Gore, who read the final, final draft and made 350+ important suggestions. Jon Land, who told me I could do it—every time I saw him. Veronica Rossi, New York Times bestselling author, and Al Garrotto whose patient support was always appreciated. To Lee Child and Robert Parker who inspired me, and Joe Finder and David Morrell who encouraged me and didn't laugh when they heard the idea.

And to my agent, Gary Brown and the team at Koru, whose enthusiasm, strategic advice and superior sales skills have made this book a reality.

Finally, to Bret Knapp, a brilliant nuclear scientist, for whom reading a book is normally a several-week, less-than-pleasant process. Bret said, "I read it in two days and wanted more. As good as any of my favorites like Reacher, Spenser, and James Bond."

No review will ever be better than that.

Following this is a great scene from
Pay, Chase & Brooke's next adventure in New York City.

*"Smile, walk confidently and project
an occasional aura of irrational menace."*

Pay

REVENGE SCHOOL — NEW YORK

Book #2 in the Revenge School Series featuring
Pay, Chase, & Brooke and the Revenge Team

By
Myles Knapp

"Oh, goody."

Chase glanced up from the luggage he was wrestling down the curb's handicap cutout. He recognized the look in Pay's eyes. Someone had or was about to mess up. "Ignore it. We've got more important things to do."

"Ten o'clock." The intensity of Pay's eyes drifted from corner to corner. He seemed to be focused on a small cluster of men, early twenties, wearing cheap, off the rack suits, laughing and joking outside Morton's Steakhouse.

"I say, again, ignore them. We came to New York to get Morano. Those guys just look like a bunch of entry level business guys out for a rowdy Sunday night."

"Rowdy Sunday my butt. If it was they wouldn't be wearing suits. Worse, their suits look brand new. And they look like they were tailored by a blind guy, or someone who'd never seen the guys who were going to wear them."

"You can't kill a bunch of guys for going to a bad tailor."

"Entry level business guys don't go to Morton's. And what are the odds of several early twenties males leaving a steakhouse at nearly eleven on a three-day weekend Sunday night sober? If they are young business guys, you can call me a racist if you want to, shouldn't there be at least one older, probably white, senior executive in the mix? Some guy who's there to pick up the check and represent management? Somebody who's got an expense account and credit card that can handle a tab that had to be at least a couple grand?"

Chase, Pay's best friend, was black. And Chase knew Pay was no racist. "Maybe it's a bachelor party that's just getting started. Or a few guys from AA celebrating someone's first year of sobriety. It's New York City for Christ's sake. But it is sort of strange that only one of them has a backpack. Guys that young usually carry backpacks, not briefcases."

"And it's not the guys in suits that worry me the most."

"Well, then what does?"

"See the three Latino guys panhandling, one on each corner except this one?"

Chase scanned the corners. "Now that you mention it that would worry me, too. I don't think New York is that much different than San Francisco."

"And what do we never see?"

"Latinos or Asians sitting on corners with signs or cups begging. That's always you white guys and us black folk. But I'm going to say it again. We agreed to maintain a low profile in New York. Those guys aren't doing anything wrong. Please, let's not go looking for trouble."

The guy standing on the far left, closest to Pay, maybe sixty feet away, tugged at his too small collar and rolled his head side to side. He grimaced, yanked his tie down about eight inches, jerked the three top buttons on his white dress shirt open and began to scratch the spot where a wife beater undershirt rested on his collarbone. One of the city's recently installed LED street lights showed a blotchy, oozing, red rash and the letters PCS tattooed on the back of his wrist.

"Panchito gang member hanging out at Morton's isn't right either."

"I'm at risk of repeating myself, but you can't kill someone for having a rash. Or an ugly tattoo. Or being a gang member. Or pan handling. Let's get moving and find a place to stay. When we find him, you can kill Morano. There are plenty of good reasons for that." Chase pushed their luggage down the handicap cut out in the curb and headed across the street.

"Yeah. Priorities. Priorities." Pay shook his head and turned his attention toward helping with the luggage.

Bam.

Bam.

Gunshots.

Screams.

Chase dropped flat to the ground pulling a nine mm Colt auto from the sandwich holster in the small of his back. "Where'd that come from?"

"Over there. By the guys you told me were just civilians." Pay snorted. Crouched behind a fireplug, in his left hand was a forty-five Judge Revolver. His right held a police baton he wore in a concealed arm holster up his jacket sleeve. Both extremely effective weapons, but useless at the current distance.

"Guess that trophy wife bleeding out on Morton's sidewalk is a pretty solid clue."

"Yeah, but maybe I'm just being overly cautious. It being New York and all." Pay's feral eyes never left the scene.

Chase could see the pulse in Pay's throat accelerate as he decided who to kill first.

The team's low-profile New York City trip was about to make headlines and there was nothing Chase could do about it. No one could stop Pay from delivering instant, painful justice to anyone who clearly deserved it.

Justifiable violence was Pay's drug of choice.

"On three."

Chase rolled to his knees behind the trolley and pulled his ankle carry, a nine mm Ruger from his boot.

Bam. Bam. The banger beside rash man shot and missed a rotund, black man in an elegant, pinstripe suit but his bullets struck down a silver haired woman carrying a teacup poodle in her pink, designer handbag. The dog yipped as the guy in the suit dashed in a zig-zag down the street. Panic pushed his middle-aged-plus-fat-guy-waddle almost into a run.

"Three." Pay exploded from his crouch angling slightly left, giving Chase about a six-inch firing window.

Bam. A bullet from Chase's Colt whistled past Pay's right shoulder and rash man's throat exploded.

Bam. The slightly softer sound of the Ruger rang in Pay's ear and a second banger grabbed at his shoulder.

Chase shouted, "Right corner." The sound of his shots changed as he targeted other gunmen.

Running full speed, two hundred and eighty pounds of muscle moving at near NFL speeds was enough to scare almost anyone in Pay's path, but it made accurate shooting nearly impossible, especially when he was shooting left handed. So, Pay always filled his Judge revolver with buckshot. He didn't have to aim much to hit anything and what he did hit was going down.

The shortest banger screamed, pulled a sawed-off shotgun from his briefcase and turned toward Pay who didn't even bother to shoot. His right arm whipped the police baton forward. It's twenty-six-inch, flat black, solid lead handle slammed into the shooter's right eye. He spun, slammed face first into the wall and hung there, unconscious, his chin suspended from a window ledge.

Pay scanned the area. Panhandlers on the corners down. Chase running toward him. Two suited bad guys down, one running like hell away. There didn't appear to be any reinforcements on the way.

Surprisingly, baton guy was moving. Rubbing at the blood streaming from his eye, he stumbled toward the only friend he still had alive. The guy with the backpack, the one Chase had shot in the shoulder, lay moaning on the ground, wrestling with something close to his body.

"Grenade." Chase screamed.

Chase seldom screamed.

Pay knew he was moments from death.

But if he shot, the Judge's buckshot load could kill innocent people. Leaping over a dead banger, he seized baton man with his left hand and heaved him at the guy with the grenade. Baton man crashed to the sidewalk, bounced and rolled up against grenade man's back.

Pay dove, and flew, like a huge, cape less Superman, toward the guy with the grenade. The Judge revolver brought him to a screeching halt when it slammed between baton man's shoulder blades. Pulling the trigger twice, Pay prayed his bullets killed both bangers before grenade man could pull the pin.

BOOM!

Pay's last thought was that he was too late.

And now he was dead.

Made in the USA
Middletown, DE
15 May 2022

65781330R00130